Archipelago

by

E. William Podojil

The Herb Society Mysteries

Cover Art by *Lea Schizas*

The Wild Rose Press, Inc.
PO Box 708
Adams Basin, NY 14410-0708
Visit us at www.thewildrosepress.com

Publishing History
First Edition, 2025
Trade Paperback ISBN 978-1-5092-6066-9
Digital ISBN 978-1-5092-6067-6

The Herb Society Mysteries
Published in the United States of America

Dedication

To my husband, fellow traveler, adventurer and partner
of twenty-five years, Joe Schlesinger

If youth only knew and age only could.
                    Robert Louis Stevenson

Chapter 1

Eleven months ago

John and Molly Halloran cuddled on their outdoor sofa. It was dark outside, and the stars and planets pierced the black sky with hopeful sparkles of light. Coyotes howled in the distance and the desert was alive with hungry predators and frightened prey. A sliver of moonlight was an added bonus since the night sky was now a velvety showcase for millions of stars and planets. A translucent ribbon flowed like a celestial river above. Before they moved to Tucson, the Milky Way was more a hypothetical concept. Cloud cover, rapidly changing weather, and the light pollution emanating from eight million inhabitants of the greater Chicago area cloaked the beauty of the outer limits of our own galaxy.

Reflections of flames danced on their faces as dry logs burned in their screen-covered fire pit at the center of their terrace. Even with a relatively wet summer, there was always a fire risk. Even the rain that fell at night would be steamed into vapor by noon the next day.

"It's nights like this that I'm glad we built this house," John said to his wife.

Molly hugged his arm. "Me too," she said, her head cocked backward and staring up at the sparkling stars. "I'm always amazed when I remember that the starlight we see today could have come from a star that died millions of years ago."

"You're the scientist, dear," John teased her. "Imagine how lackeys like me feel. It hurts my head to even think about the vastness of time and space." He took a sip of a Malbec they had picked up years ago while visiting Argentina and Chile. "I can't believe I'm approaching eighty," he said out of the blue.

"You're seventy-six," she said. "You've been approaching eighty your whole life. You're just closer to it now," she explained matter-of-factly.

John chuckled. "You are, too."

Molly softly slapped his arm. "I didn't ask for that reminder, thank you. I still feel like I'm in my forties."

"And still looking as sexy as ever," John complimented her.

"I don't miss being young, but sometimes I miss *looking* young," Molly added. "I know that sounds horribly shallow, but it's weird to be considered an elderly person when I still feel I've got another hundred years in me."

"Youth is certainly wasted on the young," John quoted.

"And wisdom sometimes feels like it's wasted on the old. Two sides of the same coin, I suppose," Molly told him. Out of the corner of her eye, she saw a shooting star streak the sky.

"It's amazing how it all goes so fast, you know? Sometimes I wish I could live another hundred years," he explained. "Then other times, I'm excited what the next phase brings."

"Next phase?" Molly asked. "You mean after we

croak?"

John nodded. "Yeah. Whatever happens, it's probably not anything we can fathom."

"What if it's nothing?" Molly continued.

"Then it's nothing. I've had a good life. I used to be terrified of death when I was younger. I'm at peace with whatever happens."

"We've both had a good life." Molly stood. "And we have a lot more of it to live, but before that, I need to use the lady's room. My bladder must react to deeply philosophical discussions." She laughed. "Want me to bring anything back for you?"

John shook his head. "I'm good. I'll be out here counting the stars."

"Be right back." She kissed him on the forehead and walked toward the house.

After using the bathroom, she walked to the kitchen and slid open the glass door.

"John, are you sure I can't bring you something?"

"How about a blanket. It's getting a bit chilly here and I'm enjoying the fire," he yelled through cupped hands.

"You got it, babe." She smiled as she blew him a kiss and turned to walk toward their bedroom.

Molly searched for the afghan her mother had crocheted more than fifty years ago. She rummaged through storage drawers and closets until she found the afghan. Outside, she heard what sounded like fireworks popping. It was probably someone using up leftover firecrackers from Independence Day two months ago. The sounds continued, and she worried about the risk of fire starting from the fireworks. It was almost September and the desert was brittle and dry after a scorching summer. She folded the afghan over her arm and headed toward the terrace to join her husband when two of the glass sliding doors shattered, creating a spiderweb of cracks across the glass. The terrace doors suddenly exploded into tiny pieces as tempered glass rained through the inside of their home. All she could think of was that a large bird or animal crashed into the doors, but Molly instinctively dropped to the floor and ducked behind a kitchen island. Her body was moving faster than her mind. *How could a bird do that?* She watched as cut glass shot across their terracotta floors like diamonds.

People were yelling outside and then she heard approaching sirens and shouting. Her mind wasn't able to connect such disparate sensations as she thought she was hallucinating. She still imagined all this was caused by an errant bird,

It became eerily quiet. Even the coyotes had stopped howling and Molly pulled herself up off the floor. As she gazed through the glass-less doors, she noticed movement on the terrace. They looked like men, all dressed in black. Still clutching the afghan, she saw one man's face in profile. A beam of light illuminated his pale white skin and bleach-blond hair briefly as the man pulled the balaclava back over his head. He carried a small pistol in his right hand. Molly would remember that pistol, toy-like, comically small, and resembling a squirt gun. Confusing beams of light danced across their terrace like they were advertising Hollywood movie premieres. Molly somehow counted four men that had been dressed in black. One half of her brain was hyper focused on details, like the gun, the man's profile, and other things she saw that didn't add up. The other half of her brain was emotionally collapsing as Molly began to realize what was happening. *This is an ambush*, she thought.

A man grabbed her from behind, and her combat training boiled to the surface as she spun around and punched the guy in the face. It was a police officer who sympathetically cradled Molly in his arms to protect her from danger. That was when she saw it. John's upturned hand splayed out from behind their outdoor sofa. She couldn't see his face, only a thin stream of blood trickling across his palm and a wine glass that lay just out of reach, its stem still intact and the globe shattered across spilled Malbec.

She turned to the man that held her from behind, frustrated that he wouldn't let her help John. "He fell," she said with frustration. "He cut his hand. I have to help him."

The police officer forced her head down as he whisked her deeper inside the house, away from windows. Red and blue lights swirled and strobed, which added chaos and disorientation to the situation. A woman screamed outside. Men were yelling and police officers started running toward the desert scrub in an attempt to find the alleged assailants. *What were people doing out so late?*

The fog in her mind began to clear. She watched as several police officers cordoned off parts of the terrace with yellow tape. Two men with a wheeled stretcher entered from the side of the terrace and her heart plunged while her mind fought between what she saw and what horrifying realities were slowly pushing away the clouds, leaving the aftermath of a storm she couldn't comprehend. John's body was lifted onto the stretcher as the first responders rushed him to an ambulance parked in their driveway. *He's dead,* she thought. She knew John was dead.

Her head swiveled to the right and she saw a crowd of her neighbors watching the scene. Her close friend Linda Eastman wailed and sobbed, trying desperately to get Molly's attention and let Molly know that she was there for her. The gravity of what she was just starting to realize made her heart race as part of her brain tried to convince her everything was just an illusion. Molly's knees buckled and a police officer caught her under the arms. Her head felt thick, like it was waterlogged. Sounds were distorted. Her vision blurred and she knew she was going to faint. *Maybe this is a nightmare.* She willed herself to wake up, but instead, everything around her went black.

Chapter 2

John Halloran had selected Bora Bora as an exotic location for their yearly board meeting, celebrating a record year of revenue and technology investments. Molly sat on the top deck of the yacht-shuttle, clutching her purse that contained a portion of John's ashes. He had always wanted to travel to French Polynesia, and now he was here, albeit in a different form than he originally envisioned. His wife was once again elevated to Chairman and CEO of Phoenix Equities and decided to honor her husband by going ahead with the board meeting as planned. The last year had been a blur since John's death. Molly called it his assassination, a crime she fully believed but could not prove. His official cause of death was listed as cardiac arrest, most likely brought on by stress he experienced during the violent ambush and attack on their home.

The perpetrators had never been caught, and the fact that they left no fingerprints or DNA samples behind led Molly to believe that they were professionals and this had been a targeted hit. John had just passed a cardiopulmonary stress test two days before the assault, so she had doubts on the official cause of his death. She knew in her gut that it was something more sinister. The Arizona police and even the FBI concluded that it was a home invasion most likely by migrants. Molly remembered the Caucasian features of one of the black-clad men. Then there was the odd small pistol. If these were migrant attackers, then they had help. The gun, the men. *Migrants don't wear balaclavas*, she thought. *Assassins do.*

John likely had enemies and many of his business associates didn't trust her, either. Although it had been fifty years earlier, Molly remembered her CIA training on multiple assignments enough to know a professional job when she saw one. The local media jumped on the hype bandwagon, fanning the flames that this was a brutal home invasion by a gang of migrants seeking to rob a wealthy white couple. *Those men were not migrants*, she thought. They were trained, precise and fast. The entire attack lasted just shy of three minutes, by her estimation. A blink of an eye and her life was flipped upside down.

Despite well-intentioned advice from family and friends, Molly decided to stay in the house they both designed and built, despite the negative memories of the attack. Ocotillo Ridge was home, at least for the foreseeable future, and she didn't want the killers to think they scared her away. This trip to French Polynesia was her first major trip without her husband, not counting the many CIA missions she and her friends kept secret from almost everyone. As the yacht-shuttle passed five-star resorts in the distance, she once again gazed upward at the blackest sky, still twinkling with stars, and the Milky Way, positioned differently than it looked at home, displayed its cloudy ribbon of countless stars that existed in the galaxy. They had crossed the equator and flew due south to the idyllic island paradise. The stars burned like infinite beacons that mesmerized her. Lukas, Taylor, and the others sat on the main deck below, but she liked being closer to the sky. The unending blackness held the secrets to so many things, and she wondered if John was watching her from heaven.

She heard the yacht's engines reverse and rumble as they approached the dock. When they disembarked, the yacht crew loaded the passengers and their luggage onto two stretched electric carts and escorted each of the guests to their cabins. Molly's bungalow sat between Lukas and Taylor's and the one shared by Tory and her boyfriend, Giuseppe. The lagoon was still like a black mirror, occasionally interrupted by a fish plunking back to the water after jumping for its dinner. When Molly entered her beautiful bungalow, she tipped the porter and walked the lit path to her front door. Each bungalow was the size of a small home in Tucson, and she instantly felt guilty for having this to herself. She unpacked and took a shower before collapsing on the plush king-sized bed. Once again, she would sleep alone as grief lashed her from the inside. She was used to living behind her facade of strength and composure, but now that she was alone, she wept. Even here, thousands of miles from home, the emptiness remained her constant companion, like a lapdog who could never leave her alone. As she lay there in her huge bed, she reminded herself of all the positive things in her life in an effort to chase away the sadness she felt. Sometimes this worked, but most of the time, it didn't. She'd eventually fall asleep only to awaken the next day, don her uniform of strength and positivity, and go marching ahead as she always had.

Molly was now in her mid-seventies and she was grateful for her health, having survived cancer many years earlier. She wondered how long she had left to live. Not out of fear, but practicality. Her kids said it was morbid, which she knew was easy to think when you had decades of life ahead of you. Molly and her friends had reunited, reviving their foursome as *The Herb Society,* a name they used nearly fifty years earlier as a cover for their counter-terrorism work with the CIA. Linda, Donna, and Betty had joined her on this trip to the archipelago of French Polynesia.

Her son Lukas was now on the board of Phoenix Equities, succeeding his mother's seat when she became CEO. He and his husband, Taylor were also here, having delayed their honeymoon for over a year due to John's death. Taylor's daughter Tory, and her Italian boyfriend, Pepe, were staying in their own bungalow. Each dwelling was separated by a thirty-foot wide channel of lagoon. The only one missing was John, and she reminded herself that part of him was tucked into a small plastic container still lodged in her purse. She knew what she had to do and after grabbing her purse, walked out onto the deck of their overwater bungalow. There was no need for lights, as the stars and the bright crescent moon sufficed. She took a pinch of John's ashes and sprinkled them into the lagoon below. Even at night, the water was clear and reflected the dancing moonbeams that striated the sea. For some reason, she felt comfort knowing that John was a part of this place.

Chapter 3

Sun crept in through the sheer curtains that filtered the early morning light. Lukas Pastore-Halloran had been awake for some time, his head resting on the muscular pectorals of his husband, Taylor. It was their honeymoon and the islands had long been on Lukas' bucket list to visit with his spouse. They had flown in late the previous night after an almost nine-hour flight from Tucson, their first long trip together on their Spectrum 7 business jet. Piloted by Taylor, his daughter Tory, and a family friend, Donna Rivera, they made the trip in one shot, touching down on Bora Bora. The San Rafael hotel staff greeted them upon arrival with flower leis and chilled hand towels. A glass of cool champagne was also an appreciated reward for the long trip.

The magnificence of the island was not visible when they arrived, except for the lighted buildings and the fortress-like mega yachts that bobbed in the lagoon. Lukas rolled his feet onto the bungalow's polished teak floors and stood. Taylor unconsciously rolled onto his stomach, now that his body was no longer pinned down by Lukas' head. The edge of a down-filled comforter and the Egyptian cotton bed sheets covered everything below Taylor's muscled back and the upper part of his sculpted buttocks. Lukas had adopted Taylor's practice of sleeping in the nude, something he originally found uncomfortable, but now it seemed completely natural.

He walked into the sitting room of their overwater bungalow, a luxury compared to the last time he'd been in French Polynesia. Lukas and his then boyfriend, Drew, sailed around several larger islands while piloting a rented boat for weeks. Most of the islands were too expensive for them to stay in a hotel, so they slept and ate on their sailboat. The relationship ended and left Lukas heartbroken, but now he was married to Taylor, a man he loved, respected, and desired more than anyone.

After he brewed a quick double espresso, he walked naked outside onto the massive wooden deck perched over stunning blue water. Even outside, Lukas felt a sense of freedom and privacy, the sides of the deck covered by an artistic privacy screen made of woven palm fronds. He had no view of the neighboring bungalows, and they had no view of him. He sipped his espresso au naturel, something he'd never done before, and something he could get used to. Taylor liked to be naked at home and outside on their penthouse terrace back home in Arlington, Virginia. He had no hangups about his body or any shame in showing it. Lukas wasn't wired the same way, and despite being in great physical shape, he felt awkward displaying nudity beyond the confines of home or their fitness center's locker room. He leaned back on his towel-covered chaise lounge and tried to relax, despite his fear of getting burned in sensitive areas not used to sun exposure.

It was just shy of seven a.m. and still too early for breakfast, despite his rumbling stomach. He and Taylor had planned to meet up with his mom and their friends who hitched a ride on their jet, promising not to encroach upon the newlyweds on their honeymoon. He and Taylor had already been married for nearly two years now. Their original honeymoon was canceled after his father died, so they leveraged the board meeting trip as a good way to enjoy the tropics, get some work done, and write everything off as a business expense.

This year's meeting would be Lukas' first, something that slightly intimidated him. Lukas was the CEO of his own company, but being on the board of his parents' company was a different matter. He knew some people resented Lukas for becoming an active member on the board. It was a fair viewpoint as Lukas avoided any kind of involvement with Phoenix Equities and heard rumors he was labeled a *nepo-baby*, which was fair, because he was.

As he stared at the clear blue water, Lukas chuckled and thought, *Well, Dad. You got your wish and I'm part of the company now*. It had never been Lukas' plan to join Phoenix, despite his father's wishes and more than occasional pressure and guilt tripping, Lukas held firm on not joining the company owned by his parents. The last thing he wanted was to be his father's son *and* employee. He was fiercely independent and didn't want to be in his father's shadow back then. Lukas always felt he had to prove himself to his father. Now that he was involved in the company, he was embarrassed by his youthful pride. He would give just about anything to see his dad one more time.

Taylor's adult daughter Tory and her boyfriend, Pepe, stayed a couple of cabins away. There were a total of nine people in their party, but Taylor and Lukas planned to spend much of it together, just the two of them. He grieved for his father and worried about his mother, whom he knew was doing her best to keep a stiff upper lip. Lukas walked to the edge of their deck, placed his empty espresso cup on the railing, and stared into the blue-green water that surrounded them. Taylor surprised him from behind as he put his arms around Lukas.

"Morning, babe." Taylor yawned. "Never seen so many shades of blue in one place." His emerald eyes beautifully complemented the surrounding lagoon and lush vegetation.

"It's surreal." Lukas smiled, reminded again by how handsome his husband was. He returned his gaze at the jagged rocks on the main island's dominant feature, Mount Otemanu, a long-dormant volcanic cone, eroded by wind, water, and the abundant plant life that clung to its cliffs. "I could look at this forever," Lukas mentioned, remembering the photo he sent to his dad of Otemanu. He chuckled at a memory of his father trying to pronounce Otemanu and butchering the name in so many ways, Lukas started to think he did it on purpose for a laugh.

Lukas felt Taylor's readiness pressing into his thigh. "Do you wanna take a swim? Either that or I need a cold shower," Taylor asked as he circled his arms around Lukas' torso.

Lukas gazed at dark, kite-shaped objects stealthily moving below the shimmering surface of the water like mini stealth bombers. "I've never seen so many stingrays," Lukas commented. "It's a bit intimidating."

"Just don't step on them, and you'll be all right." Taylor confidently descended the stairs to a water-level dock platform and dove into the turquoise lagoon.

"Feels great! Water is nice and warm!" He smiled.

"You're naked! What if my mom sees you?" Lukas called out.

"Then she'll see how lucky her son is to have married me!" Taylor laughed. "Come on. Jump in!"

Lukas hesitated and by habit looked around for prying eyes before jumping in. The splash calmed to rippling waves. "I never swam naked before!"

"Seriously?" Taylor joked, "What did you guys do in those hot Chicago summers?"

"Sweated our asses off, mostly." Lukas laughed as he looked over at the neighboring bungalow and saw his mother emerge, waving like she hadn't seen her boy for weeks. "How's the water, boys?" Molly Halloran called out. "Are you guys naked?"

Lukas rolled his eyes knowing most of the island probably heard his mom. "Yes, we are, Ma! Taylor made me do it. It's okay; we're married!" He laughed.

"Well it's not anything I haven't seen before!" Molly responded. "I'll leave you nudists in peace and meet you at breakfast in an hour. Sound good?"

Lukas treaded water with one hand, responding with a thumbs up with the other.

Another dark shadow moved beneath them before swimming to the surface, its dorsal fin cutting through the water's surface. "Shit! We've got company!" Lukas called out.

"It's a reef shark. They're pretty harmless," Taylor told him.

"I hope he's not hungry! I'm feeling a bit exposed at the moment." Lukas laughed.

"He better not touch that or there'll be hell to pay. Ready to get out?"

Lukas and Taylor pulled themselves up a chrome ladder and onto the deck. Taylor glanced at Lukas' naked body, dripping with salty water. "Everything's still intact." He smiled.

"I'll race you to the shower." Taylor turned as Lukas watched his naked white butt scampering up the stairs to their bedroom.

****

The group of nine sat at a long rectangular table, dressed in a crisp, white tablecloth and the center adorned with a bouquet of flowers native to French Polynesia. Overhead, a veranda shaded the restaurant with a roof of thatched palm leaves. With no side walls, the restaurant was otherwise open air, allowing fragrant air to fan throughout the restaurant. A tall, attentive man in his fifties eagerly approached the group, a plumeria blossom tucked behind one ear. Hands clasped behind his waist as everyone gave their order. "*La Orana*," he sang happily. "My name is Hani. You can call me Hani or Honey. I answer to both," he quipped. He stood with his hands clasped behind his back as the table gave their individual orders. Hani repeated each order from memory, and hearing no corrections, made small talk with the group seated at his table.

Taylor and Lukas quietly discussed their afternoon plans when Hani interrupted them with a twinge of bitterness. "And you two must be the happy couple I've heard about. Mr. and Mr. Pastore-Halloran, right?"

Lukas and Taylor nodded.

"Well congratulations to you both. I never got so lucky." Hani sighed. "But I'm happy for you." His attitude told otherwise. "We have lots of couples visit us here. I often wonder what happens to them when they get back home."

"Thank you, Hani." Lukas tried to change the subject. "Anything you recommend we do while we're here?"

"You must get a massage," Hani responded. "Ask for Gael. He's amazing, and rumor has it he plays for our team. His sister, Kailani, is also good for facials and stuff like that. They are not here all the time, so your timing is perfect. Before you do that, take a trip around the island. Don't get sunburned or your facial and massage will be painful, if you know what I mean."

Taylor's lack of response and side-eye glance at Lukas indicated he didn't understand the *if you know what I mean* phrase.

"A VIP will be anchoring in the lagoon in the next day or so," Hani added. "And he will request Gael and Kailani come aboard for the week he's here. The San Rafael management complies, as if they have a choice."

"Who's the VIP?" Lukas asked rhetorically, knowing it was Pierre Baptiste. He sensed Hani was begging to be asked, and although Lukas already knew the answer, he decided to play along.

Hani flicked a virtual zipper across his lips. "Sorry," he said, hoping for more questions that neither Lukas nor Taylor asked.

After breakfast, Taylor and Lukas walked toward the spa.

"That Hani guy was a trip," Taylor commented. "He seemed nervous."

"Maybe he's lonely and got chatty with two gay guys," Lukas replied. "I did get the feeling he was bitter about something."

After booking massages at *Aqua*, the hotel's

renowned spa, they decided to explore the grounds and find some activities. They arranged a high-speed catamaran to sail around and circumnavigate the island's lagoon. The group arranged to meet up for dinner that evening and went their separate ways to enjoy the island and its beauty. Taylor, Lukas, Tory, and Pepe opted for the fast catamaran to sail out to one of the reefs for snorkeling in crystal clear water.

Molly and her three friends, Donna, Linda, and Betty, tried to find a joint activity, but settled on each doing what they wanted. Each member of the Herb Society was now in her seventies and was fortunate enough to be healthy and cognitively sharp. Donna and her wife Wilma decided to paddleboard around the island. Linda and Betty opted to join Molly for a spa day.

After ascending to Chairman and CEO of Phoenix Equities, Molly jumped into her role so that she better understood the company's investments and strategy. For the last six months, she was all-in and engaged in her new role. One of Phoenix's board members had suggested the board meet on Bora Bora in homage to John. Pierre Baptiste, a self-made billionaire and lover of everything Polynesian, suggested they meet aboard his new mega-yacht, *Juventus,* and was on his way to Bora Bora. Molly was not thrilled about visiting Pierre, as she knew the entrepreneur had ulterior motives, but she decided it was a better strategy to feign an alliance with Pierre than to risk him becoming an enemy. She knew Pierre was still bitter about Molly's surprise takeover of the company after John was kidnapped in Dubai. Molly also believed Pierre was involved in, or at least aware of, the attempted takeover of the Poseidon technology. She had no proof, but her instincts were usually directionally correct.

Placing Lukas on the board was both a short term and long-term strategic move. She still hoped Lukas would eventually succeed her in order to keep the family in executive control of the company, but she didn't push it. Pierre had huge financial clout and more than enough money to buy Phoenix Equities, but John Halloran's vision and knack for spotting nascent technology in which to invest was something Molly knew was not her strength. Lukas had the ability, but not the desire to eventually be CEO. Until that decision was finalized, she would never cede control of the company. One crack in their alliance could mean the non-family board members would vote to have Pierre Baptiste buy the company, resulting in massive payouts to the owners and board members. Against her better judgment, she agreed to Baptiste's request to have the board meeting on his yacht. Molly grew more suspicious when she learned that the other board members would be on video conference instead of being there in person, no doubt at Baptiste's insistence.

She was not Pierre Baptiste's fan and once told John, "Pierre is an acquired taste. And I haven't acquired it."

Chapter 4

Fleshy, pale feet splashed through the warm water that lapped his veined white legs with feathery waves. No matter what he tried, he couldn't make his feet look younger. His father once told him, *"People's shoes tell you how rich they are. People's feet tell you how old they are."* Papa had certainly been correct about that.

Dirty seafoam shivered like it was alive as it clung to the crushed coral beach. A reef surrounded the island like a necklace, reducing the angry ocean swells to harmless ripples that flowed on the island's lagoon. Kiva Oa was like many atolls in the South Pacific, a ring of white sand islets surrounding an impossibly turquoise lagoon. A jagged peak towered above the lagoon, the remnants of an ancient volcano that erupted here eons ago. Solidified magma had weathered, cracked, and dropped into the lagoon, leaving a core of crumbling basalt that leaned like a rusty smokestack at an abandoned steelyard. Whatever power that volcano unleashed, it was not evident today. Soft trade winds fanned the island and coconut palms grew out of the sand, ripe with fruit the locals cut down with rusty machetes.

Pierre Baptiste kicked through the rippling waves, his head covered with a wide-brimmed hat that covered his delicate skin and recent hair transplants. His skin used to droop with wrinkles and jowls that resembled those of a French bulldog. At seventy-six years old, Pierre fought the aging process with gusto. Although his age was publicly known, one meeting him for the first time would assume he was in his early fifties. He tried cosmetic surgery once and he was unsatisfied with the results. Fillers, injectable toxins, skin peels, and other procedures helped him maintain his appearance, but it was his skin care regimen that was the most impactful. He found methods unknown throughout most of the world, but his product worked, and he was planning to make a fortune on it. His next treatment would be transformational.

As he climbed up a boulder protruding from the white sand, he took in the view and reminded himself that he owned this paradise island. In the distance, Pierre heard the loud barking of his dog, and he knew Marcel had found something. At ten years old, Marcel maintained the energy and agility of a puppy, and behaved like every trip to the beach was his first. Marcel was a chocolate brown Barbet, a frisky water dog named for the French word for *beard*. Marcel's fur would grow curly and unruly, requiring regular grooming. Baptiste had several of the breed during his lifetime, each of them named Marcel. The current Marcel was the first one with a bright white chest of fur. Built for swimming and retrieving hunted game, the dog was both intelligent and friendly, and Pierre often referred to the dog as his only true friend. His associates believed this to be accurate, as the Pierre Baptiste they knew was a man devoid of friends and confidantes.

Marcel's barking intensified. *He found something,* Pierre thought to himself, assuming it was likely a washed-up fish or a feisty crab. The dog appeared from the underbrush, excitedly barking still. Pierre grabbed a piece of driftwood to play fetch with the dog and to break his attention with a game. Colorful fish darted in the shallow waters and the menacing silhouettes of stingrays lurked on the sandy bottom. He used to worry if they would attack Marcel, but dog and fish mutually co-existed with each oblivious to the other. Pierre threw the stick and it soared over Marcel's head and splashed into the turquoise water, but Marcel didn't move and only continued his insistent barking. The dog started to run in the opposite direction, glancing back at Pierre to make sure he followed. Normally, the dog would plunge into the water, rescue the stick, and bring it proudly back to his master. But not today.

"What is it, Marcel?" He said in French. "What did you find now?"

Marcel's insistence continued. "*Mon Dieu.*" Pierre exhaled in exasperation and followed the sand prints to determine his excited companion's discovery. He was in no particular hurry and soon found another piece of driftwood he attempted to have Marcel fetch. No luck. Pierre and Marcel enjoyed their daily beach walks, but it had never been like this. Pierre's mind suddenly started to race. *What did Marcel find? Hopefully it's not from Juventus*, he thought, thinking back to the time a waste container was accidentally ejected from the ship and created a health crisis at one of his other islands.

Moving away from the gentle lapping waves, Pierre climbed up the slope of the beach, the soft pinkish sand yielding to his weight, the remnants of coral and volcanic rock pulverized eons ago. As he rounded a gently scalloped contour of the shore, he saw

Marcel's silhouette circling something that had washed ashore.

"Merde," he muttered to himself when he saw the tangled, fleshy mass around which Marcel circled. Someone made a mistake and Marcel found it.

****

Unlike most mornings, Pierre didn't enjoy today's stroll on the beach. After leashing Marcel and dragging him back to his residential compound, Baptiste sulked in his open-air office. Ceiling fans lazily spun above as he sat in a bamboo and wicker chair. Marcel panted and stretched out on the cool teak floor. Pierre's desk was immaculately clean, matching everything else on his compound. His staff spent untold hours cleaning and re-cleaning every surface until it glowed as nobody wanted to witness Pierre visiting unannounced and finding his domicile in a state of unkempt chaos.

Small geckos scampered up the bamboo poles that held up the palm-thatched roof. Crabs tickled the teak floor as they explored Pierre's office. He sipped his macchiato and thumbed through a large book of maps showing details of neighboring islands that made up the ten-island archipelago he owned. Modern tribal sculptures, weathered by the sea air, stood guard like totems. His sizable collection of antique Polynesian art was locked behind the doors of his island home. He straightened his arms to assist his ancient knees, unable to lift his weight alone.

As his eyes squinted and scanned the horizon, his attention was drawn to his floating fortress moored offshore, *Juventus*. Like most billionaires, Pierre owned dozens of properties around the world, including on Kiva Oa. But *Juventus* was where he felt most at home.

She was his fourth yacht and the first to be created exclusively for him. *Juventus* was unique in many ways. Propelled by a proprietary technology based upon the prototypes of molten salt reactors, *Juventus* was the first motor-driven ship to utilize this safe, sustainable, infinite, and emission-free clean energy source. It was not a new technology, but governments had not been able to quell their internal squabbling enough to develop the concept to fruition. Baptiste had impatiently sought out scientists from around the world and within two years they had successfully scaled the technology that now powered his massive vessel.

Pierre wanted his ship fully mobile so he could escape the nightmares currently facing the world. Nuclear war, another pandemic, or a civil apocalypse could be left behind on land, while he rode it out on the high seas with *Juventus.* Her unique hull design was able to cut through the waves at nearly eighty miles per hour indefinitely, assisted by a super advanced autopilot feature that used satellite navigation combined with sensor technology. This allowed *Juventus* to maneuver through dark seas at high speed and avoid obstacles like floating debris, sea life, land, and other vessels.

Rather than boast publicly about his ship, Pierre decided to take a quieter approach, while proving-out the technology in his mega-yacht. The Chinese, Russian, and United States defense departments expressed interest, yet Baptiste remained coy, his scarcity only increasing his value to them. As a board member of Phoenix Equities, Baptiste was in the catbird's seat as entrepreneurs begged for investment to support their fledgling inventions, one of which was the molten salt reactor, which now hummed in his vessel's engine room.

Designed and built by a well-known shipyard in Rotterdam, *Juventus* stretched over nine-hundred feet in length. She was his floating palace of speed, luxury, technology, exploration, and Avant Garde design that caught the public's eye wherever she moored. A crew of twenty permanently lived onboard and was ready to serve the many VIPs that Pierre invited. Of the more than forty rooms, twenty were designated as staterooms for guests. The remainder of the rooms included dining lounges, a well-equipped fitness center, spa, movie theater, mini medical center, and lounges. Crew quarters were out of view, tucked away on the lower decks. Pierre had a private suite consisting of three bedrooms, an office, a media room, and a private dining area that spanned the beam of the yacht. Retractable balconies were extended whenever the ship moored or when Pierre authorized it while sailing. His intent was to keep *Juventus* as streamlined as a bullet.

Multiple celebrities clamored for photo opportunities on board Baptiste's showpiece. Whomever graced magazines as the latest *it boy* or *it girl*, they were bound to be spotted on Baptiste's yacht. He spent much of the year aboard this floating fortress, while his dozens of properties sat empty and awaiting visitors. He connected with his executive team, attended board meetings, and even sat for televised interviews virtually. While he enjoyed the celebrity status he gleaned off of his famous visitors, he also craved privacy and alone time. The more he withdrew from society, the more valuable he became.

****

Heels clicking on his marble floors snapped him

out of his daydream. A tall woman strode boldly toward him, a worried look etched on her face. She knew what was coming.

"We have a problem." He scowled.

"Yes, sir," the woman replied. "I've been informed."

"He was badly decomposed. How long was he out there?"

The woman nodded. "One of our crew, he…"

"I know!" Baptiste exploded. "I saw the goddamn nametag on his uniform and what remained of his torso. How could you be so stupid? He was supposed to be stripped and weighted down and with no goddamned identifiers like a fucking uniform. Did you place his passport in his pocket to aid in identification?" Baptiste sneered with sarcasm.

"My apologies, sir," she offered. "I'll make sure it is taken care of."

"The media went rabid when news reports, undoubtedly leaked from your staff, raved about my Ivy League intern who disappeared from *Juventus* over a month ago," Baptiste growled. "I blamed homesickness that drove him to suicide, lost to the depths of the sea. And now I find him rotting at my front door. Thank God nobody else is here to witness your incompetence."

The woman said nothing but nodded briefly to acknowledge the error.

"I expect more from your crew, Captain Kepler. When I say I want no loose ends, that includes no fucking corpses washing up on my beach!" he mocked her.

"I will see to it personally," she replied, her cheeks

burning with embarrassment.

"Make fish food out of him, for chrissakes!" Baptiste commanded. "Nothing is to be left behind, or I'll make fish food out of you, too."

"I understand, sir," she mumbled, eyes facing the polished floor.

Baptiste smiled. "I know you do, Captain Kepler. But also understand that I can throw you back on the streets where I found you."

****

Kepler skulked with her tail between her legs and Baptiste felt invigorated. It had been a while since he chewed out a subordinate. He reflected back to his years living on the streets of Marseille where he did what he could to survive after losing both his parents. As an unapologetic bisexual, he leveraged his Mediterranean looks to woo whatever and whomever he could to claw his way from the gutter to rich people's bedrooms. He remembered these times fondly, but also remembered the terror of living in squalor, not having enough to eat, and general loneliness that comes with being a street hustler. But those dark days made him resilient and creative, putting him on the path to becoming the billionaire he was now.

He yearned for the movie-star looks he had as a young man. He tried, in vain, to leverage surgery and other cosmetic procedures to slow the inevitable slope toward aging. Baptiste would often lament that it took him half a century to become rich. Why would he only have two to three decades to enjoy it? But for him, it wasn't about longevity; it was about retaining his youthful appearance, and he believed he had a way to make that happen.

****

The following morning, Baptiste strode across the deck of his yacht, breathing in the fresh air. The deck rumbled as the anchor retracted and *Juventus* set out for her next rendezvous point, which would take most of the day, depending on the seas. Marcel whined as he saw the island move into the distance but was quickly distracted by Pierre walking toward him on the large outside seating area gracing the stern of the ship. He estimated he would arrive the following day mid-afternoon.

Pierre looked forward to seeing Molly Halloran, Lukas, and their guests at the San Rafael. He was not able to attend Lukas' wedding, but he planned to celebrate with them onboard *Juventus* and had already decided with the hotel to pay everyone's hotel expenses, a gesture that would likely oblige them to come aboard the yacht and have all their belongings transferred onto the ship. Not only would they have a free vacation, but they would also be his guests on one of the world's most famous yachts as it cruised around the Pacific. *What good is having money if you can't use it to get what you want?* Pierre often told himself.

As *Juventus* cut through the sea, Pierre smiled at her speed and stability, with movement barely perceptible due to the advanced gyroscopic stabilizing technology. Pierre paced the length of his cabin. At full speed, it was too windy to sit outside, so the large balconies were already retracted. A chime indicated there was someone outside his door. He was greeted by a clean-cut man clad in the uniform worn by cabin staff, his only distinguishing adornment a piercing of his eyebrow. Baptiste hated tattoos and other forms of body art and used to forbid any staff from having a visual marking, but while there was a labor shortage, he had to relax this requirement or he wouldn't have any staff. He gave him an up and down evaluation, and his eyes communicated approval.

"You're a new one." Baptiste eyed the young man up and down. "Who are you?"

"Marc Hammer," he introduced himself awkwardly. "You called for me, sir?"

"Where is that accent from? Kiwi? South Africa? I don't know if I'm aroused or disgusted," Baptiste mocked him.

"South Africa, sir. I'm from Joburg. I just came aboard a week ago," Marc Hammer replied. "I appreciate the opportunity to intern with you and your crew."

"Johannesburg is a shit hole," Baptiste commented. "I prefer Cape Town."

Hammer masked the slight toward his hometown behind a smile that could grace a magazine cover.

"You Rik Hammer's kid?"

Marcus nodded. "Yes sir, he said he…"

"I've heard you're quite effective at the tasks that have been assigned to you. Nice to have you as part of the team, Marc Hammer," Baptiste replied. "Please make arrangements to have the two spa workers I requested brought on board tonight," Pierre told the attendant. "We will be arriving by sixteen-hundred hours. I need some work done on me before dinner."

"Yes, sir," the attendant responded. "I attended some physical therapy classes, so I may be able to help you in the meantime."

Pierre approached the young man. "I bet you

could," he said a bit too closely to Marc's face. Hammer recoiled uncomfortably. "If Marc Hammer up to the task?"

Marc's chest inflated as he prepared for battle. He had heard the rumors about Baptiste and his initiation of new cabin staff. "Yes, sir," he answered as he begrudgingly entered Baptiste's salon.

Chapter 5

A black racing catamaran razored through the waves, its sails billowing with humid air blowing in from the ocean. The captain, a sailor from Algeria who now called Bora Bora home, had unfurled the jib moments earlier, increasing their speed to the point that it felt like they were nearly airborne. Taylor, Tory, Pepe, and Lukas hung on by their feet, snugly fastened by straps woven into the trampoline deck stretched between the two knife-like hulls. Betty got bored in the spa, so begged to join them on their trip to the reefs. The boat glided toward a small alcove where they would be able to snorkel over the reef and possibly see manta rays.

"Well, let's see if it's changed since last time I was here," Lukas mentioned, referring to his prior visit to Bora Bora when he was younger. Drew had been his first love, their first trip together a sailing adventure through the South Pacific islands. Lukas had never felt so free and in love—the two men exploring the islands as well as each other. Drew had been the one who introduced him to the freedom and uninhibited passion of young love. Lukas had defied his father's instruction to immediately start looking for a job and followed his boyfriend on the trip that became a defining moment of his twenties. It was the awakening of his sexual experiences and removing the smothering expectations his father held over him. The best times of his life were soon replaced by heartbreak when Drew informed Lukas that he didn't want to be tied down, only to tie himself down with another man with whom he moved to Europe.

"I could swim with the fish every day and never get sick of it," Taylor responded, shaking Lukas out of his memories. He glanced at this husband who squeezed on some fins and flashed him a toothy smile before jumping off the boat. *I don't deserve him*, Lukas thought, as Taylor's muscled shoulders propelled him toward his daughter's boyfriend, Pepe, who struggled with his own mask and snorkel. Lukas, Betty, and Tory eased themselves in, checked their masks, and swam toward a huge forest of coral less than fifty feet away. Lukas led his group toward a massive barrel coral teeming with fish. He pointed toward an intimidating drop off, its color deepening to an infinite dark blue. While they snorkeled on the surface, they occasionally dove deeper to inspect the animals who called the reef home.

Lukas floated just above the sandy bottom in order to get a relatively close view of a stingray that lazily flapped its wings in order to hide itself in the sand. Being mindful of the deadly tail barb, Lukas kept a safe distance from the ray, whose unblinking black eyes were motionless as stone. As if an eclipse occurred, the light was suddenly dimmed. Lukas noticed four manta rays swimming above him like stealth bombers blocking out the sun. In the distance, Betty and Tory signaled their excitement with a thumbs up before Lukas swam to the surface.

"Wow! That was amazing!" Lukas exclaimed.

"Unbelievable. So graceful," Betty repeated excitedly. "They look like giant birds."

"I think they were young. I've seen much larger ones last time I was here," Lukas stated.

"Sounds like a fish story. Maybe you were smaller," Betty joked.

"I hope my dad saw them!" Tory said, her head swiveling to find him.

Mine, too, Lukas thought, as a bolt of sadness shot through his chest. A pinch of John's ashes had already become part of the lagoon after Molly sprinkled them into the rippling water surrounding her bungalow the previous night.

A finger whistle snapped him back to attention as the catamaran's captain yelled at two swimmers drifting away from them. Orange snorkels and Taylor's blond hair identified them as his husband and his daughter's boyfriend blatantly ignoring the whistles. *Nice to see them hanging out together*, Lukas thought.

After a gentle reprimand for swimming astray, Taylor and Pepe sheepishly agreed to follow the rules and stay with the group. They made a few more snorkeling stops and eventually landed on a small *motu*—the native word for sand island. As the captain passed out drinks and cut fruit, dark clouds swirled closer toward them. Wind increased to the point that the captain lowered the sails to prevent the boat from blowing away. The speed with which the squall moved was intimidating.

"Prepare for showers!" The captain laughed as the wall of rain slammed into them.

The heavy raindrops fell hard, and the warm rain's force was so strong it looked like a special effects team had arranged it for a movie set. Smiles and laughter welcomed the brief deluge as the rain cooled the air and washed residual salt off the snorkelers' skin. Taylor and Lukas, both shirtless, embraced the rain, mouths open and arms outstretched. Tory and Pepe embraced and kissed, and Betty snapped photos of the event. As soon as the squall appeared, it stopped, and the clouds parted. The sun's rays returned and within seconds, everything returned to normal like awakening from a surrealistic dream.

Later that afternoon, Lukas and Taylor lay outstretched on chaise lounges, shaded by majestic coconut palms. Dressed in robes, they sipped herbal tea, awaiting their spa appointments.

"Pepe asked me for permission to propose to Tory today," Taylor told his husband, his tone emotionless or shocked. Lukas couldn't tell which.

"I was wondering why you two were snorkeling together and breaking the rules. How do you feel about it?" Lukas asked him as he studied Taylor's muscular chest visible between the V created by the half-opened robe. *So intrepid, yet so vulnerable,* Lukas thought, reminding himself of the traits that attracted him to Taylor.

"Tory is her own woman. The decision is not up to me," Taylor stated.

"That doesn't sound very positive," Lukas responded.

Taylor scratched his chin. "I didn't mean it like that. I really like Pepe, and he treats Tory well and as an equal."

"I wouldn't expect Tory to accept anything less." Lukas laughed. "You taught her to be independent, go for what she wants, and be a badass like her dad." He noticed a tear roll down Taylor's handsome face. "Are you crying?" he asked as he reached for his husband's hand.

"Maybe a little." Taylor chuckled. "It just hit me how fast life happens. Tory doesn't need anyone to take care of her, so when Pepe asked me, I wasn't sure what to say. *Take care of my little girl,* sounds antiquated and chauvinistic, so I just smiled like an idiot."

Lukas swung his legs and planted them on the soft grass as he faced Taylor. "You are and have been an amazing father, baby. You raised a strong, confident daughter who can take care of herself. That kind of independence scares off a lot of guys, but it's what Pepe loves about her. I think that speaks volumes about how your future son-in-law is going to live his life with Tory—as an equal partner."

"We could be grandparents this time next year." Taylor said matter-of-factly.

"Okay, now I'm depressed. Thanks." Lukas chuckled with sarcasm and some reality. He had found several gray hairs that morning, coincidentally.

Taylor exhaled and nodded. "Pepe took me by surprise, which isn't his fault. I could tell he was nervous."

"And you were surrounded by sharks, so you were vulnerable," Lukas joked.

"Thanks, babe." He reached to hold Lukas' face in his hands and kissed him. "What would I do without you?"

Foreheads touching, they smiled at each other. "Tory's not allowed to have a baby until we do, of course." Lukas said in jest. "It would mess up the whole timing thing and just be confusing for both kids." He smiled.

Out of the corner of his eye, Lukas saw a figure approach and turned to notice it was two people, a man and a woman who introduced themselves as their spa therapists. Kailani was tall and graceful, her black hair held back by a hibiscus blossom tucked behind her ear. She carried herself with grace that bordered on being regal. Her soft disposition was backed by self-assuredness and confidence. Gael wore nothing but a colorful pa'u', a type of Polynesian kilt wrapped tightly around his waist. Both Taylor and Lukas blushed as they noticed Gael's toned body and indigo tattoos that lined one arm from shoulder to elbow. His face was equally distinct with flawless skin, dark eyes, and a smile that displayed a perfect set of white teeth. Lukas noticed both Gael and Kailani each wore the identical necklace, a leather cord threading what looked like an iridescent blue pearl. Taylor noticed it, too.

"I've never seen a pearl that color," Taylor commented. "Are they native to this area?"

Gael fingered the pearl and smiled. "They are very rare. Blue pearls have special qualities for health and healing. They are only found in an archipelago where I come from."

Kailani nodded in agreement. "Our culture says that the blue pearl is a gift from the gods who protect the oceans. We wear the pearl to honor them, and some say there are blue pearls that have special powers."

Lukas thought, "Special powers for what?"

Gael interjected. "Legends say many things, mostly about health, fertility, and long life." Gael uttered something to Kailani they couldn't understand. "We should get started on your treatments."

Gael led Lukas while Kailani directed Taylor toward her treatment room. Taylor winked at Lukas as he got up to follow Gael, duck walking awkwardly in spa-issued slippers. He and Lukas had been together for over four years and were comfortable talking with each other about attractive men they happened to come across. Many of their partnered friends had their own arrangements that worked for them: open, poly, sharing their bed with an occasional third, or remained fully monogamous. Lukas and Taylor decided that monogamy worked for them, and if something happened down the road, they would communicate openly about it. Relationships evolved and neither could bear the thought of the other with someone else, so they clearly defined their limits.

During the massage, Lukas felt energy radiating from Gael's hands. It wasn't heat energy; it felt like power, clarity, and like every cell in his body rejuvenating. It was erotic but not sexual, healing and draining simultaneously. Lukas had never felt so many sensations and emotions at the same time, almost like an out-of-body experience while every sensation reminded him he was very much in his body. The ninety-minute treatment left Lukas physically spent, but more energized than he'd ever felt. After Lukas dressed, Gael led him to a sitting area and poured him some water while he waited for Kailani. He noticed Taylor shuffling toward him, his pupils dilated and his face relaxed and smooth, like ten years were taken off. Lukas saw that Taylor experienced something profound and the two men stared at each other, unable to communicate beyond a few words.

"Gentlemen," Gael announced, "we will get the rooms ready for you and be back to collect you in a few minutes." Gael and Kailani exited toward their separate rooms.

"From the look on your face, he was good," Taylor said softly.

"I can't describe it actually. How was your facial?" Lukas asked.

Taylor struggled to find the right words. "I've never felt anything like that. It was like she got beneath my skin and somehow rejuvenated everything. I don't know if I was dreaming or hallucinating. Like she repaired my skin from the inside. I feel younger."

"You look amazing, babe," Lukas commented. "My massage was a spiritual experience, and I'll leave it at that. I feel unreal."

Gael and Kailani returned and escorted their clients to their second treatment experiences. Lukas arrived in a dimly-lit room lit by candles. The scent of tropical flowers, lavender, and what smelled like vanilla created an environment of cozy relaxation.

****

Molly and John Halloran lay side by side. John twirled Molly's hair around his fingers, something he often did after lovemaking ever since their early days. Their bungalow contained a shaded, outdoor bed that was partially secluded, but still excitedly outside. Afternoon sun had warmed the surrounding lagoon. A light breeze fluttered the woven palm fronds that made up the privacy walls.

"You always liked to make love outside." Molly rolled onto her side to place her head on John's chest.

"Still a thrill after all these years. I don't think we

ever did it in a place quite like this, though." He kissed his wife on her forehead. Molly's attention was drawn to movement a few feet away. *Somebody is watching*, she thought. Suddenly, a man in a dark hoodie approached. She saw he was lighter skinned and was mesmerized by penetrating black eyes, the only features visible, the rest of his face masked by a balaclava. Molly felt malevolence. John had fallen asleep on her arm, and she couldn't move. She pulled to free her arm, but now John was already dead, his face decaying rapidly as she tried to get away. Panic overtook her as she knew what was going to happen. She covered herself with the afghan, hoping to hide, but she was pinned by John's dead weight. Her heart raced knowing how this would end, but she was powerless to do anything about it.

The ringing phone startled her awake. Disoriented, her mind struggled to transition from her dream to reality. She'd fallen asleep on a luxurious chaise lounge atop the outside deck that ringed the overwater bungalow. It was the same nightmare again. Her eyes welled, remembering the joy she felt in John's presence, replaced by the terror of the man in the balaclava. These nightmares plagued her daily for the last several months. She answered the phone, a call from the front desk.

She chalked her daily nightmares to the grieving process, her mind desperate to make sense of what had happened. Molly often reflected on that evening almost a year and a half ago. A beautiful evening, then an innocent task to fetch an afghan spared her life. The sound of shattering glass followed by the rain of tempered shards showering her. The figures vaulting over the stone wall before disappearing into the desert. Her memory vacillated on the number of attackers, but it was the one in the balaclava that she remembered most. Maybe because of his bleach-blond hair, which she later discovered was from a wig. Her experience in the CIA led her to believe this had been an organized job, possibly a hit. She still maintained that John had been assassinated, planned by someone that wanted John punished, or just gone. It vexed her still, both awake and in dreams. Her cell phone pinged.

—*Just stopped by, I think you were sleeping. Remember we have dinner with Pierre tonight*— Molly's phone buzzed with a text from Linda.

Molly cocked her head and cracked a smile.

—*Yay. I can't wait*—she typed back with deadpan sarcasm.

—*Betty can't wait to see Baptiste's yacht*—Linda texted with a smiley face.

Molly's eyes grew suspicious.

—*I think it's you that can't wait to see his yacht. Actually it's more like an aircraft carrier. Have you seen pictures of it? It's a fortress.*—

—*It's just dinner. Did he invite Lukas and Taylor, too?*— Linda texted.

—*Yeah. But I'm not sure where they are so I sent a message to their bungalow and one of the concierges will also look for them on the property.*— Molly replied.

—*I'm going to play nice with Pierre tonight. He's an investor and board member in our company. He's behind many of the most profitable investments Phoenix Equities enjoys today.*—

—*That's noble of you.*—Linda texted with a

laughing emoji.

*—I'll do my part for king and country.—*Molly texted back stoically.

Chapter 6

Taylor and Lukas entered their air-conditioned over-water sanctuary. A bottle of champagne, two crystal flutes, and a tray of strawberries sat on their dining room table. There was also a note, but the two men didn't notice it. They were too consumed with shucking their clothes and diving onto their massive bed. Something about their treatments left them energized and feeling like a decade younger. Their libidos were already healthy, but now they could hardly make it inside before devouring each other. An unseen small boat motored past their bungalow, sending ripples against the pylons suspending the dwelling over the aquamarine lagoon. Lukas lay on his back as Taylor kissed his neck, shoulders, and chest and smiled when he saw a small gecko peering at them from the top of the thatched ceiling.

"We've got a spy." Lukas laughed when he saw Taylor notice the small reptile.

"Let's give him a show, then." Taylor was already primed for round two as was Lukas.

****

They awoke an hour later to a ringing doorbell. Lukas jumped out of bed, naked and scrambling to find something to throw on his body. In his haste, he slipped on the polished floor, his leg gashed by a metal corner of a coffee table.

"Fuck!" He winced in pain. "Taylor, can you get the door? I just wiped out."

Lukas noticed the cut from his shin to his calf was starting to bleed. His arm throbbed from the weight of his fall.

Taylor hurtled over Lukas and made it to the door where he found a European-looking man wearing a San Rafael butler uniform. The butler handed him a note, averting his eyes from Taylor's naked torso and bath towel around his waist. *No need to make this more awkward*, Taylor thought.

"It's an invitation and a reminder to please join Mr. Baptiste for dinner on his yacht," the butler stated formally.

"When are we supposed to meet?" Lukas shouted from the floor.

"The yacht-tender arrives in twenty minutes," the butler answered, confused about where the other male voice originated as Lukas remained on the floor, hidden by a sofa.

"Shit," Lukas commented. "Tell them to wait for us. I've got to clean the cut before we go. We'll be at the dock in less than thirty minutes," he yelled to the butler who smiled and left the bungalow.

"I've never had dinner with a billionaire on a superyacht," Taylor commented.

"You're not the only one," Lukas responded. "He's here early for the board meeting. We better get moving. My mom needs us for emotional support."

****

At the dock, Linda and Betty also showed up. Donna and Wilma decided on a quiet night in their bungalow.

"We're crashing your party," Betty joked, dressed in a tennis skirt and pullover. "Mr. Baptiste's minions hand-delivered invitations to each of us an hour ago. This is the nicest thing I packed."

"I always pack for at least one formal occasion," Linda bragged. She was dressed in a slim-fitting silk dress cut just below the knee. Her ears and neck dripped with jewels. "Don't get excited. They're fake."

"The diamonds or your breasts?" Betty teased an annoyed Linda.

Molly smiled. "I'm glad you're all coming. I'll have entertainment watching you two."

Lukas eyed the large ship moored offshore. It was dusk and Baptiste's yacht glowed ominously, moored in the lagoon. The sky burned a fiery pink as the sun was swallowed by the horizon. A smaller craft, silhouetted by the dimmed atmosphere, buzzed toward them.

"I think our ride is here," Taylor mentioned.

"Where are Tory and Pepe?" Molly asked after silently counting their number of passengers.

"Tory and Pepe have a special date tonight," Taylor replied. "Pepe told me about it earlier today."

"No! Is it what I think it is?" Linda exclaimed in surprise.

"Pepe asked me if he could propose to Tory," Taylor answered.

"Let's hope he's better than that Diego guy." Betty scowled, remembering Tory's ex-boyfriend they had encountered during their Dubai adventure.

"Pepe's definitely an upgrade." Taylor laughed.

"I think it's good that they're alone together." Molly changed the subject. "Nobody needs the whole family around when you're making the biggest decision of your life!"

"Like all of you were when Taylor proposed to me?" Lukas reminded them.

"That was different," Linda interjected. "Taylor had already saved our lives so that made him automatically part of the family regardless of Lukas' answer."

The sleek boat approached quietly, its electric motor eerily silent. No captain was onboard to pilot, yet the boat was able to perfectly parallel park at the dock using sensors and autopilot controls that maneuvered it. A young male crew member, dressed in uniform, threw nautical ropes around the bollards to hold the boat steady for people to board. Taylor, experienced with autopilot in aircraft, had never seen it on a boat. He noticed Taylor's interest in the autonomous watercraft that still needed a human to moor it.

"Only a matter of time before autopilot can do my job, too," he laughed. "I'm Aleks. I'll escort you to *Juventus.*" He held out his hand to Taylor, Lukas, and the rest of the boarding party.

Aleks Borisov spoke with an accent that sounded Eastern European, like Russian or from one of the former Soviet republics. His eyes were mesmerizing and distracting, like those of a Siberian husky. He had sharp Slavic features that added to his intrigue. Lukas wondered what his story was—how did he end up working for Pierre Baptiste? Taylor informed him that he was born in Russia and adopted by his American parents. Even with Taylor's disclosure, Aleks showed little emotion nor shared any personal information in return.

"I don't think a robot can do what you're doing.

Too many variables!" Taylor smiled as he boarded the boat. Aleks kindly escorted Linda, Betty, and Molly onto the boat. Lukas insisted he board on his own.

The inside of the shuttle boat glowed a calming blue from under-seat LED lights. The only sound was the sloshing of harbor ripples as the electric boat made its way toward the mothership. Throughout the lagoon, large yachts bobbed in the gentle waves. They were dwarfed by Baptiste's massive *Juventus* that loomed ahead, its enormity growing as the shuttle boat approached. There was something both majestic and menacing about the sleek, modern ship. Both the hull and the superstructure were a rich cobalt blue. Inside lights glowed through portholes.

"It reminds me of a spaceship," Taylor mentioned. "It's all hull with minimal decks."

"Look how wide it is," Linda pointed out. "Looks like the nautical version of a stealth bomber."

"The X-Bow means she's pretty fast in the waves," Taylor explained, pointing out the reverse-sloped bow that gave the ship its futuristic appearance, "and super stable with a very wide beam," he continued to evaluate. "Stability, speed, and aquadynamic."

The shuttle slowed as it approached the yacht, positioned perpendicular to the sleek long ship. Balconies jutted out from the ship like open cabinet drawers.

"He has retractable balconies. I've never seen them in real life," Taylor observed as the yacht-tender maneuvered itself to a parallel position with the massive ship.

"Where's the door? Are we supposed to scale up the hull with ropes?" Lukas joked as he looked at the towering ship above him. The hull's exterior was smooth and aerodynamic, like the fuselage of an airplane. "This ship is huge. I've never seen anything like it."

Suddenly, two panels on the hull opened, exposing what looked like a dry-dock inside the ship. The shuttle remained still while two large mechanical arms extended from the ship and gently lifted the small boat out of the water and tucked it safely into the docking bay inside the vessel. The panel door closed, and the room buzzed with low-tint blue lighting that gave the bay an oddly impersonal feel.

"Feels like we just entered an alien spaceship," Linda exclaimed.

"Welcome aboard *Juventus*." A tall, athletic-looking man in his late twenties, dressed in the ship's uniform, approached them with his hand extended. "I'm Marc Hammer, Chief Purser." he said proudly as he led the group to follow him through a passageway and up a flight of metal stairs. The group's clanging shoes echoed throughout the metal stairway as they climbed, eventually landing at a luxurious lounge with comfortable seating.

Marc offered beverages and cool face towels. There were no takers.

A flat-screen television lowered from a slot in the ceiling before it quickly brightened to life. "I'll need you to review this short safety video," he instructed them. "It's a regulation so that if there is an emergency on board, you'll know what to do."

Taylor had not seen lifeboats visible on *Juventus* and the video displayed they were embedded within the superstructure walls. Inflatable like an airline safety chute, the lifeboats were constructed of puncture-proof materials already fitted with built-in navigation and safety systems plus enough food and fresh water for fifty passengers. Each life raft looked to be about thirty feet long, from the video demonstration, each boat also complete with a protective weather covering.

"These rafts are very high-tech," Taylor observed. "Each one is the size of a small yacht itself."

"Yes, sir," Marc responded. "Each raft can theoretically support fifty people, but that's a bit tight if you ask me. Most *Juventus* crew are on shore leave, so it's just you and minimal staff." He forced a chuckle. "There is plenty of room if we have an emergency, plus we have a few escape pods for Mr. Baptiste and his VIP guests."

"I'd like to reserve one of the pods, just in case." Lukas unsuccessfully attempted to get a laugh from their handsome Purser.

Taylor stared at Marc's eyebrow piercing. "What is that?" he asked.

"It's a trident, sir," Marc responded. His eyes caught Taylor's before purposely averting his eyes.

"Any significance?" Taylor explored further.

Marc paused before responding. "I like the water, and I think it's cool"

"It's also the symbol of Pisces, ruled by Neptune," Taylor provoked him. "Or Poseidon if you're into Greek mythology."

"I am a Pisces," Marc lied. "Let's get back to the briefing."

The video continued to show how two mini submarines were also on board and could be used for excursions or a quick escape if needed. A stern-looking, statuesque woman entered the room. Dressed in a crisp blue captain's uniform, she stood with hands behind her back, her dark hair pulled into a chignon. "Good evening. I'm Captain Diana Kepler." She extended her hand to each of the guests who recently boarded. "Welcome aboard *Juventus.*"

Captain Kepler's severe features and thin body gave her an exotic appearance common in runway models and drug addicts. Her uniform was form-fitting and accentuated what few curves she had throughout her athletic build. Her aquiline nose was subtle and gave her an air of authority and dominance. "You are dismissed, Purser," she said to Marc, with a smile that Taylor thought looked a bit too familiar.

"I think Baptiste recruited the crewmembers from runways in Paris or Milan," Lukas whispered to Taylor.

"I haven't seen so many lithe, beautiful people in one place in a long time," Taylor softly replied. "Including our resident Pisces."

"Good to see you again, Mrs. Halloran," Kepler commented. "We met previously on Mr. Baptiste's former yacht, *Borealis,* I believe."

"Yes, we did. New Zealand about five years ago," Molly replied and smiled in acknowledgement. "Fortunately, I was able to attend the New Zealand board meeting. I usually hover closer to home to help with my grandchildren."

"Important work, Mrs. Halloran," Kepler replied. "*Borealis* was the predecessor to this ship, but *Juventus* is a different vessel entirely."

"*Juventus* is certainly unique," Molly replied, not sure of what else to say.

"My condolences on the loss of your husband," she

said, her voice chilly and business-like.

"Thank you, Captain," was all Molly could say in response. Every time someone acknowledged John's death, the momentary lift of appreciation was clouded over by the constant reminder that her husband was not here.

Captain Kepler nodded curtly, signaling the end of her personal conversation. "Mr. Baptiste has asked me to give a brief tour of this vessel. Cocktails will be served in thirty minutes."

Captain Diana Kepler had worked for Pierre Baptiste for a decade. As a teenager, she was a troubled kid who dabbled in drugs, theft, and general mischief before being sent away to a "wilderness camp" by her wealthy parents who had no interest in watching their only daughter unravel before their eyes. Diana was a blight on their family name, had pierced and tattooed her body, and nearly dropped out of high school. After three trips to juvenile detention and a stint at rehab, her parents wanted her gone, at least from their Bel Air mansion. At seventeen, Diana hadn't traveled much beyond their Southern California bubble, but after a few days at sea, she knew this was what she wanted to do. The passion she felt for ships snapped her out of her funk. She graduated from both high school and college and returned to the helm of ships ever since. Diana's father was a major motion picture producer and asked his friend, Pierre Baptiste, if he knew of anyone looking for a yacht captain, and Pierre jumped at the chance to hire her on as a first mate, and eventually she was promoted to captain.

Captain Kepler led the guests down the flight of stairs, galvanized metal painted with non-slip coating to prevent mishaps, the clanging of the steel echoing through the stairwell.

"We'll start with the engine room," she announced. She waved her hand toward a non-descript white box the size of two refrigerators sitting side by side.

"You may have heard that *Juventus* is the only private vessel powered by a molten salt reactor."

"Captain," Linda Eastman replied, "We worked for the Department of Energy at Argonne years ago, so we're familiar with the overall reactor design, but it is wonderful to see one in action. But tell me, how is it so small?"

Kepler replied, "Yes, Mr. Baptiste told me about you all. I'm very impressed by what you ladies were able to accomplish back then, considering the environment at the time."

"You mean that women shouldn't be in science?" Betty added.

"God forbid we be anything other than teachers, secretaries, or nurses," Linda commented. "Although in fairness, we did become teachers eventually."

"Yes," Captain Kepler answered. "Women like you helped pave the way for women like me. There are not many female ship captains even today, but it's becoming more common."

Linda winked at Molly and mouthed, *"She's so nice."*

Explaining in detail how the molten salt reactor provided an almost endless supply of clean energy, Kepler also stressed how it was safer than traditional water-cooled reactors. "Mr. Baptiste's team was able to create a smaller version of the reactor." Kepler pointed at the gleaming machine. "This little box makes

Juventus fast, safe, and it operates without emissions. Mr. Baptiste bought the intellectual property from the inventor."

Molly's interest piqued at this last statement, before she disregarded it and continued looking around the spotless engine room. "Now I'll show you the lower decks." Kepler confidently strode toward a metal door and after opening it, waved to have the group follow her.

Lukas and Taylor were the first to reach the room behind Captain Kepler. Their eyes wide and mouths agape, they studied the views from the underwater observation deck. *Juventus* had underwater spotlights that illuminated the surrounding lagoon. A giant manta ray swam by, curious about the lights, its black wings spanning at least ten feet across. Two other mantas joined, swimming closer to the glass observatory to study the people in it. Their mouths and gills gulped with excitement. Colorful fish bobbed excitedly as more and more small fish joined to view the ship's inhabitants, who stared back at them. *Juventus* was the place to be for humans and fish this evening.

"This is unbelievable," Lukas stated in amazement. "It feels like we're the ones in the aquarium and the fish are watching us." A small shark explored the transparent windows, baring sharp teeth or smiling, Lukas couldn't tell.

"Wait until you see the view in deep water," Captain Kepler continued. "It's like a window into another world. I'll let Mr. Baptiste explain more about that."

Molly's brow furled again. *Deep water? What was the captain talking about?*

Just then, a loud voice echoed through the dark, tranquil chamber. "How do you like my fishies? They're my only friends, I'm afraid, other than Marcel, of course." Pierre Baptiste grinned, arms outstretched as he welcomed his guests. "Welcome aboard my investment in sustainable ocean exploration," he stated proudly.

Pierre went to each of his guests and welcomed them by name, even the ones he'd never met before. He'd obviously done some research on his guests. Linda and Betty both eyed him suspiciously.

"This handsome man must be Taylor." He hugged Lukas' husband and unexpectedly kissed him on the cheeks and then his lips, a move that was too familiar, too soon. "I'm sorry I couldn't make your wedding." He reached for Lukas' face and held it in his hands, his forehead pressed to Lukas as the latter maneuvered from being kissed, as well. "How's my favorite nephew? Lukas, it's so good to see you," he said, a bit too friendly, considering Baptiste was not part of the family.

"I'm doing well, Pierre. You haven't changed a bit since I last saw you."

"Ten nephew points for Dr. Halloran." Baptiste laughed, flopping his arm around Lukas' shoulder. His smile faded when he noticed a red streak of dried blood on the inside of Lukas' arm. "What have you done to yourself, dear Lukas? You're bleeding."

Confused, Lukas immediately raised his pant leg to see his injury from the fall. The bandage was still in place. "Underside of your arm, Lukas," Baptiste directed.

"Ah, shit," Lukas exclaimed when he saw the gash

in his skin. "It must have happened when I fell earlier. I didn't see it."

"Well, I hope you are okay. I can call Dr. Nevon, the ship's doctor if…"

"Not necessary, Pierre, but thank you." Lukas blushed. "I'm just a klutz."

Baptiste spotted Molly standing next to the captain, engaged in conversation. "There's my nemesis." He interrupted them as he went in for a kiss on both of Molly's cheeks. "You're looking stunning as ever."

Molly gritted as she smiled back at him. "Why on earth would you think I'm your nemesis, Pierre?" Her calm demeanor cloaked her dislike and distrust. "Just because I implemented an emergency succession clause when John died doesn't mean I'm your nemesis," she lied. She didn't trust him one bit, her icy veneer fooling no one.

"You're a shrewd businesswoman," he commented back. "I still can't believe John is gone. Such a violent tragedy. Americans and their guns. It's like a plague. I read they believe the attackers were illegal immigrants."

"We don't know who John's killers are, Pierre. Let's not get into speculation as to who the assailants were." She pivoted around a potential political argument despite Baptiste's predisposition toward speculation. "It's still an open investigation."

"Oh dear," Baptiste responded. "I thought John died of cardiac arrest."

"That's the official cause of death, but I was there and believe differently," Molly asserted.

"Well, I hope they find the rascals," Pierre commented. "Good luck to you."

Rascals? Molly thought. It wasn't a word normally used to describe cold-blooded killers, but she didn't have the interest or the energy to get into a debate with Pierre Baptiste.

"We'll dine in due course, but I'd first like to show you a few more things," Pierre continued as he led them into another room. It was a laboratory, spotless and sterile. It looked like an operating room rather than a lab. "The ship has four labs in total, plus a medical clinic," he explained.

"What kinds of tests can you do onboard?" Linda asked.

"Basic water analysis—temperature, salinity, toxicity," Pierre explained. "Plant, animal life, soil analysis, geological tests, carbon dating, DNA…"

"Carbon dating?" Molly asked. "Do you come across artifacts?"

"Short answer is yes, Molly," Pierre answered. "We find artifacts on the islands and sometimes under the water. We do preliminary tests only—just to verify if something qualifies as an ancient relic. If so, we'll notify the local government, and they can do whatever they want with it." Molly glanced at Pierre, her eyebrows raised with skepticism. "Our current interest is studying potential new minerals and elements that may be lurking in the deep."

"Why do you need to do DNA tests?" Betty asked.

A team of waiters carrying trays of cocktails quietly infiltrated the laboratory. "I decided to have the cocktails down here, if you don't mind," Pierre stated, evading Betty's question. "I have one more thing I want to show you." Betty raised her eyebrows, noting his snub to her question.

Pierre led them down a corridor that stopped at a thick metal door. Baptiste's key card and biometric scanner unlocked the vault-like door, and the group entered what looked like a small atrium. The clank of the door closing startled them. Donna and Linda downed their drinks and grabbed another one as Pierre Baptiste walked around the room, proudly showing off the inner workings of *Juventus*.

"I'm a bit disoriented," Lukas commented. "I assume we are below the waterline?"

Pierre touched a screen and two large doors covering the central part of the floor began to separate, exposing the sloshing water below. "Actually, we are *at* the waterline, Lukas," Pierre answered him while entering commands on the touch screen. An orange light flashed while an ominous tone sounded three times. Overhead, Lukas saw a smaller vessel, the size of a minivan, being lowered onto a platform in front of them. It was a submersible vehicle, designed for deep water exploration and outfitted with dual pontoons attached on either side. The name *Jeune 1* was elegantly painted on its hull. "Its sibling *Jeune 2* is out on a joy ride."

"Young?" Lukas translated.

"Yes," Pierre explained. "I've wanted a submarine since I was a boy. Now I have two."

"How deep can it go?" Taylor asked.

"It can operate safely to a depth of five-hundred meters," Pierre answered. "But we rarely take it that deep. It's far too dark down there for what we need to do."

"May I look inside?"

"Of course." Pierre guided Taylor over to the sub

as Taylor peered inside. "It can carry up to six people, but four is more comfortable."

"Looks like an aircraft cockpit up front," he observed.

"Similar controls." Baptiste smiled. "But fully autonomous for planned missions. Technically, we can program the entire journey to undertake with or without a pilot."

"Do you have extra pilots as a backup?" Taylor asked.

"Astute of you, Taylor. Yes, we do have pilots, but they are on shore leave. They like to take the subs free-wheeling when they have the opportunity."

"What kind of free-wheeling missions do you do?" Molly asked skeptically.

"We are explorers, my dear," Baptiste responded. "We need to search and investigate. Sometimes we don't know what we're looking for. Artificial intelligence hasn't been able to replicate curiosity and wonder."

"The cockpit reminds me of a helicopter's," Taylor noticed, still searching the *Jeune 1* with enthusiasm. Lukas smiled at his excitement. Like a kid on Christmas morning.

"Can you fly a helicopter, Taylor?" Baptiste asked.

"I can fly just about anything," Taylor stated confidently.

Chapter 7

Long drapes flowed over windows and ambient lighting glowed to provide just enough light to add a sensual mystery to the room. They entered the salon of Pierre Baptiste's private stateroom, which seemed too large to be onboard a ship. Expensive art hung on the walls and spotlights accented sculptures ranging from ancient Polynesian to a dark bronze Botero statue of a genderless human form. Colored lights glowed from inside a floor-to-ceiling aquarium that covered a wall where Pierre showcased some of his lethal sea creatures. Besides tropical salt-water fish, there were starfish, eels, and what looked like a sea cucumber. Two of the world's most venomous animals, a box jellyfish and a tiny blue-ringed octopus, skulked in opposing corners of the aquarium. A third lethal specimen, a juvenile yellow-bellied sea snake, attempted to mimic a piece of seagrass, similar to the actual ones growing from the aquarium floor.

"It's my deadly trifecta," Pierre boasted. "A bite from any of these three animals can be fatal within minutes, or sometimes seconds."

"Lovely creatures," Lukas said without sarcasm. "Your pets?"

"Their venom paralyzes the central nervous system and diaphragm muscles, rendering the victim unable to breathe," Pierre informed them. "They are all native to the South Pacific. It fascinates me how the loveliest seas contain the deadliest sea life."

Marcel the dog galloped into Pierre's salon, his tail wagging happily as he nudged the visitors for affection.

"Which number in the line of Marcels is…?" Molly checked the dog's gender, "he?"

"Number five." Pierre smiled through gritted teeth. "I don't like to talk about his predecessors. He understands French and English and knows what we talk about."

Taylor stared outside one of the large windows and saw burning tiki torches bathing the grounds of the San Rafael in a fire-generated light that flickered and cast long shadows. The tambor of beating drums echoed across the lagoon and indicated a Polynesian luau was underway on land. He focused his eyes across the dancing shadows and hoped to see his daughter Tory. *I wonder if she said yes,* he thought.

Baptiste explained details about his art that nobody had asked him about, and how he had one of the most expensive art collections to grace a ship, showcasing some prized sculptures ranging from a Greek kouros to Rodin and complemented by Polynesian totems and tribal art. A long, sleek, and transparent table stretched across the room. Lukas quickly counted the place settings adorned with fine china and crystal. He calculated the number of guests, plus Baptiste and there were two extra place settings. *Who else is coming to dinner?* he thought to himself as he perused original Gauguin, Degas, Warhol, and lesser-known artists' paintings. Pacific Islander figures were carved into the high backs of eleven dining chairs. Their mother-of-pearl eyes seemed to move or change. Carved wooden eyes of the tribal sculptures danced, illuminated by the flickering votives atop the table. Each chair was unique but consisted of faces with mournful eyes staring in anguish or ecstasy. Lukas made a mental note to ask Pierre more about them.

A large Basquiat painting, exploding with color, anger, and humor, captivated Taylor who seemed lost in the meaning behind it.

"This could be about Heaven, Hell, the Garden of Eden, who knows?" Baptiste commented. "Many of Jean-Michel Basquiat's works depict meanings known only to him. He died so young we may never know."

Taylor continued to study it. "What's your take on it?" he asked Pierre.

"I don't know," Pierre continued. "It reminds me of Adam and Eve, the expulsion from paradise, the death and destruction wrought upon the world."

Taylor's eyes widened. "Oh, a happy painting."

Baptiste snickered. "Most good art is borne from pain."

Their attention was drawn to a stately couple entering the dining salon. Taylor and Lukas recognized them both, despite the context in which they met. They both approached the handsome pair.

"Gael, Kailani, what a nice surprise to see you again!" Lukas truly was surprised, but happy to see them.

Captain Diana Kepler brushed by Gael, a sly smile on her lips. Kailani looked downward, maybe in shyness. Probably in disgust.

"Mr. Baptiste requests us when he visits the island," Gael explained.

"I can see why," Taylor added. "You both have

magic in your hands. Truly a gift. Lukas and I felt like we were ten years younger after our sessions."

"Massage is part of our culture," Kailani explained. "Gael and I grew up learning these techniques, how to detect energy, manipulate it. The energy is already yours; we simply find it and move it to a place where you can use it."

Lukas cocked his head and smiled at Taylor. *Well we certainly used it!* he thought. Taylor smiled back, a reference understood without verbalizing it. "When did you both come on board?" he asked the couple.

"You were our last appointment. Mr. Baptiste sent a boat for us soon after," Kailani responded.

"Your blue pearls look even more intense tonight." Lukas wondered if they were actually glowing.

"It's because they know we are on the water," Kailani commented. "Closer to their home."

"The islanders where we are from wear them every day until they die," Gael elaborated. "Then they are passed to the next generation."

Pierre clapped his hands, summoning everyone to the table. Uniformed attendants ushered the women into their seats and then repeated with the men. Captain Kepler sat directly to Pierre's right. Frosted flutes of champagne were delivered to each guest.

"While we wait for our first course, I want to thank you for coming aboard and agreeing to have dinner with me." Baptiste raised a glass to his guests. "I'd also like to welcome Gael and Kailani to the party and appreciate all they have done for me. And especially, what I need you to do next." Gael smiled uncomfortably, apparently unaware of what this may be. Kailani stared coolly at Pierre.

Lukas, seated next to his husband, leaned over and discreetly spoke to Taylor. "I have a weird feeling about this. Feels random, but very staged."

Taylor nodded in agreement. "Maybe it's a billionaire thing. World revolves around him so he's showing us his toys."

"Impressive toys." Lukas chuckled nervously as he caught a glimpse of his mother whose placid face masked something. He'd seen that look many times. Was it surprise, fear, or some other emotion she intentionally tried to hide? He still could not discern her simple boredom with something or whether she was absolutely furious. Something was going on and his mother sensed it, too.

****

Lively chatter filled the salon as several conversations went on at once. A well-known chef had whipped up a four-course masterpiece they enjoyed immensely. A simple sorbet, made from native kelp, filled silver bowls ceremoniously placed before each guest.

"That was a delicious dinner, Pierre," Lukas complimented his host.

"I hire only the best chefs in the world, often from Michelin-star restaurants. I pay them handsomely, as you can imagine."

Molly subtly rolled her eyes before wait staff rapidly collected the fine china they had used. Crumbs swept into receptacles and napkins refolded, water glasses refilled. It was like a fine restaurant, each move coordinated and choreographed.

Baptiste interrupted the casual conversation by clinking a glass with his spoon. The soft rumbling of voices drifted off until there was silence. Pierre sat alone at the head of the table as he waited for his guests' attention to be focused on him.

"Thank you for joining me on my floating home. I hope dinner was to your liking."

"It was wonderful, Pierre," Linda responded as heads nodded in agreement.

"It's getting late, and we should be returning back to shore soon," Betty added. "I have an early yoga class I want to attend."

Baptiste smiled. "I have something I want to show you first. It's a prelude to my current project."

The salon lights suddenly dimmed and a large cube, completely transparent, emerged from the room's floor. It was not a television, but a cube made of four sides of a rigid, transparent film. It glowed a light blue and appeared to be hovering above the table. The salon was suddenly flooded with color. Marcel stirred and grunted, unphased by the interruption to his nap. Within seconds, the salon's walls and ceiling seemingly disappeared. Wild colors, flashes of light and swirling colorful graphics created an alternate reality where Pierre's salon disappeared.

Lukas felt vaguely sick to his stomach.

"Close your eyes," Taylor told him. "It's only an illusion, but your eyes think it's real."

"Great, virtual motion sickness." Lukas closed his eyes as Taylor instructed and he began to lose the sense of vertigo. The lights dimmed and suddenly, the salon's ceiling morphed into the night sky. Stars, constellations, and planets twinkled against the blackness. A crescent moon hovered in the sky. Somehow, they were surrounded by a virtual sea that rocked beneath the twinkling black sky. The room dramatically morphed into what felt like the inside of a volcano. Virtual magma bubbled in the distance. Taylor wondered what happened to the priceless art on the walls, as the walls were replaced by sheets of lava pouring from the ceiling and down the walls, puddling onto the floor. The visual effect showed the molten lava enveloping virtual stone pillars, and primitive relics were swallowed by a sea of oozing orange. *If Hell is real, this is what it must look like*, Taylor thought.

Linda reflexively lifted her feet off the bubbling floor hologram. The program was choreographed to resemble the destruction of an ancient city, completely engulfed in magma. The visual simulation started to darken, representing the cooling of blackened underwater lava. The visual realism of the holographic images left the guests with open mouths and wide eyes. Computer-generated sea life now swam between them, as if the entire salon was now underwater. Holographic fish and sea life appeared to float in front of the guests' eyes. Molly grabbed at one of the fish, only to swipe at a mirage. A large tiger shark bared its teeth as it rushed toward Betty, who instinctively covered her head beneath her arms. The three-dimensional images were so realistic it was disconcerting—especially when the sharks and moray eels floated among them.

Next, the coffered ceiling appeared to change into a giant glass dome, from which they appeared to be underwater looking upward toward the surface. Silhouettes of whales and large sharks appeared to swim overhead. The dazzling display, made realistic by CGI and holographic technology, captivated the audience.

"Shit, that's unbelievable," Taylor called to Lukas as he watched the incredulous expressions on the faces around their table. A vibrant coral reef materialized next, teeming with brightly-colored fish and a moray eel so realistic some guests sat on their hands as it slithered between virtual cubby holes it called home.

"It feels like we actually went underwater," Betty exclaimed.

"This is so amazing," Linda added, "I have goosebumps."

Baptiste beamed as the choreographed graphic display captivated his guests. The details were so intricate and realistic, even the CGI fish had scars and other injuries that made them look authentic. The underwater scene then morphed into a vast subsurface plateau. Tiny underwater volcanoes spewed bubbles that reached for the surface. In the fast-moving film these grew into massive cones that peaked above the ocean waves and gradually became lush, tropical islands. Ahead of them lay a virtual deep-sea trench that plunged into blackened depths. The editing of the three-dimensional projection rivaled a Hollywood blockbuster in terms of realism and drama. In the distance, all they could see was murky blue ocean.

"It's the birth of a chain of islands," Taylor whispered to Lukas.

"It'll be prime island real estate in a couple million years." Lukas smiled.

"Baptiste is probably waiting for that to happen."

"How do you do this, Pierre?" Linda asked, entranced by the technology that created such realism.

"An upgrade I added for my personal enjoyment, and I wanted to share it with you. It's basically a wild combination of digital film projectors, holograms, surround-sound, LED technology, lasers, computer-generated imaging, and the best cinematographers money can buy."

"It's spectacular," Betty exclaimed. "Like I've experienced those images in real life."

"Your brain may agree with you," Pierre replied. "This technology has physiological impacts like your body experienced the real thing…adrenaline, cortisol…your balance."

"So why are you showing us this?" Molly said with an impatient edge to her voice.

"Consider it a prelude to my current project I wanted to share with you," Pierre replied. "I have searched for years, and I believe I've found something so big, so transformational it could rewrite our history and shatter many things we have always assumed true."

The guests hung in anticipation, waiting for Pierre to reveal his discovery.

"What would you say if I told you that human beings may have originated from a place that nobody knows about and those that do, never discuss it? That many of civilization's great stories and legends had their origins in a landmass known as Zealandia."

"Zealandia?" Molly clarified. "I thought that was only a myth."

"And where is this landmass, as you call it?" Lukas asked.

The floating film glowed with a video that depicted the word *Zealandia* sank beneath the waves.

Taylor rubbed his temples. "I'm confused. What exactly is Zealandia?"

"I'm going to explain that to you all, ladies and

gentlemen," Baptiste replied. "The fun stuff is just beginning."

The floating screen turned fiery red, animated with volcanic explosions and magma forming thick rivers of glowing hot lava. Lukas focused on the title of the film.

Zealandia - The Lost Continent.

Chapter 8

Elaborate holograms, brilliant colors, and animation left Pierre's guests feeling like they had experienced a physical journey through an undersea world. Lukas pinched the bridge of his nose, his eyeglasses dangling in his other hand. "That was a bit overstimulating," Lukas said to Taylor. "That hologram experience gave me a headache and mild vertigo." The salon's ceiling was illuminated again like the night sky, with bright stars shining through a blackened sky.

"This is the same sky sailors navigated by for millennia," Pierre pondered. "Not much has changed. Same stars and same planets, even when the eighth continent flourished."

"Were the Zealandians, if that's what they're called, a seafaring people?"

"Not sure," Pierre answered. "I assume that if they were, they used the stars to navigate like mariners do to this day."

"Betty," Lukas asked. "You're the expert on stars and constellations. Would the night sky have looked similarly as it does currently?"

"Linda is the resident expert on the cosmos, not I," Betty stated, re-directing the question.

"Nothing we can be certain about, Lukas," Linda added. "We have no proof of what the sky looked like that far back. We're talking about at least five thousand years before the early Egyptians started recording history. A staggering amount of time has passed, but if I were to guess, I would say our solar system and galaxy are fundamentally the same."

"True, Linda," Pierre replied. "But I'm more curious about the celestial bodies outside our solar system."

"Curious how?" Linda asked.

"I believe Earth holds many secrets still yet to be discovered," Pierre told the group. "But how do we know what to look for? We have to start in the present day and look back in time, collecting clues and investigating what happened."

"What are we looking for?" Lukas asked.

"A map. An image. A chronicled history that helps us follow the breadcrumbs."

"Pierre, I'm not following you," Molly told him, the same edge to her voice. "What does this have to do with a lost city at the bottom of the Pacific Ocean?"

Pierre breathed deeply so he didn't emotionally respond to Molly's sarcastic undertone.

"Zealandia was not a city, my dear. It was a continent, a massive landmass that occupied much of what now lies beneath the Pacific Ocean. If it truly was the cradle of humanity, it likely took those secrets to the bottom of the sea."

Taylor jumped in. "I've never heard of anything like this in any of my ancient history studies. How did you learn about it?"

Pierre chuckled. "My billionaire peers are busy flying into outer space and designing civilizations on the moon. Very noble of them, but I'm more interested in learning about the planet we currently inhabit. Did you know that oceans cover about seventy percent of the earth, and that only five percent of the oceans have actually been explored?"

Heads shook in disbelief.

"We don't understand the planet upon which we live," Pierre pontificated. "How many secrets do our oceans hold?"

The group sat in silence, not sure whether to answer Baptiste's rhetorical question.

"I actually learned about Zealandia while I was searching for something else. I asked Gael and Kailani to visit with us tonight so they can explain this lost world from their culture's point of view."

Gael cleared his throat, not sure of where to start. He had a charming disposition between nervousness and confidence that made Lukas and Taylor want to see him succeed.

"Gael should be a model. He's absolutely gorgeous," Lukas whispered. "Not that I noticed or anything."

"Yeah, me neither," Taylor joked.

"What Mr. Baptiste has told you is accurate with our culture's legends of lost land swallowed by the sea," Gael began. "It is well-known history for us."

Betty asked, "I never heard about Zealandia when I lived in Asia. What can you tell us about it?"

"Well," Gael continued. "We were taught that Zealandia was the cradle of all people. It was the land of Eden, home of the gods and other stories from antiquity. Mr. Baptiste, can you show the image of the map?"

Captain Kepler lounged on a light-colored sofa, legs crossed and eyes hungrily focused on Gael and her

Purser, Marc Hammer. Lukas thought he saw her wink at the handsome masseur standing before them. An image appeared that displayed the western coasts of North and South America and Eastern Asia. A landmass slowly came into focus on the screen, filling much of the Pacific basin with a continent about half the size of Australia.

"That's Zealandia?" Lukas asked. "It's huge!"

"It is, Dr. Lukas," Gael replied formally. "Five million square kilometers in size."

Taylor gasped. "Was it part of Australia? I noticed that New Zealand is part of it."

"Zealandia actually broke off from Antarctica, not Australia," Pierre added. "Gondwana, the supercontinent that preceded Pangea, was the original landmass, so by studying soil and rock samples, we know how the continents split."

"And how does a continent sink?" Lukas asked.

Molly jumped in. "It doesn't, at least not all at one time. There are a number of things to consider, were this to be true. Like when did this landmass exist?"

"Estimates are that Zealandia began to sink close to seventy million years ago. I'll explain more about that later. I believe that the remaining chunks of the continent began to break off and sink as late as seven to ten thousand years ago. Maybe longer," Pierre jumped in.

"So humans would have been living on whatever remained of the continent then," Linda surmised.

Pierre nodded. "They most likely migrated slowly to what is now New Zealand, Fiji, Tonga, Vanuatu, and other islands in the vicinity."

"But don't forget the effects of the ice age," Molly

interrupted. "At roughly the same period, Earth was experiencing what we call the Ice Age in the northern hemisphere. That means a huge amount of Earth's water was tied up in glacial ice, and as we learned from Poseidon, the amount of water on earth has stayed relatively constant for millennia."

"So those glaciers would have drawn from the ocean water, so sea levels would have been lower than today?" Taylor asked.

"Significantly lower," Molly responded. "Ocean levels then were estimated to have been between five-hundred to eight-hundred feet lower than where they are currently."

"That's similar to the height of a large office tower," Lukas added.

"This would have dramatically shifted the landscape across the globe. Places like the Maldives would have been considerably higher relative to the sea level of the time. Imagine the Pacific islands today, larger and more plentiful. The Aleutian Islands provided an accessible land bridge from Asia to the Americas. The world looked very different back then," Molly concluded.

Linda jumped in. "And imagine how the deluge of water changed everything when the glaciers started to melt at the end of the Ice Age. Your beachfront tiki hut was suddenly hundreds of feet under water. To the people of that time who never knew the science and geography behind these dynamics, it must have felt totally unexpected and sudden."

"Like a punishment from the gods," Gael concluded.

"The melting ice would be coming from far away

in a different hemisphere," Taylor added.

"Even with all our modern technology, we still can't hold back the oceans," Molly commented. "It must have felt like the end of the world."

"That's what I added to the simulation." Pierre demonstrated, pointing to the map of Zealandia. He tapped the screen and added virtual water level changes in increments of thirty meters. "Look at what happens."

The Zealandian hills started to disappear as the virtual water filled in the mapped land. By the time Pierre had filled one hundred seventy meters of virtual water across the map, the result was surprising. What had been a contiguous landmass known as Zealandia now appeared as chains of islands.

"The South Pacific archipelago," Lukas pointed out, before he directed a question back to Gael and Kailani. "So what do your legends say about how Zealandia disappeared?"

Gael nodded at Kailani, who stood to speak. "The legends say that Zealandia was destroyed in a day," she told the group. "Waves swallowed the land as it sank into the ocean. Only people with boats were able to escape," Kailani concluded the story.

"How does a landmass sink so fast?" Betty asked. "That would have to be a dramatic catastrophic event."

"The short answer is that it didn't, like Molly said," Baptiste reminded them. "The sinking likely took place before there was a significant population of people. By the time humans arrived, the remaining bits of Zealandia were inhabited, but surrounded by peril."

"Unbridled seismic activity kept the place a hotspot of volcanic activity," Betty suggested. "Think of the folklore that developed. Volcanoes, rivers of fire, magma, great floods. It must have been a terrifying time to be alive. History and religions used stories like these to keep their people in line through fear."

"The ring of fire," Lukas commented.

"And one of those volcanoes could have been massive, like Vesuvius, right?" Molly theorized.

"Think bigger," Pierre countered.

"Technically, if Zealandia was the size Gael is talking about…" Linda paused, calculating something in her head. "It would take super volcanoes," Linda emphasized the plural, "at least three to have been interconnected, sharing a magma source, and collapsing at roughly the same time."

"So, Linda, you're suggesting it would take massive volcanic activity combined with rising sea levels to…" Lukas' thought was interrupted by Taylor.

"What is the structural integrity of a volcano?" he asked.

"I think it depends, but flowing lava would create hollow pockets we call lava tubes," Molly replied. "But it would be the caldera that would ultimately sink, leaving the remaining lava column still above the surface, like Mount Otemanu here on Bora Bora." Molly glanced at her watch. "Speaking of which we are probably overstaying our welcome."

"No, no," Baptiste waved his hand. "I'm fascinated by the conversation amongst such smart people."

"So to answer your question, Taylor," Molly continued. "Think of a volcano as having lots of air pockets inside it, lava tubes, gas pockets, things like that. Over time, the weight of the cone and everything on it like water, vegetation, and things, gets so heavy the structure collapses and creates a caldera, like Crater

Lake, for example."

"Who would like to join me for some expensive French cognac as a nightcap?" Pierre interrupted as he counted the raised hands and signaled to the wait staff to fetch the drinks.

"As you can imagine, gravity always wins and the honeycomb of lava rock starts to implode like a giant sinkhole, bringing everything down with it. Of course, all of this is hypothetical." Molly continued, "Gael, your legends say Zealandia disappeared in one day. Do you know of any records or drawings that detail this event?"

Gael shook his head. "Just the stories."

"So, no known record to prove anything, so this was information passed from one generation to the next," Molly continued. "I agree with Baptiste. It probably took thousands of years to actually occur. Even two centuries is a very long game of telephone, also known as folklore. I'm sure stories got bigger and more dramatic as time went on."

"Pierre," Lukas asked. "A lot of these themes sound familiar; a sunken civilization like Atlantis, a great flood that Noah experienced, rivers of fire from Hades. Do you see a connection?"

"I do, Lukas," Pierre answered. "We have no idea what kind of technology the Zealandian civilizations had, nor how the story of the sunken Pacific continent traveled all the way to the Mediterranean, India, and other parts of the world. Perhaps, Zealandia and Atlantis refer to the same historical and geological stories; one actual and one an allegory used in folklore."

"So which one do you believe is the actual?"

Taylor asked.

Pierre tapped his chin in thought. "Zealandia would have existed far before Atlantis, going by Plato's telling of the account. There's no way to know for certain unless we find something to prove either's existence."

Three waiters interrupted the discussion, balancing glasses of warm cognac on heated trays. They placed a glass in front of each guest. Pierre raised his glass, and the others followed.

Lukas stood to select a drink. He suddenly felt light-headed and appeared to lose his balance.

"You okay, babe?" Taylor asked.

Lukas nodded. "It felt like I was on an elevator for a second. Kind of wobbly."

"Even on large yachts like *Juventus*, we are still a mere speck in the mass of the ocean," Baptiste commented. "The value and power of water always amazes me."

Molly turned her head toward Pierre as she processed that comment. *Like the Poseidon technology*, she thought.

"To the legend of Zealandia and the treasures it may hold." Pierre Baptiste raised his glass for a toast. "May the world one day know its secrets."

Each guest took a sip of the cognac. Captain Kepler abstained. "I'm driving tonight," she joked. At the same time, she held Gael's gaze until he looked away. She smiled, triumphantly.

"Pierre, this is absolutely amazing," Lukas complimented him.

"Thank you, Lukas." He nodded. "And here's to you and your husband. May many fun adventures be in your future."

"To old friends and new friends." Pierre raised the glass toward Molly and the Herb Society.

"And absent friends," Taylor added.

Linda and Betty swished the cognac in their mouths. Linda smiled and sat back onto the sofa. Betty grimaced and offered the rest of her glass to anyone.

"Not a cognac fan, eh?" Pierre commented, as a waiter whispered something into his ear. Baptiste looked perplexed.

"It's a bit strong for me, but thank you," Betty replied.

"Tell me what you would like instead," he said to Betty. "I have a well-stocked liquor and wine cellar onboard *Juventus*. Just tell one of the attendants what you'd like. Fruit juice or anything else we have for you."

A waiter returned with a frosted glass of fruit juice. "Would you like some rum in this?"

Betty smiled and gestured she would take a pinch of rum.

****

After a second glass of cognac, the conversation moved to the plush sofas, where the guests were more relaxed, pliable, and informal. Lukas stretched out on his back, his head in Taylor's lap. Gael gently massaged his feet which sent waves of warmth up through Lukas' legs. Kailani worked on each of The Herb Society ladies while Taylor snored softly, still adjusting for jet lag.

Lukas stared at Gael working on his feet and lower legs, his buttoned shirt flopped open exposing his flawless skin and muscular chest as Gael looked up at him. He then moved to Lukas' temples, hair, and jawline, his eyes already closed and feeling like he was completely relaxed. Gael then approached his husband and started massaging Taylor's feet and legs. Lukas drifted deeper, his thoughts becoming more vivid and surreal. He felt like he was in a mildly psychedelic dream, his vision going in and out of focus, his limbs heavy. Erotic fantasies played through his mind. Taylor's arousal was evident as Lukas' head was cradled in his lap. He smiled that his husband was experiencing something similar, and he couldn't wait to get naked with him. It had been a wonderful night and Lukas hadn't felt so relaxed and happy in a long time. His mother, Linda, and Betty were already asleep. Gael squeezed himself next to Taylor and stroked Lukas' hair as he moved his head to rest on Taylor's chest. Lukas smiled and rolled on his side and began stroking Gael's hair, his own eyes droopy as he scanned the room. Marc Hammer watched intently at what was unfolding, as if a bacchanalian festival was underway and Lukas was the entertainment.

Pierre sat straight in his chair, observing what was transpiring with his sleepy, happy dinner guests. Lukas' vision blurred as he drifted in and out of lucidity. Every care he had was magically replaced by happy thoughts and well-being. Gael's head, tipped backward in a sleepy haze, now rested in Taylor's crotch. Taylor's arms draped over Gael's shoulders. Lukas struggled to focus, but the sight of his husband lounging suggestively with another man didn't bother him. He normally would react with jealousy or anger, but for some reason, all felt good.

Lukas felt two strong arms suddenly lift him from his armpits, someone else lifted his feet. He thought he was floating, but he was being carried, suspended between Marc Hammer and another sailor. *What was going on?* Lukas thought he felt hands paw his bare chest and stomach. He then caught a glimpse of Hammer and Aleks. The two men dropped him onto a soft bed, undressed him, and tucked Lukas beneath the sheets and left the cabin. Lukas' eyes darted as he searched for Taylor and a twinge of jealousy pinched him remembering the sight of Gael so close to his husband. But as quickly as it came, the envy vaporized and he was happy again.

Chapter 9

Bright sun radiated slivers of light throughout the stateroom where Lukas and Taylor slept, naked with cool white bed sheets wrapped around their limbs. Lukas opened a disoriented eye that searched the environment for something familiar. He had no recollection of where he was. His head pounded and the sunlight felt like a laser directed into his brain. He fought queasiness. Cotton-mouth reminded him of his overindulgence the night before, but he really didn't drink that much. Lukas had scattered visual memories from the previous night, but otherwise, he remembered nothing.

Lukas glanced over at Taylor, lying on his back, his forearm flopped over his eyes, his body uncovered and naked. Instinctively, he ran his hand over the injuries on his leg and arm, certain that he opened the wound during a night of partying. As he flopped the covers off his leg, he noticed taut, unblemished skin with no sign of injury. A quick check of his wounded arm also found no sign of injury. He pulled at his skin; there wasn't a mark anywhere. No scab or scar. The wound had vanished somehow. *Did I dream I had those cuts?* he thought. His short-term memory struggled to remember, but all he could recall were fuzzy snippets.

At the foot of the bed, the comforter was pulled and bunched into a small mountain of fluff and fabric.

Two feet that didn't belong to his husband stuck out from underneath the Egyptian cotton pile. *Who the fuck is that?* Lukas thought.

He rustled Taylor awake, while instinctively covering up his husband's privates with a blanket. Taylor stirred, his eyes fluttering open. His dry tongue tried to moisten his dry lips and Lukas could tell Taylor had the same cotton-mouth he had. Cotton-mouth, dehydrated from the prior evening. Taylor's eyes were wide with confusion and disorientation.

"Where are we?" he asked Lukas, before recoiling to a seated position after seeing the disembodied feet sticking out of the comforter mountain.

"Jesus, who is that?" Taylor exclaimed. "Why are we naked?"

"I don't know. I think we passed out and we're on Baptiste's ship," Lukas replied as he scrambled to the stateroom window, naked as the day he was born. Attempting to open the window shades, he searched for a control switch, found it, and opened the shades.

"What do you see?" Taylor asked.

"We're not at Bora Bora anymore, I can tell you that." Lukas noticed their bed mate's feet start to stir. "Shit, what did we do last night?"

A tattooed, muscled arm emerged from under the comforter before a dark-haired head was exposed as Lukas pulled back the sheets. "Oh fuck," was all he could say as he continued to expose their guest inch by inch. Lukas' stomach clenched when he revealed Gael, asleep on his stomach and like them, completely unclothed, his rhythmic breathing starting to quicken.

Taylor, mouth agape, sat in stunned silence. "I don't remember...anything," trying to recall. "Do you?"

"No, Taylor. Of course not." Lukas' heart sank as he shook his head. "We would have talked about this first, right? I mean, crap, it's our first…"

"Yeah." Taylor said bluntly. "On our fucking honeymoon."

Lukas combed his bed hair with his fingers like, trying to recall anything. "I remember he was giving us foot massages. I was lying in your lap…"

"And the back of his head was between your legs. You seemed to be enjoying yourself," Lukas retorted. Gael stirred. His eyes fluttered open as he studied the two naked men in front of him. He reached for his blue pearl necklace. It was missing and he jumped up, leapt out of bed, and frantically started to search through the sheets to find it, unaware of his bedmates. Taylor and Lukas watched him, half asleep, on a search mission and like them, completely naked. Not finding the necklace, Gael snapped into consciousness, and realized he and his two clients were gawking at each other. Gael's face twisted in confusion. "What is going on? What am I doing in here? Where is Kailani?" he asked in a panic, his chiseled, handsome face drawn and haggard.

"We woke up right before you," Lukas answered. "We're trying to figure everything out, too. Do you remember how you got," he paused uncomfortably, "into our bed? Where are our clothes?"

Gael's eyes wildly darted around the room. The bed and the naked men were the last of his concerns at the moment. "I've got to find my pearl."

"I feel like I was drugged," Taylor commented.

Lukas sympathized. "Seriously, babe…I'm as

confused as you are."

Gael continued to search the bed and pulled out the leather strip that held his blue pearl. He held it out. "It's been cut." Taylor reached for one of the blankets to cover himself up as Lukas walked stark naked toward the stateroom closet in search of clothes. He angrily threw open the closet doors and searched for his underwear at the very least. Three robes, emblazoned with a logo indicating Baptiste's company, hung from satin hangers. Three sets of slip-on sandals sat on the closet floor.

"Where are our clothes?" Lukas demanded. His brain was in overdrive as he paced the stateroom talking to himself. The naked problem solver jumped into action.

"Lukas," Taylor called to his husband, "the wound on your leg is gone."

"Yeah, I know. I thought maybe I dreamt it."

"Check your arm," Taylor called out to him as Lukas replied he already had. No trace of any cut, gash, or wound was there either.

"That's really weird," Taylor remembered. "It was bleeding pretty heavily so it was deep." Taylor walked toward the small dresser, his bed sheet wrapped around him, following behind like a royal robe or bridal train. Still no clothes.

"Nothing in here," he said as he opened and closed the dresser drawers. "Shit. What the hell is going on?"

Gael rubbed the back of his neck, habitually searching for his phantom necklace.

"Good morning, sleepy-heads," a French-accented voice announced through the speakers. "Please meet us in my salon. An attendant will be with you shortly." It was Pierre Baptiste's voice. "And I see you've found your robes. It's up to you if you want to wear them."

"We're being recorded," Gael stated.

"Probably video and audio," Taylor commented. "He's been watching us."

Lukas dropped his face into his hands. "I don't even want to know…"

Pierre's disembodied voice interrupted. "We're in international waters, Lukas, but I'll personally make sure you get proceeds from any video that goes viral." He laughed at his own sick joke. Lukas whipped around, not sure where the camera was hidden. He was furious.

"Of course, I'm only joking," Pierre cooed. "I've known you since you were a toddler." He stopped mid-statement. "Forgive me. That didn't come out correctly. I'll personally see to it that all video on board is wiped. Unless someone intentionally saves it without my knowledge."

A knock echoed off the cabin door. "Your escort is here," Pierre sang. "See you boys in a few minutes."

The three men hastily threw the robes on and slipped their feet into the sandals.

"This is fucking ridiculous," Taylor whispered.

They heard the door unlatch and slowly open. Marc Hammer and Aleks stood there, arms crossed, waiting for the men. Dressed in the yacht's uniforms, the men brusquely escorted Lukas, Taylor, and Gael out of their stateroom. Lukas noticed a judgmental smirk on Aleks's face as they guided the three of them toward Baptiste's salon. When they entered, bright sun shone down through the massive skylight spanning most of the ceiling. Betty and Molly wore similar robes. Each of them appeared confused and agitated. Lukas noticed his mother's facial expression and felt a twist in his stomach. He knew that look on his mother's face. She was furious.

Betty Bao was the first to acknowledge their arrival. "I can see Jacques Cousteau took your clothes, too," she sarcastically welcomed them.

"My head is pounding," Linda commented. "What did we drink last night?"

Gael cursed something in a language no one recognized, his face etched with anger.

The thin-film projection cube appeared again, now hovering in front of the seating area where they currently were. Like the night before, the screen glowed a rich turquoise color before a face appeared. It was the cartoon-like face of what appeared to be a Roman or Greek god. The voice was that of Pierre Baptiste.

"Hello, dear friends," he welcomed them. "I hope you all had an enjoyable evening. That cognac was one hundred years old."

"How old was the sedative you laced it with?" Molly spat. "We want to get off this boat."

Baptiste chuckled sarcastically. "I'm afraid that isn't possible at the moment. And there was something in your drink, but it was not a sedative."

Molly growled, not sure where to begin. "You're holding us against our will. You've taken our clothes, phones, and documents. What did you drug us with?"

Baptiste's avatar held up its hand. "No more questions for the moment. I need to tell you all what is happening."

"Why do I feel I'm not gonna like this?" Lukas said, as Taylor reached for his hand. Lukas was crestfallen as he reflected on the morning events. Guilt crept over him knowing he had been extremely attracted to Gael but horrified that he potentially acted on it. His stomach was in knots, and he wondered what Taylor was thinking.

Baptiste confirmed they had been drugged, but there was no clarity as to what laced their cognacs. Both he and Taylor had found Gael extremely attractive, but he felt sullied, and with Pierre's admission, all of them had been drugged with something. Having a three-way on his honeymoon wasn't something he'd ever planned, especially this early in their relationship. They hadn't even talked about it. Lukas' stomach flipped with guilt and anger. He felt violated in a way he couldn't articulate. *Maybe nothing happened and we just went to sleep*, he tried to comfort his racing mind.

"First things first," Pierre announced. "I have booked spa appointments for each of you. Gael and Kailani will assist you with the times. It's something you should experience. It will give you something to do in the meantime. I insist upon it."

Taylor and Lukas looked at each other in confusion, not knowing what Baptiste meant.

"Last night, I told you about the lost continent of Zealandia," Pierre began. "Today, we are approaching the eighth continent's edge, which I believe is part of the land that was consumed by the ocean."

"Where are we, Pierre?" Linda asked pointedly. "I looked out the window and saw some other island that isn't Bora Bora."

"That is correct, Linda. We are no longer in French Polynesia," Pierre replied. "We have changed our position because there's something more to the story of Zealandia."

"So where are we, then?" Taylor asked.

Pierre ignored Taylor's question. "One of our research ships has found ruins submerged about forty-five meters below the surface of the ocean. There are stone carvings, possibly glyphs that could be related to some other ruins we believe were also from Zealandia."

"When did you become an archaeologist, Pierre?" Molly sneered.

Pierre's face curled with a mischievous grin. "I'm not an archaeologist, Molly. It's not the ruins that interest me. It's what they are made of."

"I have no idea what you're talking about," Betty commented. "Stone, Pierre. They are made from stone like most ruins."

"Bridge!" he barked. "Run the visuals on the ruins."

The transparent screen fluttered from Pierre's face to an underwater scene. Divers swam around what looked like a sunken altar, their bubbles rising rapidly to the surface.

"Oh good," Baptiste commented. "Looks like it's not too deep."

"Thirty-five meters, sir. The divers have not descended past twenty-six meters," Captain Kepler's voice replied over the speakers.

"One hundred twenty feet is close to a diver's limit," Lukas calculated. "The ruins look relatively intact, considering their age, but why are we looking at these?"

Gael glared at the images on screen. His jaw clenched, he said nothing. Molly noticed the shift in

Gael's deportment. "What is it, Gael?"

"I know this place."

Taylor studied the unique color of some of the ruins. The material was smooth, like marble or porcelain. In the flickering light beneath the waves, the material appeared to be luminescent and slightly blue-green in color. He noticed Gael reach for his absent pearl, discreetly lowering his hand when he remembered the pearl was missing.

"That material glows slightly, like your pearl did when we boarded *Juventus*," Lukas remembered. Gael remained uncomfortably stoic.

"Gael," Baptiste interrupted. "Would you like to give a brief explanation for what we have found?"

Gael, his eyes cast downward, took in a deep breath. "We have found ruins from an ancient city that once stood. *Pierre de lune* is what we call the material. *Moonstone* is the English translation. It is specific to this archipelago. It is nowhere else on earth."

"How is this material related to the blue pearls?" Lukas asked.

"The pearls we wear are special and come from oysters in this region. Much of the moonstone exists in solid form, like stone or rocks. But some has been reduced to sand. It's this sand that becomes part of the pearl."

"I've never heard of a material with that name. What kind of stone is it?" Molly asked, still furious at her captivity.

"I'll get to that shortly, Molly," Pierre added.

"We have always kept this a secret, until Mr. Baptiste learned of it," Gael added. "All we know is that it only comes from our islands."

Molly processed Baptiste's chess moves. *He knows exactly what he's doing, the prick,* she thought.

She approached the screen that now projected Pierre Baptiste's face. Molly knew she needed to keep her cool as Baptiste loved it when he got under someone's skin.

"Pierre," she asked calmly. "Where have you taken us?"

Pierre shook his head. "No, no, no. You'll ruin the surprise."

Molly maintained her composure, and Lukas could see she was about to erupt

"My dear," Baptiste attempted to reassure her. "I promise you and your friends are safe as can be."

"They're not my friends, Baptiste. They're my family," she calmly clarified.

"Point taken," Pierre mocked. "I can assure you that we are on the precipice of an exciting discovery, and I want you all to be part of it."

"How long will we be at sea?" Lukas asked. "Taylor would like to get back to see his daughter."

Pierre looked visibly confused by Lukas' comment. He switched off the video part of the screen and only communicated by audio. "I wasn't aware you had more in your party. My apologies."

"I don't think we're going back," Taylor muttered under his breath.

"We've had to travel some distance, I'm afraid," Pierre attempted to soothe them. "You all slept for two days, so you must be hungry."

Molly's face burned red. "Two days? Where the hell are we, Baptiste?"

"It's a massive ocean," Baptiste said. "And as I

told you, *Juventus* is the fastest passenger vessel ever built, so we were able to travel quite far."

Taylor, frustrated that he could not communicate with his daughter, stormed toward the screen that displayed Baptiste's smug avatar-face. "You're a businessman, a visionary of new technology. Why are you chasing lost continents and, more importantly, why are we involved?"

"Taylor, do you actually think I would put you in harm's way?" Baptiste asked. "Quite the opposite really."

"So why are we even here? Are you giving us the official word that we've been kidnapped?" Lukas asked, visibly irritated.

Pierre's disembodied voice paused. "So, Lukas," Pierre asked calmly. "How are those nasty gashes on your leg and arm doing today?"

Lukas paused, surprised by the question. "They're gone."

Baptiste nodded confidently. "Yes, they are indeed."

"Stop avoiding our questions, Baptiste!" Molly shouted.

"My question to Lukas is pertinent to our destination," Baptiste replied calmly. "Lukas, as you slept, your wounds were treated with moonstone."

Molly stormed toward the transparent screen displaying Pierre's smug face. "I demand to know where we are!"

Pierre feigned indignity. "Molly, there is no need to make demands. As you wish, I'll show you where we are."

Lukas shook his head. "What did you mean about

my injuries? How did they disappear?"

Suddenly, the walls and the ceiling of the salon changed color, the lights dimming briefly as a new image came into focus. The guests gasped as the room's walls and ceiling transformed to deep shades of shimmering blues and greens. Before them were the ruins they had just seen on the screen.

"Thanks for the aquarium projection, Pierre. I'd rather know where we are than enjoy another one of your performances," Molly said.

Taylor put his hand on Lukas' shoulder. "What's that?"

In front of them stood a series of light-colored mounds of boulders resting on the seafloor. They looked vaguely out of place against the relative flatness of the ocean plateau surrounding them. One of the mounds was especially large, like a giant ball buried half-way in the sand. Except this ball looked to be fifty feet high. Tiny figures propelled themselves with small sea scooters while chipping blocks of the stone away and dropping them into their baskets.

"What are the divers doing?" Taylor asked Baptiste.

"They work for me," Pierre responded flatly. "They are collecting more moonstone to bring back to the ship."

Lukas pointed to another object approaching them. "That looks like one of the mini-subs we saw in dry dock."

"How do you get a video like this under water?" Linda asked.

"It's not a video, Linda," Baptiste stated proudly. "You are looking at *Jeune 1* returning to *Juventus* after a mission."

Molly approached for a closer look, her mouth agape as realization collided with her reality. "It can't be…"

Pierre chuckled. "I assure you it can and is." Pierre watched as each of his guests came to the same realization. They were watching this live. The pixelated room that entertained them with the story of Zealandia now transformed into a massive clear observation bubble.

Lukas' eyes widened when he realized what was happening. "How do you do this?"

"Another proprietary technology I'm testing," Baptiste bragged. "It's based upon virtual and augmented reality. Much of what you've all experienced since being on board has not been real, but a compilation collected by digital cameras surrounding every property I own, including *Juventus*."

"So how much of the last day has been real?" Molly asked.

"All of it has been real. Real conversations, real food, real people. The art collection you saw was actually a hologram of the gallery in my home on Kiva Oa."

"How are you getting images of us positioned underwater? The perspective looks like we are at the same level as the divers and sea mounds."

A wicked smile curled on Baptiste's lips. "That's because we actually are in that position, so the perspective is correct. We are underwater."

A light bulb went off in Taylor's mind. "That can't be possible."

Baptiste chuckled because nobody had figured it

out until now. "Surprise," Baptiste snickered sarcastically. "We are resting more than one hundred feet below the surface of the Pacific Ocean."

"How did you do…?" Molly didn't finish her thought as she was speechless.

Pierre chuckled. "*Juventus* is more than the most highly advanced mega-yacht in the world. She's also the fastest, most luxurious submarine ever built."

Chapter 10

Tory lay in bed, her arm extended, as she surveyed the diamond engagement ring sparkling in the early morning sunbeams filtering through their windows. Her new fiancé was sleeping gently next to her, his arm unconsciously flopped over her abdomen. She smiled as she watched the gentle rise and fall of his muscled back. Pepe was the man she wanted to be with for the rest of her life. She gently pried Pepe's arm off of her and stood up to put on a robe. Like Pepe, she was naked having fallen asleep after a furious round of lovemaking the night before. Tory had always been attracted to men from other countries or cultures. It was something about their passion for life, independence, and confidence that attracted her. Giuseppe, whom she nicknamed Pepe, was no different. Born in a small mountain village in Italy, he had all of the above, plus a great sense of style, a sarcastic sense of humor, an athletic toned body, and a smile she found irresistible.

She couldn't wait to tell her dad Taylor about her big news, even though she knew Pepe asked for his permission to propose while they snorkeled. She had to explain to Pepe that's what was expected of American men, to ask a woman's father for her hand. Pepe thought it was archaic, arguing that she wasn't a piece of property. He believed any woman should make her own decisions. Tory begged him to do it anyway and he complied. Taylor told him he thought it was a ridiculously archaic tradition, as well, and the two men bonded over how strong of a person Tory was. For Tory, she wanted everything to be perfect. Her last serious relationship ended in a surprising, humiliating manner. She didn't want to leave anything to chance.

She and Pepe showered, distracted again, and delayed by another sexual romp. They dressed and got ready to head to breakfast to meet with her dad and Lukas. She called him on her mobile to let him know she'd be a few minutes late. The call went immediately to voicemail, so she texted him and awaited his response. Since Tory was old enough to have her own phone, Taylor always made sure that he was available by text. Even his fleet of jets had Wi-Fi so that texting would work even at cruising altitudes.

"They are probably at breakfast," Pepe told Tory. "Let's go meet them."

When they arrived at the breakfast place, they noticed Donna and Wilma sitting alone at a table, quietly chatting. Donna immediately waved when she saw the couple.

"Hey, sleepyheads!" Donna smiled. "How was your evening?"

Tory held out her hand to display her engagement ring. Neither Wilma nor Donna had any knowledge of Pepe's impending proposal and were truly shocked.

"Girl, you are gonna be a beautiful bride," Wilma told her. "Have you guys set a date?"

Tory shook her head. "Haven't yet. Still getting my head around being a future wife to this sexy Italian dude."

"You both make an adorable couple," Donna told

them. "I'm so happy for you."

"Have either of you seen my dads?" she asked them, referring to both Taylor and Lukas as her dads, despite growing up as a daughter of single-parent Taylor. Tory was so happy for Taylor finding Lukas and she told both of them that she was changing her last name to Pastore-Halloran, just like Taylor did.

"I belong to both of you now," she teased them. "So you better stick together if you don't want a custody battle."

Taylor thought it was cute, but Lukas knew Tory was serious. She once told him that she wanted two parents, and her future children wanted both grandparents. "I've got it all figured out, so don't screw it up," she told them continuously.

Tory tried to call her dad. Again, it went directly to his voicemail. *That's odd*, she thought. "Do you ladies mind if we join you?" she asked Donna and Wilma.

"Of course not," Wilma replied as she massaged sunscreen onto her face. "Black skin burns, too. I also don't want to age before my time."

"I don't think you have anything to worry about there," Pepe complimented her. "Each of the Herb Society women looks about twenty years younger than you actually are."

"Who told you my age?" Wilma teased back. "Maybe I'm only thirty-five."

"I'd believe it if you told me that." Pepe winked.

"Just so you know, we have a tennis court reserved in thirty minutes, so we'll bug out before that," Donna announced.

"You ladies are active. Always doing something." Pepe observed. "I admire your energy."

"Wilma used to be a women's basketball coach," Donna explained. "Now she holds fitness classes and does personal training for the old ladies where we live."

After exchanging pleasantries and each other's plans for the day, Donna and Wilma excused themselves to head to the tennis court. Pepe observed that Tory seemed preoccupied and reached for her hand. "*Stai bene, cara?*" Tory glanced at her handsome fiancé and smiled. She loved when he spoke affectionate Italian to her.

"I'm fine, babe. Just find it weird that I can't find my dads. I was so excited to tell them."

Pepe gazed at her. His eyes sparkled when he smiled. His face exuded confidence and compassion. She loved that he was so laid back and good in his own skin. *I can't believe he's mine,* she often thought.

"*Cara*, they will still be excited. Maybe they're out snorkeling again," he reassured her. "We can walk by their bungalow after breakfast, yes?"

Tory smiled and nodded, still too shy to try out her fledgling Italian skills. "*Grazie.*"

After breakfast, they wandered the palm-lined path that led to the overwater bungalows, and soon stopped at her dads' place. Tory approached the door and knocked a few times. Nobody answered. She then pushed a doorbell, and again, no answer. As they turned to walk away, she heard the door open and turned around. Standing in the door was a San Rafael housekeeper smiling back. "*La Orana,*" she seemed to sing the Tahitian greeting. "May I help you?"

"I was just looking for my dads," Tory explained to her. "I'll come back later."

"Oh, your fathers checked out of this bungalow last

night."

Pepe and Tory stood in surprise. "Did they move to another bungalow?" Tory asked.

"I'm sorry, but I do not know. You can ask the reception. *La Orana*," she said as she closed the door to Taylor and Lukas' former bungalow.

Pepe held Tory's hand as they walked down the path that connected the overwater villas with the rest of the San Rafael property. They stopped to watch birds play in the swaying coconut palms and then watched as a school of stingrays swam under a bridge they crossed.

"I could live here," Pepe stated. "It's like a paradise."

Tory smiled faintly, preoccupied by why her dads had checked out and didn't tell her. When they entered the reception area of the San Rafael, they were given a refreshing fruit juice. Lazy ceiling fans turned slowly above, just enough to circulate the air. She approached the front desk. "Hi, I'm looking for my fathers. They were staying in bungalow 22W, and I went to visit them, and the housekeeper told me they moved."

The front desk clerk searched her computer for records.

"I see them here. Mr. Taylor and Mr. Lukas Pastore-Halloran, right?"

A sense of relief washed over Tory. "Yes, that's them."

"Hmm. They checked out this morning and their bill has been paid in full."

Tory's eyes popped with surprise. "You mean they left the hotel?"

"It appears so. Their luggage was transferred to a private boat, compliments of the CEO of San Rafael

Hotels."

Tory shook her head. "He wouldn't have checked out without telling me. Did they take your yacht shuttle back to the airport?"

More computer typing. "I have no record of them taking the yacht shuttle."

Tory continued to check the status of the other guests in their party. "Mrs. Halloran checked out this morning. Linda Eastman and Betty Bao also checked out this morning." The clerk paused. "That's strange. They all checked out at the same time—2:58 a.m. local time."

"What?" Tory exclaimed. "That's not something they would do without telling us. We all flew here together…"

Pepe picked up her thought. "The *Goose*! We need to see if the jet is still at the airport, and if they flew away on it, that opens up another load of questions."

"How soon can we get the shuttle to the airport?" Tory asked the agent, who was rattled by the news and tried to make sense of what was going on.

"I'm holding it for you now. It's right outside. Hurry, they'll bring you back, too."

****

Thirty minutes later, the San Rafael's yacht shuttle pulled into the dock slip for Bora Bora airport. There were a number of private jets parked on the tarmac, so Tory and Pepe ran off the yacht and started searching for her dads' plane. Within a few minutes, they found the Spectrum 7 business jet they affectionately called the *Goose 2*. Its sleek body and pearlescent paint job reflected a blinding burst of sunlight that made it stand out from the other jets.

"At least we know they didn't leave the island. But where would they go if they checked out of our hotel already?"

The departure horn bellowed from the San Rafael yacht, so they ran toward it and jumped aboard just as it was pulling away with a load of new hotel guests.

"I wonder where they could be?" Tory asked Pepe, who was deep in thought.

"Maybe they left the island another way," Pepe pointed out. Pepe had served his compulsory military service in his early twenties. He opted to join the *Guardia Costiera*, the Italian coast guard, and served for three years, mostly assisting with immigrant rescues in the Mediterranean and Adriatic seas. He had basic knowledge of flying a helicopter, performing helicopter rescues, and piloting rescue boats, so he had another theory. "Perhaps they left by ship."

Tory shook her head. "He would have told me."

"*Si, cara.* You're right. Your father knew I was going to propose to you last night so he wouldn't have left. He told me the night before that they'd meet us for breakfast. He and Lukas wanted to see your ring and congratulate us. It just doesn't make sense!"

"So you think they rented a boat, Pepe?"

"No." Pepe scratched his head. "But I wonder if someone who had a boat took them without telling anyone."

Chapter 11

Lukas paced the floor of the salon, occasionally glancing briefly at the panoramic view surrounding *Juventus*. While he was intrigued by mounds of shimmering moonstone, he struggled to avoid the panic attack that was erupting to the surface. Realizing he was trapped underwater, his claustrophobia was kicking into high gear. Taylor noticed beads of sweat on Lukas' forehead and he knew what was happening as he watched his husband flop into a sofa, his knees drawn, curled into a ball. Taylor sat beside him and gently rubbed Lukas' back.

"Just breathe, babe," Taylor instructed Lukas. "Focus on your breath. Remember, this feeling always passes." Lukas struggled to regain control of his breathing, his eyes squeezed shut as his body reacted to a phantom terror that threw him into a panic attack. Lukas' mind struggled as one side of his brain went into panic and the other side struggled to calm him. His claustrophobia, or as he called it, situational claustrophobia, was something he'd struggled with most of his life. He could ride in an elevator or fly in a plane for fifteen hours and be fine. It wasn't about the size of the space; it was the situation that tipped him over the edge. His biggest fear was being trapped underwater, and now he was living it. Lukas knew the panic would pass. He had to logically talk himself through the irrational fear that gripped him. The question was when his nerves came somewhat back to normal. Taylor was a calming force for him and kept physical contact as he rode out the cycle. Inside Lukas' brain, extreme analytical logic clashed with vividly imagined death and disaster scenarios.

This will pass. I'm feeling calm. Hold it together, Lukas, he kept reassuring himself

Suddenly, the pixelated walls and ceiling reverted back to their original display, which instantly started to reduce Lukas' anxiety. Molly Halloran angrily called out to Pierre Baptiste.

"Enough of the games, Baptiste. Why the hell have you brought us into this?"

Pierre dismissed her emotion. "You think I'm really interested in a lost continent and whatever the hell happened to it?" He pointed and glared at Gael. "That may be his motivation, but it's not mine. You should know me better than that."

"So what's your motivation?" Lukas asked Gael.

Gael glared at Pierre's on-screen avatar. "My interest is learning more about my culture and my ancestors." Gael tried to sound convincing. "Zealandia is part of who I am. Kailani, too. Mr. Baptiste told us he was searching for it, and he asked us to help." Gael then remained silent. His stoic face showed a twinge of anger.

"That sounds like bullshit to me," Linda shouted. "None of·us are archaeologists, so why do you need us and not oceanographers who have knowledge of this Zealandia place?"

Betty was equally frustrated at Baptiste's passive-aggressive demeanor, and now Gael. She walked over to Gael, with her finger pointed at him. "Stop with the bullshit, Gael. You can drop the *learning my cultural history* crap. You're in this for another reason."

Baptiste chuckled and nodded sympathetically at their confusion. "I like you, Betty. You're quite direct."

"Why are you talking through a monitor and not in person?" Betty questioned him. "You're like a stupid old Bond villain. You're a coward."

"Ouch! But it is one of my favorite movie franchises," Pierre responded blithely. "I will be there, in person, for dinner. I'm having some work done. We can talk more about the project then."

Baptiste's avatar disappeared and the thin-film screen retracted back into the ceiling.

"Bastard!" Betty cursed. "Nice business associates you got there, Molly."

****

Several hours later, Pierre lay in a private spa room. Kailani worked a cream into his facial skin while Gael looked on. Hanging on the wall was a framed black and white photograph displaying a scene of two young men, probably in their late twenties, horseplaying on the beach. Baptiste smiled at the memory and remembered when the photo was taken. A much younger Pierre Baptiste, frozen in time, youthful beauty and strength radiating from his handsome Mediterranean face. He had just started to build his business empire and had his whole life ahead of him. The other man, Gael, looked exactly like he looked currently. Perfect skin, body, and muscle tone, like an ageless Polynesian god.

"It's been ages since we first met," Pierre whispered to Gael. "You're still the same beautiful man

I met on the beach almost fifty years ago, and you haven't changed a bit."

Gael smiled, knowing he could not say the same thing back. Not yet at least.

"I've loved you ever since that day. Thank you for everything you've done for me," Gael said, his eyes twinkling.

"I'm just a rich old man who would sell his kingdom to look young again." Baptiste sighed.

"I love you the way you are," Gael insisted. "It doesn't matter to me.

"Well, it matters to me. I want to be young like you," Baptiste replied.

"I'm not young, I just look young." Gael smiled back.

"You're young where it counts," Pierre said playfully. "How are you feeling about all of this?"

"Kailani and I will work on your guests in the spa, so they will see the effects by dinner and then we'll present the new you."

"My extreme makeover," Pierre commented.

"They will see your new look and will want to know more."

"And I plan to tell them more," Pierre answered him. "Everything. Well, just about."

"I'm worried we won't have enough for the islanders," Gael lamented. "Have you learned how to make more?"

"Not quite yet but getting there," Baptiste answered as he started to pull off his clothes to prepare for the procedure. "Why do you keep asking me?"

"Because of the guilt and shame I feel," Gael explained. "My people depend upon moonstone. I sometimes wish I never mentioned it."

Baptiste reached down and took Gael's concerned face in his hands. "Your secret is safe with me. And don't worry. I'll still make you one of the richest men in the Pacific."

****

Below deck, Molly, Linda, and Betty stretched back in plush treatment chairs. Across from them, Lukas and Taylor sat in their chairs. Nobody knew what to expect. Baptiste wasn't kidding when he said he insisted upon them using the spa. Each one had been escorted to the treatment rooms and awaited what was next.

Gael and Kailani stood, each wearing native clothing. Gael was naked from the waist up, his lower half covered in a traditional *lava-lava* or *pa'u'* depending on which language was used to describe it. Lukas noticed his blue pearl, apparently found, hung around his neck. He felt intimidated by Gael's beauty and youth. Lukas also couldn't get the picture out of his mind of Gael and Taylor sleeping together on the sofa while they sipped cognac.

Kailani wore the female version draped across her body. The spa lights had been dimmed and soft music played in the background. They heard occasional rain showers that sounded so realistic, they believed they were truly outside.

"We will now start your treatments," Kailani announced quietly as she and Gael placed cucumber slices over each of their eyes. "Today, we will be working on your shoulders, neck, and head."

"Please try and relax. We will start with your shoulders," Gael informed them.

Behind all five of them, Gael and Kailani massaged their shoulders and upper arms. Muscles were tense due to Baptiste's cat and mouse game and leaving their whereabouts a mystery. All they knew was that they were far from where they boarded *Juventus*, the mega-yacht and luxury submarine combination. Their hands kneaded out knots and smoothed stringy muscles until each of the five patients were relaxed. Both Gael and Kailani had the gift of energy rejuvenation after years of training. It seemed to be working.

"Next, we will apply a cream to your necks," Kailani softly whispered. "It may be a bit chilly at first."

Gael and Kailani continued to massage their necks, not only the back, but also the front where older skin tended to droop and wrinkle. Lukas had noticed it on his own neck, and he had just recently turned forty. The Herb Society, being women in their seventies, had a bit more wrinkling and what Betty called *turkey necks*.

Lukas felt an odd sensation where Gael had applied the cream. He couldn't describe it, but his skin felt cool on the surface but much warmer sub-dermally. There was also a slight feeling of pin-pricks, but with an oddly sexual-like tingling, similar to how he felt on the sofa with Taylor and Gael. His brain struggled to put the sensations into words, but overall they were puzzlingly pleasant.

"Finally," Gael announced, "we will work on your faces. This may take some time, so I hope you enjoy the sensation."

Sensation? Molly thought it was an odd way to describe a facial, but she couldn't think of a better word, since she'd never felt anything like this.

Whatever this cream was, it felt like it was healing her skin from the inside-out. Her cucumber-covered eyelids felt heavy as she was lulled into a sense of pure relaxation, along with the feeling in her skin she couldn't describe. As Kailani did her work, Molly drifted into a dream-like state. She wasn't aware, but her companions were also in the same condition.

Chapter 12

With their treatments complete, Kailani gently shook each of their guests awake as Gael adjusted the cucumber slices to completely cover their eyes again.

"How do you all feel?" Gael asked the group, each of whom confirmed they felt extremely relaxed and refreshed.

Large mirrors faced the back of each treatment chair, the reason for which they would soon discover. "Your chairs will be turning one-hundred-eighty degrees and you will be facing a mirror. We want you to see yourself in the mirror, so the lights will be dimmed until your chairs are repositioned," Gael instructed.

Kailani depressed a button, and each guest felt their treatment chair swivel and then stop. Lukas could see through the underside of a cucumber slice that the lights were slowly being brought up.

"On the count of three, we will ask you to remove the cucumber slices from your eyes," Kailani instructed. "Gael will collect the slices from you afterward."

"One, two," Gael counted down, purposely stalling at the last number. "Three."

As they opened their eyes, they were met with disbelief at what was reflected back. Nobody said anything, but each person touched their face and necks in amazement.

"Do you like what you see?" Gael asked, already knowing the answer.

"But how?" Linda was speechless.

"I look twenty years younger, maybe thirty," Molly exclaimed.

A thirty-year-old Lukas Halloran stared back at him, his reflection almost surreal. "You look great baby," Taylor commented. "Not that you didn't before."

He stared at his own face in disbelief. The thirty-year-old Air Force pilot was in the mirror. "I forgot how hot I was." He laughed. "Wrinkles are gone."

"You're still hot," Lukas commented. "But yes, you're hot at thirty, as well."

For several moments, the women and men stretched their skin and made crazy faces in the mirror, as if doing these things would confirm the reality of their refreshed images.

"Your treatments are compliments of Mr. Baptiste," Kailani told them. "He has requested each of you back to his salon."

"Now you have experienced firsthand the miracles of moonstone." Gael smiled triumphantly as the others still stared at themselves in disbelief.

****

Pierre Baptiste enjoyed the theatrics of a big surprise. As a successful tycoon and one of the world's richest men, he'd seen and done just about everything. Watching a person's reaction to something big and unexpected could keep him entertained forever, like an endless loop of the Christmas mornings he was never able to experience as a child born into poverty.

Before they reported back to the salon, they shed their robes and put on silky crew uniforms. Pierre planned to reveal the final piece of the puzzle to them before he appeared for dinner.

"We look ridiculous," Molly commented. "I feel like I'm in third grade at Saint Mary's school. Pierre's gone off his rocker. Something's happened to him," she told Betty. Taylor and Lukas had not arrived, nor had Linda. The entire situation made her very uneasy as her subconscious mind started to connect dots she hadn't known were there.

Lukas and Taylor walked slowly down the hall, farther apart than usual and tension still hanging between them. "You seriously look at least a decade younger." Taylor's attempt at breaking the ice was not successful.

They continued to walk in silence.

"Lukas," Taylor started. "We need to talk about whatever is bothering you. We're hostages. Again. We can't have this Gael thing hanging over us, and I'm not even sure what happened."

Lukas stopped and grabbed one of Taylor's hands. "If something happened, it did because I wasn't aware of my actions. I would never do anything like that to you. But the thought of you and Gael together kind of freaked me out."

"I have no memory of that night, either. We were both drugged and both woke up together with Gael in our bed," Taylor commented, his tone direct and slightly agitated. "You blamed me, Lukas. Like I had planned it out and decided to do something like that. You were in that bed, too, and I know we both found Gael attractive, and he was rather flirty. If we did

110

anything with him, it isn't something I consciously decided as my memories are blank."

Lukas sighed. "You're right. Sorry. I get jealous pretty easily and I let it get the best of me."

Taylor grabbed his husband's shoulders. "I hate to remind you, sir, that even though you look thirty, you aren't, and you're stuck with me for life, whether you like it or not," Taylor replied. "You are who I love. Nobody else. Got it?"

Lukas nodded. "I got it."

Taylor grabbed him by the shoulders and kissed him. "Jerk," he mumbled.

Lukas mumbled back, "I don't know what got into me."

Taylor eyed him sarcastically. "Hopefully not Gael, but I'll love you anyway if he did."

"I feel like an idiot."

"Forgiven. You can make it up to me when we get some privacy away from this goddamned boat...submarine, whatever the hell it is," Taylor told him. "Let's put this behind us and get out of this weird situation with *Dr. Evil*, as soon as we fucking can."

"If he's petting a cat on his lap, I'm jumping overboard."

"Good plan," Taylor answered. He interlaced his fingers with Lukas'.

"At least we got our rings back," Lukas observed. "The security goons discovered they are not mini-tracking devices."

"Do they even make those?"

"I don't know. I'll look it up on the internet if I ever get my computer or phone back."

"That should teach you not to bring your laptop on

your honeymoon." Taylor laughed.

****

It was their second large dinner and Baptiste was ready for more showmanship. Nobody had much of an appetite. Lukas picked at his plate, and Taylor pulled apart dinner rolls while his meal continued to get cold.

"I've got to say, this guy has good food on board," Betty commented, as she gulped a glass of mango juice after wolfing down her dinner. "I was starving."

Behind them, Lukas felt the presence of someone entering the room yet resisted the urge to acknowledge the person. As he assumed, it was Pierre Baptiste who scurried around the table to take the seat at its head.

"I hope you've all enjoyed dinner,"

He smiled when he saw the delicious expressions of shock on his guests' faces. Pierre Baptiste had transformed into a forty-something, chiseled Mediterranean god. Wavy dark hair was effortlessly slicked back over a perfect head. His tan face was graced with deep-set dark eyes that twinkled with mischief. White teeth gleamed bright. Baptiste's skin was taut, but not pampered. His athletic build made him tall and strong. Pierre's guests stared at him, speechless.

"I know you have questions and I'm here to answer them, but let me start with the continuation of our story about Zealandia." Pierre waited for any reaction, but all he received were the angry stares of his passengers. "I must say that you are all looking extraordinarily refreshed." Not one of his guests acknowledged his comment. They continued to stare at him, their eyes looking for proof of whether his appearance was another illusion, or if it was real.

"Very well." He read the room and began his story.

"We spoke about Zealandia, the eighth continent that now lies beneath the ocean. Many people have discounted the concept of sinking continents or civilizations such as Atlantis, Lemuria, Nan Madol, and others. When we talk about folklore, there are three components these mythical locations share. First, each of these places was rumored to be destroyed and sunk in a single day, even though that's nearly impossible. Second, each of these civilizations was somehow more advanced compared to the civilizations that followed. And third, the destruction of these places was somehow connected to the folklore of a vengeful god, their inhabitants punished by divine retribution, like Sodom and Gomorrah. Historians and even average people like you and me believe these things because who doesn't like a big, dramatic disaster story?"

"Pierre, you look…different." Molly interrupted. "What's going on? Is this why you've abducted us? Part of your technological light show?"

"Patience," he replied. "I'm getting to that point." Pierre paced the room. "And please don't refer to being abducted. You are my guests aboard *Juventus* and you're free to go any time. People pay twenty-five thousand dollars each for a trip on my ship. You should consider it a gift."

Molly said nothing but her stone-like expression said enough.

"For all the work being done to build the future…" He looked at the blank, uninterested stares of his guests. "You know, fuck it. I'm going to cut to the chase."

"That'll be a first," Betty whispered to Molly. Pierre's ears perked as he stifled a reaction.

"Imagine it's a thousand years from now and

humans will look back on some of our discoveries—like transportation, space travel, the internet, artificial intelligence, and other things like that. What will they think? What does the earth look like in the future, assuming there is an earth left to inhabit?

"Now think back, even less than two hundred years, and look at what has been developed since then. Imagine our ancestors from two centuries earlier looking at our world today. It's something none of them could even imagine. Yet, think of all the knowledge that is lost after one's lifetime is complete. We always assume civilization becomes smarter and more advanced as time progresses, but why do we make the same mistakes? If civilization was suddenly destroyed by war, disease, a giant asteroid, or some other calamity, how would the survivors start over? Would things just keep on progressing or would we go back to square one?"

"So you imply that people would need to step back and rebuild what had been taken for granted in daily life," Lukas stated. "We would have to go back to hunting, gathering, and farming, tribal warfare, and basically start from a new baseline."

"Exactly," Pierre answered. "And the society that was destroyed would be talked about for generations as a mythical world that was far more advanced, which is basically true, compared to the world that was building back."

Molly glared at Pierre as if knives shot out of her eyes. "The point, Pierre."

"The point is that in less than half a century, everyone in this room will be dead or so old they are just waiting for life to be over," Pierre replied. "Fifty years is nothing, and in a century, nobody will know we ever existed. That's the human life cycle that's been going on for eons."

A map of the seafloor glowed on the transparent cube. "We have proof that Zealandia exists." Pierre circled what looked like trenches and submerged mountain ranges. "These are fault zones." He pointed to a boundary of trenches that clearly delineated a submerged plateau. "This is the New Hebrides trench and to the right of it is the North Fiji basin, which is close to where we are currently located."

"We're in Fiji?" Molly shouted as Pierre attempted to calm her.

The guests squinted to see what Pierre was talking about. "This is part of what we now call the Ring of Fire. The plates are constantly moving, creating volcanic activity, earthquakes, and land that both rises and falls. I believe this is the northern boundary of Zealandia."

"Interesting, Pierre." Betty sat, arms crossed, unimpressed.

"I'm getting to the good part," Pierre responded.

"How do you know that's the northern part of Zealandia? It could just be a deviation in the ocean floor, not beachfront property on a lost continent," Taylor commented.

Baptiste paused. "It's the crust that tells us. There are two types of crust on earth: seafloor crust and continental crust. Continental is much thicker and has a different structure, unique rocks, and minerals. My team aboard has found that in this area," Pierre circled the undersea plateau, "which indicates that this plateau is part of the continent and the deep trenches have probably always been submerged. The strange thing is that the continental crust I showed you abuts the seafloor crust." Pierre circled the convergence. "I believe a large part of the continent somehow broke off and sank right about where we sit now."

"Okay," Lukas stated. "That's interesting, but how does a chunk of a continent suddenly break off like a cracker or something?"

"You raise an interesting question, Lukas. I believe there was another kind of catastrophic event that happened. Not only what we've already spoken about, but something else." He waited for someone to ask him. Nobody did.

"Very well, I'll share my theory," he proclaimed with irritation. "Something big happened, as we all know. Continents don't sink every day, and a major force would have been needed in order to create such a cataclysmic event."

"Or events," Betty commented. "It could have been a combination of things, right?"

Pierre smiled in agreement. "Most likely multiple things, Betty. We have no proof, so all of these are theories only. We can only speculate based upon the available geological data."

"And what does the data say?" Taylor asked.

"Not much, really. We can tell from the types of crust, as I mentioned earlier. There is also tectonic plate history that could have contributed to Zealandia's demise," Pierre concluded. "Zealandia's crust was extremely thin, literally stretched by opposing tectonic plates. This can lead to additional stress on the landmass."

"I'm from Chicago," Molly stated. "I know the

difference between types of crust."

"I was waiting for you to say that, Ma," Lukas mumbled.

"There had to be other factors at play," Baptiste continued.

"Such as?" Molly asked.

"I'll get to that, but think about the mechanics of a landmass sinking. When was the last time you saw land sink? Those alive at the time probably thought it sank, but I think something else happened."

"We're all ears, Pierre," Molly responded flatly.

"I think the continental crust collapsed. I've mentioned tectonic activity," Pierre started. "We've discussed rising water levels due to the Ice Age melting phase that would have raised sea levels significantly. The only other thing is…" he paused, satisfied he'd captivated everyone's curiosity. "An impact."

Chapter 13

Lukas had been fascinated by astronomy since he was five years old and memorized recorded asteroid hits from around the world. *An asteroid that could sink a continent?* he thought, imagining the size, trajectory, and speed of something that destructive and pulling on his memory of strikes from the area in which they currently sat.

Pierre noticed the wheels turning inside Lukas' head. "Lukas, how big would an asteroid need to be in order to sink a large chunk of Zealandia? Just a rough estimate."

Lukas shook his head. "I don't know, but even Chicxulub wasn't big enough to destroy the Yucatan Peninsula, let alone the North American continent, but it caused utter destruction anyway."

"Water levels were lower then," Betty interrupted, "but even so, there were massive tsunamis around the world."

"Yes," Baptiste agreed. "And Chicxulub's crater is both on land and at the bottom of the Gulf of Mexico, yet the Yucatan didn't sink. Why is that?"

"Are you asking us for an answer or posing a rhetorical question?" Lukas answered, growing tired of whatever game Pierre was playing.

"Chicxulub was a catalyst to mass extinction, as far as we know. A cloud of debris plunged Earth into a two-year global winter, and some say it was longer. This created the ultimate battle for survival among dwindling resources, but there are no fossil records of a global cataclysm prior to Chicxulub, nor after. I'm not saying it didn't happen, but these kinds of events usually leave some kind of evidence behind. Any ideas?" Pierre posed the question with drama.

Taylor noticed Pierre's smug expression. *He knows something*, he thought. "Pierre, what do you think happened? Have you heard about a planetary impact the rest of the scientific community has not?"

"Everything is just a theory, with various degrees of proof," he responded. "I have doubts on whether Zealandia was hit by an asteroid, yet the moonstone intrigues me. Could there have been a trifecta of events which hastened its destruction?"

Molly jumped in. "Even if a volcano and an asteroid were active at roughly the same time, why wouldn't we have fossil or soil records that prove that?"

"Maybe it wasn't just one volcano, or one asteroid," Linda theorized. "We are at the perimeter of the Ring of Fire, so there could have been more than one volcano."

Baptiste agreed. "That's where my mind goes, as well. For all we know it could have been a super volcano."

Betty jumped in. "An asteroid strike could theoretically activate multiple magma chambers at once, leading to a massive explosion and…"

"Possible destabilization of the crust to make a large landmass collapse into the ocean," Lukas completed Betty's thought. "Wow, but I'm still unclear on the striking asteroid."

"Maybe it wasn't an asteroid, Lukas." Pierre offered it as a possibility. "Perhaps it was something else. Something faster, perhaps denser and heavier that triggered massive destructive forces that conspired to destroy a continent."

Pierre changed the direction of the conversation. "Have you noticed anything about the crew on my ship? What about yourselves? You've witnessed my transformation in the last two days. Besides looking healthy and vigorous, do you also feel any different?"

"It's only been a few hours since our treatment," Lukas answered. "But my skin feels different, and I don't need my glasses as much."

Pierre nodded. "And you, Molly?"

She let out a big sigh. "Pierre, I don't know what was in that face cream, but I look much younger, well, my face at least. The rest of me looks like my old self."

Betty, Linda, and Taylor expressed similar feelings of revitalization, more energy, and the disappearance of wrinkles and blemishes."

"My liver spots disappeared as did some blue veins on my neck," Linda commented.

"You look fantastic, Linda," Baptiste complimented her. "All of you look amazing." Pierre chuckled and returned to his seat at the head of the table.

"Dear friends, now you see another piece of the puzzle and also why I've arranged to have you aboard. I wanted you to experience the power of moonstone personally,"

"Power of moonstone?" Molly laughed. "It's basically pumice."

Pierre remained tight-lipped and stoic. "Did you

know that the archipelagos around the South Pacific all started out as barren, lifeless piles of igneous rock? The occasional sea birds, fish, and crustaceans were the only animals. There was no plant life, until some coconuts, adrift in the Pacific from who knows where, came ashore, sprouted, likely died, and this happened for centuries. But eventually some coconuts survived, sprouted, grew, and multiplied."

"So, if I'm understanding this correctly," Lukas tried to confirm. "We have come here to discover a possible eighth continent beneath the ocean and your theories on why or how it sank, right?" Pierre nodded. "And I'm guessing you're not selling us anti-aging treatments, or are you? You had me following you, but the coconut story threw me off."

"I'm not selling you anything, Lukas, and the coconut story should make sense soon," Pierre answered.

"The eighth continent isn't the big story here if I assume correctly," Taylor commented.

"You are partially correct, Taylor," Pierre answered. "The continent and its destruction are pertinent to the discovery we are now undertaking."

"So what's the other pertinent part or parts?" Betty interjected.

Baptiste leaned back in his chair. "Friends, we are on the adventure of a lifetime as we search for what has been sought since the dawn of mankind." Pierre saw excitement and suspense in his guests' faces. "There are some who say Zealandia is the location of the true Garden of Eden. Possibly even the dawn of the human species."

"You mean the Garden of Eden where Adam and

Eve lived?" Molly asked.

"The literal dawn of humankind could have been Zealandia, before it was destroyed obviously," Pierre stated. "For millennia scientists and archaeologists have theorized Africa was the starting point for what evolved into *Homo sapiens*, which I am not disputing nor confirming. But what if it were somewhere else, like here?" Pierre held out his arms. "Somewhere in this vast undersea continent, the history of our species began."

"I can't even begin to fathom this," Lukas answered. "What makes you think that?"

Pierre got up and started to pace the room. "You experienced it yourselves! Magically becoming younger and more vibrant in hours. What could possibly cause that to happen?"

"I really hope this isn't more of your CGI bullshit," Lukas pointed out as he caught Linda's glance. "No offense. You look amazing." Linda winked and smiled back.

"I can assure you this is real, and I want to offer up my theory so that we can work together and trust each other." There was silence. "Very well, I'll tell you what I think."

"We're all ears, Baptiste," Molly antagonized him.

"I believe Zealandia collapsed beneath the waves due to the eruption of major volcanoes, the rising seas occurring worldwide at the time, and another important factor." He paused. "A comet."

"You think a comet hit this place? That would have certainly taken out Zealandia and most of the Pacific Ocean," Lukas said.

"Maybe even a chunk of the Earth," Betty added.

"Comets don't need to be huge. They can break up upon entry into the atmosphere and become more like…bullets. Chicxulub was like a dirty bomb and this theoretical comet would be like a sniper's bullet. They destroy what they hit, and multiple fragments of the comet could have set off a volcanic chain reaction, but there wouldn't be an extinction-level event for the rest of the planet."

"Bad luck if you lived in Zealandia, though," Taylor noted.

"I believe these comet fragments peppered the land, sparked volcanos, and potentially hit the magma chambers, which would have created a crater collapse. Our huge super volcano was likely a shield volcano— much like the volcanoes in Hawaii and even Mons Olympus on Mars. They can be massive and if there was an actual crater collapse, it would have created a caldera and maybe even an enormous sinkhole. Are you with me so far?" Pierre asked. "Now here's the crazy part. Several years ago, my scientists detected a mineral substance we have never seen before. It does not match up to anything on the periodic table or any alloys made from our base elements."

"So you believe these to be extraterrestrial materials delivered here by this comet?" Molly asked. "Do we even have proof of a comet, or fragments thereof, hitting the earth?"

Baptiste shook his head. "Molly, you're on the right track, but it's not extraterrestrial—meaning coming from our solar system."

"No way," Lukas jumped in. "You think this was an exocomet? Is that even possible?"

"We only have them in theory. No proof, I'm

afraid," Pierre answered. "But yes, this could likely have been an interstellar comet."

"From outside our solar system?" Taylor asked.

"Very possible, but it could have even originated from outside our galaxy. Comets are made from material that comes from chunks of stars and planets," Lukas added. "An interstellar exocomet, which is a wildcard and not likely, but for argument's sake, would have come from far outside any known or mapped part of the universe."

"Which sounds impossible, I know," Baptiste confessed. "Sir Arthur Conan Doyle wrote *when you have eliminated the impossible, whatever remains, however improbable, must be the truth.* An interstellar exocomet is improbable, but not impossible, so let's say a new material was somehow brought to earth and was concentrated in a very specific location near where the comet fragments impacted."

"Legends say that it came from the gods on the moon, hence the name *moonstone*," Gael explained. "Our people have known about it for lifetimes, and we wear jewelry like this." He pointed to his newly returned necklace. "Blue pearls are formed from oysters. The sand is weathered moonstone. A grain of it gets into an oyster and the oyster makes the pearl. Moonstone is quite powerful. Even a grain of moonstone sand contains its properties."

"So how does this relate to Zealandia?" Lukas asked.

"Nearly every island in the Pacific Ocean was originally formed by volcanic activity," Pierre explained. "Except my archipelago," Pierre noted. "The chain of islands is made from moonstone. We've taken core samples and they come back as a total match to the samples we talk about."

"And you believe your archipelago is made up of fragments of this interstellar comet?" Linda asked.

"I do," Pierre said confidently.

"This new material," Molly asked. "What makes it special?"

"It has a molecular structure I've never seen before," Pierre explained. "It also has some…surprising properties, some of which you experienced today."

"Like anti-aging?" Molly asked.

"The moonstone somehow can regenerate people," Gael elucidated.

"That's what makes the moonstone so unique and valuable," Kailani added.

"Gael," Pierre asked him. "Tell our guests how old you are."

Gael rested his head on his hand. His eyes darted toward Lukas and Taylor. "My next birthday, I'll be one-hundred fifty-six years old."

Molly tried to stifle a laugh. "Nice parlor trick, Baptiste. What are you getting at?"

"I'm one-hundred fifty-six, too," Kailani shouted. "It's the truth." Her conviction was palpable, as was Gael's, and they both recited their birth years without a thought.

"Kailani is my sister. My twin. We went through a ceremony as babies where we were treated with moonstone, and now we are a century and a half old."

Lukas and Taylor studied Gael. He was perfect, almost too perfect. *Could Baptiste be telling the truth?* Lukas thought.

"I can assure you I am." Baptiste responded, as

Lukas processed what he was thinking.

"You can read our minds?" Lukas choked out.

"Only some of your thoughts, Lukas." He responded. "The material has many properties. It allows for telekinetic communication, which I'm still learning. It's rumored in Gael and Kailani's culture, it can bring people back from the dead…not like zombies, but it can revive human tissue within an hour of death. I've never tried it personally. Any volunteers?" Baptiste asked sarcastically.

"And you've tried this material on yourself?" Molly asked.

"I have," Baptiste said without emotion, "as have nearly every crew member on board *Juventus*. Most take it regularly. That's why I have such a youthful and attractive crew."

"Who else knows about this?" Molly asked.

"Very few people, but spoiler alert, some sit on your board," Baptiste inferred.

Lukas' gears were spinning. "So this material, it's like a wonder drug?"

"Lukas, think about our planets. In the grand scheme of things, we are all part of a galactic archipelago. Earth can sustain life. Most planets do not. Comets are like the coconuts I mentioned earlier. Swirling around the cosmos until they land on a planet with the infinitesimal chance that they bring something unique," Baptiste stated eloquently. "This comet brought something miraculous and has been right under our noses for millennia."

Thoughts ran through Molly's head. John, her breast cancer scars, their spa rejuvenation, Gael and Kailani's ages. "Are you telling us Zealandia is the location of…?"

"Before I answer your question, think about one thing all societies have in common."

Lukas started off, "Laws, order, customs…religion."

Baptiste smiled. "And what is common within all of our religions, even paganism?"

"A higher power, I guess," Betty answered.

"A god or gods, more specifically," Taylor commented.

"Right, Taylor. Immortal gods. Unchanging for centuries. Usually youthful, always strong," Baptiste continued. "What if they walked among us, or still do?"

"Now you sound ridiculous." Molly snickered.

"Do I?" Baptiste questioned. "I want you to think about it logically. If there was a material that made someone appear forever youthful and immortal, by human lifespan's standards, how would you explain it? If these god-like beings spanned generations, were depicted in art, music, and literature, they would be unique, special."

"And I would be protective of whatever made me that way," Lukas answered honestly.

"Thanks for your honesty, Lukas," Baptiste replied. And I assume that only those deemed special would be able to use the power of this material, not anyone on the street."

There was stunned silence until Baptiste broke it. "Moonstone, only found in Zealandia, is the material likely linked to the mythical Fountain of Youth."

Chapter 14

Baptiste's guests sat stunned by the news he just delivered.

"The actual Fountain of Youth?" Taylor asked. "For real?"

"I told you the material had some other properties," Pierre gloated. "This is why I believe it came from an interstellar comet."

"And do you plan on telling us these properties?" Molly asked impatiently.

Pierre nodded. "Of course, but I must ask for your strictest discretion."

The angry group glared at him.

"The moonstone contains one more thing that is likely the source of its regenerative properties, but it is potentially quite controversial. Any guesses?" Pierre waited for a moment.

"Just tell us." Molly sighed.

"There are traces of a nuclein pattern scientists have never seen before and matches no sample of the billions stored in databases around the world. It is truly unique to my archipelago and nowhere else."

"So what is this nuclein you mentioned? Do you know what it is?" Lukas asked,

"I ran it through artificial intelligence and again, no match. Then I tried a new platform using generative AI," Pierre explained.

"Generative AI is both fascinating and scary. It utilizes massive amounts of data, existing knowledge, algorithms, patterns, and synthesizes that into a thought or idea," Lukas explained. "It works similarly to the human brain but without emotional prejudice."

"What does prejudice mean in your statement?" Betty asked.

"These AI platforms generate content, ideas, and theories based on data and possibilities, without the emotional/opinion part all humans have. It will give you a list of possibilities without ruling out things that most human minds would discount as impossible," Lukas explained.

"So I asked AI what it could be and it came up with only one possibility, which I've never seen before. Its analysis of the nuclein patterns startled me to put it mildly."

"And what did AI say it was?" Molly asked.

Baptiste paused. "It's a structure of DNA that matches nothing we have on Earth and likely has an origin outside our galaxy."

"Interstellar DNA?" Lukas asked in disbelief. "That alone would be one of the most remarkable discoveries in human history."

"Why aren't you telling the scientific community about this?" Linda asked.

"I've told several scientists, all of whom happen to work for me, with iron-clad non-disclosure agreements."

****

The group digested the information Pierre delivered. Linda pondered her own situation, her body lithe and taut, like forty years were magically erased from her biological age. "Have you tested this alien DNA to make sure it's safe?" Linda asked.

"We are right now," Baptiste responded. "You are all our guinea pigs."

"And for the record, it's not been proven to be alien DNA, and it's millions of years old so not much of it remains. My guess is that it's DNA from lifeforms that lived on a now-exploded planet somewhere outside our galaxy."

"That sounds like alien to me," Betty scoffed.

"Did you know we were going to be used as lab experiments, Baptiste?" Molly asked.

"I authorized it, if that's what you mean," Pierre replied defiantly. "I can assure you it's perfectly safe. Gael and Kailani are living proof, as are the thirty crew members on board."

"You used me as a lab animal?" Linda shouted.

"Linda, please calm yourself," Pierre said softly. "You had a minor dose, only cosmetic. It will wear off within days, which is part of its value."

"How so?" Lukas asked.

"Imagine looking twenty years younger overnight. One would continue to buy this material to keep looking that way. It's the ultimate consumable—pride and ego driving continuous use," Baptiste said proudly.

"How will you announce this to the world, Pierre?" Molly asked, suspicious of his answer.

"I could alert the scientific community, who would descend upon my archipelago and strip-mine the moonstone, or Fiji could claim domain over it, even though I bought mineral rights when I purchased the chain of islands."

"Are there other islands or archipelagoes that have

similar material?" Taylor asked.

"None of which I'm aware. It only appears to be from my *Jardin Archipelago*, that's the new official name I chose in homage to the Garden of Eden."

"So what do you plan to do?" Lukas asked.

"Think about the money we can make," Baptiste proclaimed. "This is a disruptive leap into a whole new realm of anti-aging and extended youthful beauty."

"But what about safety and long-term effects," Betty prodded. "You'll need research testing, drug trials, and legal authorization to use it."

Pierre reacted with theatrical frustration as he rolled his eyes. "Those two!" He pointed to Gael and Kailani. "That is your research!" Pierre emphasized. "Look at yourselves and my crew. That's the proof!"

"So the side-effects of moonstone are youth and beauty?" Lukas asked.

"Isn't it marvelous?" Baptiste was buoyant.

"Gael said this was a material used by his people for centuries," Linda interjected. "Are you telling us they have to keep rubbing this moonstone cream on their faces every day or they'll age like a prune?"

Gael and Kailani glanced at each other. "We were treated differently in order to have the effects more permanently," Gael explained.

"It's not something most people can experience," Pierre interrupted. "So the topical cream does the trick."

"Pierre, I understand that," Molly continued. "I don't even know what this material is or what Gael means when he mentioned being treated differently. It's one thing to be used by villagers. It's another thing to get something like that commercialized for the general public."

"Who said it's for the general public?" Pierre asked. "That's not what I was suggesting."

Molly chuckled. "Ah, of course it's classic Baptiste. You are suggesting making this available only for the elite?"

Pierre said nothing, his silence prodding Molly to continue. "I can't imagine what you're planning to charge for this, but I'm sure you've got that all figured out already." She shook her head in disbelief. "Why would you squander something like this to be sold on the black market for the rich and powerful only?"

"It's not a cancer drug, Molly," Pierre responded. "It's about vanity. Rich and famous people would sell their souls for something like moonstone. It's not something you'd pick up at the local drug store."

"But wouldn't it be illegal?" Taylor asked. "It's basically a controlled substance that likely came from another galaxy. What if it's radioactive?"

"I don't have time for decades of approvals, "Baptiste dismissed him. "People will have to take their own risks with it. Gael and Kailani can become millionaires by training folks how to use it. All of us will become incredibly rich!"

"And how do you get the moonstone when it's one-hundred feet underwater?" Lukas asked.

"It's submerged and reachable only by a submarine." Pierre admitted. "I haven't worked out the details, but mineral rights are mine, as I mentioned."

"Coincidence, I assume," Molly said sarcastically.

"Of course, Molly," Pierre mocked her. "That's how I've made my fortune. Snapping up coincidences that randomly flutter by."

Lukas noticed Gael's clenched jaw. Something

wasn't settling right with him. "Gael, what's your thought on this?"

Gael paused. "It means less for our people if Mr. Baptiste uses our supply. He was going to try and duplicate it in a laboratory and sell that."

Betty stood to address Baptiste. "How the hell do you replicate alien DNA in a lab?" She buried her face in her hands. "Just like human history to exploit natives with lies and then take all of their riches." She looked at Gael. "I hope you're not believing this guy."

Gael looked downward and didn't respond.

"This will be like a drug cartel. You get people hooked, jack up the price, create more demand, and you've got billionaires that will pay anything for it," Linda said with emotion.

"I see you're catching on, Betty and Linda," Baptiste snapped with icy certainty. "I'm still working out the details." He glared at Linda and Betty. "I haven't quite figured out the sales channels. That's where I need assistance."

"What if Fiji claims eminent domain and confiscates the material?" Lukas asked.

"They won't want what they don't know about, Lukas," Baptiste replied flatly. "I've got plans for that scenario."

"You said this…material can not only regenerate tissues, but actually restore someone's life, correct?" Molly questioned him. "I don't understand why you wouldn't help the medical community, or first responders. Imagine being able to revive a dead child, victims from a mass shooting…anything. I guess the profits aren't there for humanitarian uses."

"Molly, we have not proven that a dead person can

be brought back to life," Baptiste furthered his argument. "That information came from folklore told by Gael and Kailani. I have no reason to not believe them, but I haven't personally witnessed a Lazarus-like event."

Molly turned to Gael and Kailani. "Have you witnessed someone returning from the dead?"

Gael glanced at Baptiste before answering. "I have not," he lied.

"I have," Kailani answered. Baptiste glared at her. "A body needs to be fresh, no decomposition or rigor. But I've seen it work."

"We tried it on a crew member that drowned accidentally," Baptiste lied, referring to the dead body that washed up on his island. The young man had, in fact, not drowned, but succumbed during an experimental application of moonstone. "We were unsuccessful, unfortunately."

"Where is the moonstone exactly?" Taylor interjected, inadvertently changing the subject. "You said it's reachable by submarine. Is it down deep?"

"It's right in front of us." Pierre replied, looking at the spherical mounds and chunks of light-colored rock that littered the ocean floor. "This appears to be the mother lode. I hypothesize this was part of the comet's nucleus, obviously very solid to be able to survive impact."

"What is that on the seafloor?" Taylor asked, pointing at the sparkling sand beneath the cliffs.

"Sand, mixed with moonstone. Just a few grains of the blue sand are incredibly powerful," Baptiste answered. "As Gael pointed out, these little grains of moonstone make powerful pearls."

"Pierre, something major doesn't add up," Betty interjected. "I'm no expert on comets, but the one thing I do know is that the width of a comet's nucleus and coma is measured in kilometers, not feet. I have a hard time understanding how something this big didn't destroy life on the planet."

"The Chicxulub meteor was estimated to be ten kilometers wide," Linda chimed in. "We all know what that did. Do you think the nucleus survived an impact like that?"

"I don't know for sure, but I believe the moonstone was the nucleus that somehow broke apart while approaching earth, landed in the Pacific, and potentially took some of Zealandia with it. Let me show you what I think happened."

The video screen flickered to life, and a computer simulation showed different scenarios of how the comet entered the atmosphere and eventually impacted the ocean. "Artificial intelligence has proposed two scenarios," Baptiste began.

"Will there be a point when you use actual human intelligence?" Betty asked. "Just curious in case technology is not our ally here."

"Here is scenario one." Baptiste ignored Betty's comment and watched the simulation of the comet splitting into halves before crashing into the ocean. "And here is scenario two." The group watched the comet hit the atmosphere and split into nearly one hundred pieces. Half of them rained down upon Zealandia and created havoc with tsunamis and mega eruptions. The other bits of the comet crashed into the Pacific and correspond to the ten pieces lining up into the current shape of the Jardin Archipelago.

"And you think scenario two is what actually happened?" Lukas asked Baptiste.

Pierre nodded but said nothing.

"If your trifecta theory is correct," Linda jumped in. "Scenario two is just that."

"Overall, scenario two also suggests why this impact would have been isolated primarily to the Asia Pacific region," Pierre explained. "Imagine throwing a boulder into a swimming pool. The splash, waves, and destruction would be concentrated, much like Chicxulub. Scenario two would be more like throwing buckets of pebbles into that pool. It would still have an impact, but the energy is much more dispersed, and therefore, less impactful on a global scale.

"We have no proof of any of this, but the size of the moonstone chunks, that likely became islands, logically match that scenario and also explains why there is no impact crater."

"Would a tsunami have wiped out part of Zealandia?" Betty asked.

"No doubt," Pierre Baptiste said confidently. "It could have contributed to pushing lower-level land to be submerged. Remember, the rising oceans alone were already happening, and the volcanic eruptions were further destabilizing the ground."

"How long have you been studying this?" Molly asked.

"More than two decades. It started as a passion project that came together like a jigsaw puzzle," Pierre replied. "Part of our mission is to find out how much of the material is actually there and contained below the soil of my islands."

"Our mission?" Molly snorted. "*Your* mission,

Pierre. We are here against our will, remember?"

Baptiste blotted his lips with his napkin. "That's why I have a proposal for all of you. Help me locate and prove-out the moonstone properties and supply. I'll offer Phoenix Equities a major position in the company." He gazed at Linda, Betty, Taylor, and Lukas. "You will each be a shareholder, as well. It's a team effort, and I reward the team for success. As I mentioned, Gael and Kailani will become richer than their king."

Lukas glanced at his mother. Pursed lips and serious eyes meant Mama wasn't buying it. She glanced back at Lukas, and he could tell she was pissed and tired of Baptiste's bullshit.

"Pierre," Lukas asked. "How long can *Juventus* remain submerged?"

"Still having claustrophobia?" Baptiste asked.

"A little bit," Lukas responded professionally, although inside he burned with resentment. "It would be nice to have some fresh air."

Baptiste chuckled. "We have been slowly rising toward the surface and will soon be ready to get some fresh air, if that's what you want, Lukas. It's the least I can do."

The group was surprised by this. "*Juventus* is designed to move silently and smoothly, almost imperceptibly," Baptiste boasted. "Gyroscopic stabilization makes the ship nearly motionless, even at high speeds and in rough seas. We are almost at our destination. No reason we can't dine al fresco."

"What's our destination?" Taylor asked.

"The Jardin archipelago. You'll get to see the moonstone islands yourself."

"When do you think we will be on the surface?" Lukas asked.

"Why? Do you have an appointment somewhere?" Baptiste laughed.

Lukas shook his head, playing up the claustrophobia thing. "When do you think we can get some fresh air?"

"How about before dinner? I'll arrange for drinks and appetizers on the deck. We are actually very close to Kiva Oa now."

Taylor winked at Lukas. This meant Taylor likely had a plan.

Chapter 15

The floor-to-ceiling drapes parted and revealed a warmly-lit terrace adjacent to the salon. Water dripped from two curved plates that looked like a giant opened clamshell. Attendants were already using squeegees to dry the flooring and prevent falls. Taylor and Lukas stepped outside. The sun had nearly set on the horizon, illuminating the sky in bright pinks, reds, and oranges. *Juventus* lay still in the water, moored about five-hundred feet off the shore of Kiva Oa, Baptiste's private island residence. Molly, Linda, and Betty stood together, taking in the view of the island and Baptiste's massive home.

"It must be nice to be a billionaire," Betty said. "You've got to admit, it's a slice of paradise."

"Yeah, and it's nice to get some fresh air," Molly said. "I was starting to get claustrophobic myself. What do you ladies think about all of this?"

"I don't know Baptiste, but I think there's something he's not telling us," Linda commented.

"You're likely correct on that," Molly responded.

"He's a psycho if you ask me," Betty continued. "You see what he's doing, right?" She paused for Molly and Linda to answer. "Baptiste wants to make a fortune off this moonstone stuff. I get that, but there's something stuck in my craw."

"What do you think that is?"

"There is something about how he weaves this big story together, reeling us in about ancient ruins, the eighth continent, super volcanoes, and rising sea levels. If I strip all the bullshit away, I see a very clever marketing plan for this moonstone. It will become the ultimate anti-aging treatment that people will literally fight for. He wants to be the only source, shut us up by giving us equity in the company and probably some other things. Imagine when his customers become addicted to it."

"He'll own them," Linda commented.

"A drug lord," Molly jumped in. "Create the need, control the supply, gouge customers with high prices. It would be a cartel."

Betty and Linda nodded.

"I'm not going to lie, but I love my new face," Molly confessed. "I enjoy looking younger and feeling prettier. I could see myself getting emotionally addicted to moonstone."

"Imagine what you would pay if your career depended on your looks," Linda added.

"I guess that's why he has so many celebrities on his yacht," Betty continued. "Seeding his customer base. It's a pretty ingenious strategy actually." She looked around the open deck. "Look at all these beautiful people who work on board, and Baptiste admitted they're all taking moonstone, so they're beholden to him, too."

"We're on the ship of the lost souls," Molly kind of joked. "I wonder what Gael was talking about when he referred to the treatment he and Kailani went through as kids. I get the impression their youthful appearance is a bit more permanent."

"I thought the same thing," Linda commented. "We will have to ask Kailani—she seems the more open of the two."

"Imagine if Gael is referring to a permanent solution to aging. More extreme, most likely. Definitely more expensive," Betty hypothesized.

"There's something else going on," Molly interjected. "Baptiste is too rich and too well connected. Moonstone is only part of the story."

"What's the other part?" Linda asked.

"If I know Baptiste," Molly answered. "It's something we cannot even fathom."

****

On the other side of the deck, Taylor and Lukas chatted privately.

"According to the sky color, we should have nice weather tomorrow," Taylor told Lukas. "I need to get into an open space for at least three minutes. Can you cover for me?"

Lukas nodded as he walked with his husband. "Unless this is just another one of his illusions," Lukas mentioned. "With all his tricks we could be in the engine room imagining this."

"At least it looks real. I'm going to walk closer to the stern," Taylor replied as he walked toward the back of the ship. Lukas stared up at the flaming sky, and immediately thought of the skies in Tucson where his parents lived. He could already see stars and planets start to peek out from the dark blue sky that soon would be black. He looked forward to seeing the constellations from the southern hemisphere. Lukas took a deep breath and filled his lungs with fresh air. It was nice to not be confined to the ship.

"Lukas," a voice called from behind him. He turned to find Gael standing within inches of him. "Can we talk?"

Gael and Lukas sat on one of the plush sofas sitting on the deck. It was the first chance for them to talk since he found Gael naked and asleep in their bed. Taylor noticed the two men talking but stayed in position as he counted seconds.

"I'll be there in a minute," Taylor called to Gael.

"I'm glad you're both here," Gael started as he massaged the back of his neck. "I thought it was good that we should talk."

Lukas nodded. "Thanks. It's been on our minds."

"I don't remember anything before waking up in your bed. Do you?" Gael started.

"Taylor and I think we were drugged. Maybe our cognac was laced with something," Lukas continued. "Last thing I remember was the three of us hanging out on a sofa."

Gael acknowledged with a nod. "I think it was the moonstone powder they put in our drinks. I connected the dots when I heard about your wounds suddenly healing."

"You can consume the stuff?" Lukas asked. "I mean, I guess we did."

"It's not a good idea to consume it, but a little bit won't hurt you," Gael continued. "That was my first time ingesting it. It was almost hallucinogenic. I don't know what you guys experienced."

Awkwardness hovered over them like a cloud. "I don't remember, you know, if we did anything else. Do you?" Lukas asked, afraid of the answer.

Taylor walked over to join them. "Whatever drug it

was, the rest of the night was wiped from my memory."

"I think you both are beautiful men," Gael began. "But I don't think we did anything. I think I would somehow know in my heart if we had. I'm devoted to someone, and I don't think I would have betrayed him."

A pause hung between them. "I can't remember if we did or didn't," Taylor answered.

"Kailani is usually there to watch over me. She's technically my big sister...five minutes older, you know," Gael explained. "We've been best friends our whole lives."

"How did you get into this whole thing?" Lukas asked Gael.

"Pierre and I met on Kiva Oa fifty years ago," he said. "I've been in love with him since then, although we've never lived together, you know? We come from two very different worlds."

"I understand," Lukas commented. "High powered businessmen are constantly traveling the world. Probably not around together long enough to make a relationship work, huh?"

Gael hesitated. "I have dedicated the last fifty years to him. I don't care about his money. He doesn't want..." Gael struggled for the words. "It's because he doesn't feel comfortable with me looking young while he continues to age. People would discover something, so I never leave the island, except to go to *Juventus* or the Bora Bora San Rafael."

"Why there?"

"Pierre owns several San Rafael properties, including Bora Bora. Since he's the boss, he can hide me if he needs to," Gael explained.

"Thanks for sharing that," Taylor interjected.

Gael stated, "It was your energy and passion for each other that I sensed. I felt you were both very much into each other, and not ready to share that."

"You could sense it?" Taylor clarified.

Gael nodded. "You're beautiful to watch together, and anyone would want to be part of that energy." He paused. "You reminded me of Pierre and me when we first met decades ago. I was drawn to you both because it was something I wanted to be a part of, which is when I knew I had to distance myself. Plus, I didn't sense you were interested."

Lukas replied, "We've been together a little over four years. I'm not ready or interested in taking that step. But, Gael, you are an amazingly attractive person."

Taylor nodded. Lukas noted he was staring at Gael. "But maybe in a hundred years, we'll be more open to it."

Lukas nudged Taylor back. "I can wait."

"Gael," Taylor asked, "Why are you involved in this? Do you support Baptiste on his mission?"

Gael remained silent for a moment. "I've done something I wish I hadn't."

"What's that, Gael?" Lukas wondered.

"I shared the secrets of moonstone and now I'm worried for my people if Baptiste sells it all over the world."

Lukas and Taylor nodded but said nothing.

"Anyway," Gael continued. "It was my fault, so I stayed around to make sure I knew what's going on. Pierre promised me he was trying to copy it in a lab, but I've given up on that happening."

"Why did you tell him, Gael?" Lukas questioned.

"If you don't mind me asking."

Gael looked troubled. "I hoped he could be young again, so he felt comfortable being with me. I love him no matter what. I don't care if he looks twenty-five or eighty, and I've proven that to him. I just think he feels inferior because he looks so much older, which is ridiculous."

"How about now? The treatment has made him much younger-looking, and rather dashing," Taylor asked.

"I hope to be married to him by the end of this trip." Gael laughed. "But I know I want him more than he wants me for the rest of our lives."

"So how did you and Kailani become…like…this?" Taylor struggled to find the words.

"Certain people from our islands are chosen to be bearers of the moonstone when we are babies. It's like a kind of baptism, where we are submerged in the moonstone water so it gets into our bodies. Then we grow like normal people but stop aging at around twenty-five years old. It's been a part of our culture for as long as anyone remembers."

"So are you immortal?" Lukas asked.

"Our legends tell us the moonstone comes from another planet where people, or whatever they are, age at a different rate," Gael explained. "We still age, and we still die."

"How long?"

"The oldest person in our history lived to be approximately five-hundred years old," Gael stated. "I never got to meet him, unfortunately."

"So you've not even hit the potential half-way

point. No mid-life crisis on the horizon?" Lukas asked with a touch of irony.

"Most of us last between three hundred and four hundred years," Gael elucidated. "Many of us end our own lives due to loneliness. It is a bit of a curse."

"And why were you and Kailani chosen?" Taylor asked.

Gael thought for a moment. "Because we were twins, I think. It's not very common in our society. The religious elders selected us as *mahu*, or two-spirit people."

****

As the men continued to chat, they noticed the waves had become larger and a strong wind was blowing from the east. The stars were hidden behind swirling storm clouds and the temperature had dropped quickly. Soon, squalls of rain raked the terrace and people ran for cover. Lukas stayed on the deck, enjoying the deluge that drenched him. He took off his shirt and let the rain pelt his naked torso. He somehow knew they would not be outside much longer.

****

A bell sounded on the ship, followed by a command from Captain Kepler.

"Ladies and gentlemen, a category four typhoon is brewing about two-hundred kilometers away. While we don't expect to be hit directly, we do expect high winds and rougher seas within the hour, so *Juventus* will move to a protected harbor and ride out the storm. It is not recommended to go ashore as typhoons are quite violent should they hit closer to us. Wind and storm surge damage could be significant. We will be closing the back deck soon."

Taylor casually ran his fingers through the hair on the sides of his head. He felt the familiar bump on his scalp and shot a dripping wet Lukas a sly smile. "Let's get inside before the back shell closes," he suggested as he and Lukas helped Gael to his feet.

"The fresh air was nice while it lasted," Lukas remarked. "I hope we don't get seasick."

"According to Baptiste, he's got the gyroscope thing that keeps us stabilized," Taylor reminded him.

Marc Hammer inspected the deck with authority and gestured with a hand wave that everything was clear. A motor engaged and the moveable shell that covered the back of the ship began to move. As the shell telescoped over the aft deck terrace, orange warning lights flashed as a computer-generated female voice calmly counted down from ten until the watertight seal engaged. *Aft deck encapsulation complete*, the computer voice informed them without emotion.

Pierre Baptiste sauntered through the salon chatting with his guests. He smiled when he saw Lukas and Taylor, curious to interrupt their conversation with Gael.

"Hello friends," he began. "We should only get impacted by the outer edge of the storm, so I have asked Captain Kepler to allow anyone to disembark should they wish. I have several rooms in my compound to house all of you. We may need to take *Juventus* below the surface to ride out the storm, so I wanted to give you the option."

A quick glance to Taylor confirmed his instinct. They should get off the ship.

"I think we'll take you up on the offer," he said.

"Let us know what we need to do."

Baptiste etched a smile on his face. "Of course, weather can change our plans, but I'll make the arrangements for you and your party to stay on the island." Gael stood silently. "I will need you and Kailani to help round up the divers and process the moonstone they have brought aboard," Pierre added.

****

Lukas and Taylor walked through a corridor leading to their stateroom.

"Do you think they were able to get a clear signal?" Lukas asked. "I timed you on deck for three minutes, as you asked."

"Thanks. That should have been enough time to get picked up by a satellite. I just hope the thing still works," Taylor answered.

When they entered their rooms, they found their clothes neatly folded on top of their bed, their electronics placed gingerly on top of the pile. The men stared at their belongings, unsure of their next actions.

"What do we do?" Taylor asked his husband.

Lukas scanned the room for the cameras and microphones he knew were there, but most likely invisible to them. "We put on our clothes, I guess, then see what we do next." He fumbled with his laptop, flipped it over, and saw the battery had been removed.

"Well, this is basically useless unless Pierre happens to have a spare charger." Lukas and Taylor could read each other well, and Taylor had already caught on to the game. *Keep talking about nothing.*

Taylor continued to talk about nothing as Lukas, pretending to unfold his clothes, discreetly popped his small satellite phone into the pocket of his slacks, as he dropped his robe.

"Well, they get to see my bare ass again," Lukas announced as he scrambled to slip on his pants. "See? I'm not such a prude anymore."

"You're anything but a prude, my man." Taylor winked.

"I know, but it fits my nerdy image I try to maintain." Lukas laughed as he buttoned the fly on his lightweight jeans. "Been awhile since I've gone commando."

Taylor jumped into his clothes at the same time. "I heard Baptiste is feeding us before we disembark for the night. Something about not having food on the island."

"Seriously?" Lukas responded. "Do you think we should go then? I mean, I prefer land but I'm not a big fan of starvation. What if we get stranded if the storm is bad? We have no way of communicating for help." A thin smile appeared on his lips.

"Fine, we can stay here to see how the storm plays out." Taylor understood their new course of action. "Maybe Baptiste's chef can pack us some food to go."

****

Gael sought out Pierre. He hadn't talked to him since his transformation and decided he would congratulate him for the results. As he rounded a corner, he spotted Baptiste and Marc standing together in the hallway. Pierre kissed Marc's neck as the man attempted to rebuff him. Gael's face burned with shock and resentment, but he continued watching them until he saw Marc relent and Pierre open the door to his special room. *Their special room.* His stomach dropped as he struggled to process this while rationalizing that neither he nor Baptiste had an exclusive relationship, or technically a relationship at all. Neither man promised the other anything, but Baptiste's implication had been clear. Once he achieved youth, he would be ready to be with Gael openly.

With a deflated ego and dashed hopes, Gael turned around and walked toward his stateroom.

Chapter 16

The yacht shuttle motored back from their brief trip to Bora Bora airport. Tory and her fiancé confirmed what they needed to know—their dads' plane was parked there, untouched. Once they left the yacht, Tory and Pepe ran back to their bungalow. She had to check something on her laptop.

"How are you expecting to find them, *cara*?" Pepe asked.

"I know my dad. He would never leave like this unless it was against his will. He'll find a way to tell me where he is."

The laptop came to life and Tory pulled up a map of the Pacific basin on her screen. Pepe watched as she clicked icons of Taylor's electronic equipment and began a roaming search for any of them. "This is gonna take a while. I need to talk to Donna ASAP."

The finder swirled as it searched for each of Taylor's electronic pieces. Tory also had the signatures of Lukas' pieces but after ten minutes, she got a popup message that the items were not found. She ran the scan again, remembering the code her father gave her years ago.

"This is going to be slow," Tory told Pepe. "Want to go with me to find Donna and Wilma?"

After searching the lush San Rafael grounds, they spotted Wilma and Donna about one hundred feet offshore on stand-up paddleboards. Tory jumped up and down to get their attention, and when Donna noticed, Tory motioned for them to come back to the shore.

The lagoon upon which they paddled was mirror-still and glowed a surrealistic blue-green color common in French Polynesia's waters. Crystal clear water and crushed white coral sand conspired to make Bora Bora the most beautiful island in the world, according to a famous writer. Tory squinted as the women neared the shore, their paddleboards appearing to hover rather than float.

"What is it, honey? Everyone okay?" Donna asked, flustered.

"It's my dads. They're not here. They left." Tory breathed, trying to quell a rising panic.

"They left?" Wilma asked. "You mean they left the island?"

"The *Goose* is still at the airport, but…"

"How do you know it's at the airport? What's going on?" Donna cut to the chase.

"My dads never came home last night, at least I don't think they did," Tory stated excitedly.

"Weren't they onboard Pierre Baptiste's ship last night?" Wilma asked.

Tory nodded. "I asked the front desk, and they informed me that everyone in our party checked out except for the four of us."

"Okay, now that is weird," Donna commented. "I've known the gals since before your dads were even born, hon. It doesn't feel like typical behavior for them."

"Not for my dads, either," Tory added.

Donna didn't need any more information. She

knew Molly, Linda, and Betty like sisters, and having worked in the CIA together, they never would have disappeared without telling anyone.

"I'm looking up *Juventus* to see if there is any news on her location." Wilma's fingers tapped the keys of her laptop.

"Why do they always call a ship *she*? Donna asked rhetorically as Wilma searched. "It seems like an odd tradition. An object with a gender. Weird."

"In Italian, we have male and female words. I never really thought about it," Pepe commented. "Maybe it's from the women carved on the front of old ships."

"Figureheads," Tory replied. "Good theory."

"Bingo," Wilma exclaimed. "I have the *Juventus* website pulled up." She scrolled through it. "Nothing on here about their current location. Shit."

"I'm tracking my dad."

"How?" Donna asked. "You said he didn't have a cell signal."

"I know," Tory responded. "He has a subdermal GPS tracker. He gave me the frequency years ago in case he disappeared."

Donna laughed and shook her head. "That guy. I should have known!"

****

Over the last twenty years, branches of the United States military have offered combat and rescue personnel the option of having a subdermal tracker placed on their body. This was left as a personal decision for the service member but was offered and recommended to those involved in search, rescue, and reconnaissance missions. Taylor, having a young daughter, wanted to make it as easy as possible for him to be found either alive or dead. He never wanted his daughter to not have closure, should he be shot down or die on mission. When she got older, he gave her the frequency for the tracker and also shared it with his husband. Now, all these years later, she was hoping it was still active.

The four of them entered her bungalow where her laptop sat on the edge of their bed. The map of the Pacific Ocean from Asia to North America searched for the beacon. She still had not received a hit. The circular cursor swirled like a peppermint candy rolling through space.

"Did you get one of those implants?" Wilma asked her wife.

"Haven't you been tracking me?" Donna asked with mock surprise.

"You haven't given me a reason to," Wilma answered softly.

"Is that a challenge?" Donna joked. Wilma's deadpan face showed that the joke fell flat.

****

Tory's laptop suddenly got a hit. A loud ping sounded as the four friends waited for coordinates.

-16.990, 173.390

"That's seventeen degrees south and one hundred seventy-four degrees east," Tory called out to Pepe who entered the coordinates in his GPS finder.

"Fiji. They're somewhere near fucking Fiji!" Pepe shouted. "How far away is that?"

"Almost two-thousand miles," Wilma commented.

"How the hell did my dad get to Fiji?" Tory asked, knowing nobody knew the answer.

Chapter 17

The electric yacht-tender awaited its passengers. Lukas, Taylor, Molly, Betty, and Linda sat in the plush seats as the boat was guided out of the docking bay toward the lagoon. With Baptiste's blessing, his dog Marcel decided to accompany them on the short voyage to spend the night on Kiva Oa. Marcel recognized the island and was excited to visit, as he stood on his hind legs, his front legs balancing him on the boat's railing. Aleks would pilot the small craft once it was in the water. Robotic arms cradled the yacht-tender as they extended out from *Juventus*. Marc was in place to manually control things should the robotics not work properly, which was unlikely. The group stepped out onto the exterior launching deck as the yacht-tender moved from inside the ship. The late-afternoon sun burned red, its warmth tempered as the Earth was transitioning to a much cooler night in a few hours. Marc motioned for the group to enter the yacht-tender and he gently lowered it to the water. From the side of *Juventus* to the dock on Kiva Oa, Aleks estimated it would be a fifteen-minute ride to their sleeping location for the night. Sunset was still an hour away. The plan was that Aleks would accompany the group to Baptiste's compound, get everyone settled, and then return in the morning to bring them back to *Juventus*. Aleks estimated this would take a maximum of forty-five minutes, so Marc left the docking bay doors open for his return.

The yacht-tender bubbled silently across the lagoon toward Kiva Oa. From the watercraft, Taylor took in the tropical beauty of the island. Lukas pointed to a massive structure built into the side of a small hill. It was Baptiste's compound, their home for the night. Molly had seen photos of Pierre's massive home grace an architectural magazine, yet even the glossy photos couldn't replicate the ambience of the island and the size of the dwelling. Aleks slowed the boat as they approached a shabby wooden dock that looked out of place against the backdrop of island beauty and an architectural showpiece. Aleks idled the boat in the shallow water as Lukas and Taylor disembarked first, each helping the older women cross the wobbly deck. Marcel leapt out of the boat to follow them, which meant Aleks would need to moor the boat and fetch the dog that would likely be resistant to returning on his own.

The group trudged toward the compound, climbing gradually up a trail composed of crushed shells and stone. In the distance they heard a rumble that sounded like thunder, only louder and less natural.

"It's a beautiful island. Baptiste has good taste," Molly commented.

"I'll give him that," Linda agreed. "Think of all the famous people that have been here."

Lukas walked away from the group and reached for the satellite phone in his pocket. He held the power button for a few seconds and the phone jumped to life and searched the skies for either a satellite or cell-phone signal before typing his message to Tory. He got a satellite ping and discreetly typed out a quick message.

W Baptiste Kiva Oa Against will. WROK Ship/sub be careful

He then tapped commands for the satellites to take images of their location that he could then forward on to Tory just in case Taylor's subdermal chip didn't register. After discreetly pocketing the phone, he joined the group. Marcel, who had been excitedly sniffing every tree and bush within a twenty-foot radius, suddenly went still. His rump cowered downward, his tail tucked between his legs, and his eyes seemed to plead for something nobody could understand.

"What got into him?" Taylor asked. "Looks like he's spooked."

Another rumbling noise echoed through the air, this one louder and lasting longer.

"Sounds like thunder," Betty noticed. "Perfect timing. Let's head for cover."

They walked toward a covered gazebo to wait out the rain. Marcel didn't follow them, instead turning in a circle, agitated and sniffing the air. Aleks was the first one to notice the level of the lagoon had dropped a bit. "Tide's going out. I better get going," he told the group.

The rumbling noise returned, this time louder and followed by a large thud. Marcel continued to cower, frightened by something unseen. The water level continued to drop and suddenly, the silence was broken by the deafening sound of *Juventus'* horn. It repeated itself two more times. Aleks stood frozen as he watched the water drain away from the keel of his electric boat. Lukas glanced at Taylor and knew he suspected the same thing.

"Shit! We need to get this boat in the water,"

Taylor yelled as he, Lukas, and Aleks jumped into the now exposed sand to try and push the yacht-tender toward the shallow water. *Juventus'* horn bellowed again, and Lukas could see the crew on deck preparing to depart for a safe zone. Betty, Linda, and Molly jumped in to help the men push the boat toward the water. Although everyone knew what was happening, nobody needed to verbalize it. They just knew they had to get the hell out of there. The yacht-tender was able to float and Aleks worked to pull the women up, who held onto the boat despite being up to their shoulders in water. Taylor pulled himself up to assist Aleks and threw a ladder over the side so the women could board quickly. Lukas treaded water as he helped the women position their feet and start to climb on board. In the distance, he could see an ominous black, cylindrical column of smoke and ash pushing toward the sky.

Marcel paddled furiously and was pulled onto the yacht-tender's rear deck as Lukas finally boarded and hoisted up the ladder.

"Get us out of here!" Taylor shouted as *Juventus* started to slowly lumber toward the open ocean. Aleks aimed the yacht-tender's prow toward the gaping hole of the launching bay, its doors still wide open.

Aleks took the electrical engines up as fast as they would go, and the yacht-tender skipped over the waves to close in on *Juventus*. Molly and Linda both pointed at a massive wave in the distance. Its peak had not yet crested, but the dark blue monster approached Kiva Oa at alarming speed. Whoever was piloting *Juventus* turned her bow directly into the oncoming wave. Marc Hammer stood at the launching bay doors waving Aleks toward him. Marc lowered a flexible ladder over the side of the ship as Aleks attempted to nudge up against the huge ship.

"Mrs. Halloran, you first!" he yelled as Molly started climbing the rope ladder.

"Mrs. Eastman, you're next!" Linda was already holding the ladder steady for Molly, and Betty held it for Linda as she climbed, and then followed, herself.

The first wave hit in the distance, which meant the next one would likely hit them. With the three women on board, Lukas and Taylor argued briefly about who should go next. Lukas lost the *Rock, Scissors, Paper* game which meant he was to board next. The wave was now cresting, and Lukas had to scramble up the side of the ship before Marc pulled him to safety. From this vantage point, Lukas could see the succession of tsunami waves heading for Kiva Oa and he realized there was no way Taylor, Aleks, or Marcel would make it in time. His eyes locked with Taylor's and Lukas knew he was aware of what faced him, but neither man was able to speak. Aleks stared straight ahead, pale with fear, but unyielding, before pulling away from *Juventus* and heading straight toward the first tsunami wave.

"Get inside!" Marc yelled at Lukas. "You're gonna get sucked out when the wave hits! Launch doors won't close!"

They suddenly felt *Juventus* tip upward, its bow rising as if it were a jet taking off as the ship started up the leading edge of the wave. Lukas had never seen a tsunami in real life, and he was not surprised that the wave was massively thick, a literal mountain of water that was barreling down on anything in its path. Marc grabbed Lukas' arm and forcefully pulled him inside the landing bay as they crested the first wave.

"You'll get sucked out!" Marc yelled. "Get the women to climb up the stairwell! This is gonna be bad."

Lukas squinted to find the yacht-tender boat. No luck. His stomach sank thinking of the tiny watercraft taking on these waves and how scared they must be right now.

Marc and Lukas joined Molly, Linda, and Betty in the dry dock area where the yacht-tender normally sat. *Juventus* pitched upward again before crashing down into a trough between rows of waves. Whatever gyroscopic stabilization technology Baptiste boasted about was now not working as waves battered the ship in every direction. The group steadied themselves against the crashing surf pounding them. Stomachs churned as they held on through the rough seas.

"Ma! You and your friends need to get out of here in case we're T-boned by a wave! It'll flood the compartment. Take the stairs up!"

Molly motioned Linda and Betty to follow her to the upper decks. A wave broadsided *Juventus* and thousands of tons of water crashed through the opening and flooded the launching bay. Lukas and Marc held on to each other, the force of the water pounding them and tearing them apart. As the water receded, Lukas saw Marc being pulled out of the ship with the exiting water, disoriented and confused. Lukas dove into the water and secured his arm around Marc's torso and prevented him from being sucked outside the vessel. Lukas' shirt had been torn off his body due to the power of the waves. Another wave slammed into the ship, its immensity bludgeoning both men and throwing them across the interior deck amidst the swirling and foaming water, tossing them around without mercy. Marc pointed to a ladder.

"We need to get up higher. Follow me!"

All Lukas could think about was Taylor and how he was hopefully managing through this, but he didn't want to think about how small the boat Taylor was on actually was compared to *Juventus*.

"Where the hell did the tsunami come from?" Lukas yelled over the crashing waves and sloshing water.

"Volcano, probably," Marc replied unemotionally as if this happened every day. "Seamount that blew through the surface and all hell broke loose. There's a tsunami alert from New Zealand to Hawaii."

"Taylor's still out there!" Lukas shouted. "With Aleks and Marcel, too."

"Hang on!" Marc shouted as *Juventus* rode another mountain of water and crashed down the other side of it. The ship shuddered so violently Marc worried it would rattle apart.

"Once we get through the waves, I'll have the captain go back to look for them and also see what happened to Kiva Oa," Marc shouted.

Lukas saw the sun had lowered even more toward the horizon. "It's gonna be dark soon. We should turn back now!"

****

The water around Kiva Oa swirled with once-powerful waves that weakened once striking land. Aleks had piloted the yacht-tender through the worst of it, or so he hoped. He remembered driving the boat directly into one of the mammoth waves, rode it to the top, and then crashed back down into the trough only to repeat the sequence. At one point, a rogue wave, likely created when the tsunami wave retreated back into the ocean, swamped the small boat. It somehow didn't capsize, Taylor having helped balance the weight inside the boat to keep the keel relatively stable.

Both men could see what was left of Kiva Oa after having at least four tsunami waves pummel the island successively. Surprisingly, Baptiste's compound looked relatively intact compared to the buildings around it. The dock they used to disembark was gone. They were surrounded by a stew of destroyed buildings and vegetation. It was a miracle they were still alive.

Taylor looked on as he manually bailed water from the boat as fast as he could. Marcel shivered in one of the boat's corners, dripping wet. He had been at sea since he was a pup, so fortunately was unaffected by the rocking motion caused by the waves, yet Taylor could see the poor guy got more than he bargained for.

"Do you think that's the end of the waves?" Taylor yelled to Aleks.

Aleks nodded but said nothing, continuing to concentrate on watching out for potentially damaging debris, or even worse, whirlpools forming in the cauldron of soupy brown water.

Darkness grew as the setting sun met the horizon. Taylor feared they may be stranded on the remains of Kiva Oa or would be found by *Juventus* or another ship. Either way, he knew Lukas was probably okay and would be doing his best to find him.

"We are running low on battery power," Aleks told him. "I'm going to try and get us near the cove where we landed earlier."

"Good plan," Taylor confirmed. "I don't need to be

lost at sea indefinitely."

Aleks piloted the yacht-tender toward the shore and beached it on the sand, the only option they had with no dock or mooring lines. In the distance, they saw *Juventus* coming toward them. Her blue hull appeared black, and her windows and portholes glowed like bright stars shining through the darkness.

"I have to say I'm glad to see that ship," Taylor commented.

Again, Aleks remained quiet, only acknowledging Taylor's comment with a brief nod.

Taylor pulled out an emergency kit and found a flare gun he hoped still worked.

"I'm gonna shoot this off, okay? In case they can't see us." Taylor pulled the trigger and watched as the sky lit up in a trail of orange-red fireworks. *Juventus* confirmed receipt of the distress signal with three toots of the horn.

Within a quarter of an hour, the men heard the buzzing sound of an outboard motor coming toward them. The shape of a Zodiac with three figures inside bounced in the twilight. Marcel whined with excitement as he heard the watercraft approach. When they came into view, Taylor saw his husband at the prow of the motorized raft, with Baptiste sitting in the middle and Marc Hammer manning the engine. Their ordeal was over. At least for now.

Chapter 18

The sleek jet sliced through the darkness as they crossed miles and miles of ocean on their way to Fiji. Tory piloted the Spectrum 7 business jet, the newest addition to her father's executive jet company, Nimbus Aviation. Donna Rivero sat in the co-pilot's seat while their significant others, Pepe and Wilma, sat patiently in the cabin's buttery leather chairs, occasionally nodding off, only to startle awake again. The jet's interior was trimmed in light-colored wood, matched with light beige leather seating and recessed LED lights. Lukas had sent a cryptic email to Tory indicating that they were being held against their will, somehow submerged and without any communications ability.

Donna rubbed the back of her neck. "I think we may be going beyond FAA guidelines for pilot flying time."

"I won't tell if you won't," Tory responded, not sure if Donna was serious in making her comment. "The size of this ocean is unbelievable. We have two more hours until we touch down."

"Then what?" Donna asked.

Tory thought for a moment. "I honestly don't have the foggiest."

Pepe walked sleepily into the cockpit. "Where are we?"

Tory studied her map. "Somewhere between the

equator and Australia. About eight-hundred miles to Nadi, the main airport. Then we need to figure out where they are and how we get them."

"I don't have any contacts in the Fiji Coast Guard, but I can jump from a helicopter for a rescue mission, if you need me to," Pepe joked.

"Don't laugh," Donna responded. "She may take you up on it."

****

When they were approximately two hundred miles from Nadi, they began their descent, and almost immediately after, Fiji air traffic control called them.

"N4202 - Alpha, this is control tower."

"Fiji control, this is N4202-A approaching your airspace," Tory responded.

"Please be advised, we are under a tsunami warning due to high levels of volcanic activity midway between Fiji and Tonga. Waves are expected to be small, and they will approach from the east. However, just in case, we are making alternative landing arrangements in Vanuatu should the situation worsen, Air Traffic Fiji, out."

"Air Traffic Fiji," Tory responded. "We have limited options due to fuel levels. Estimating an eight-hundred-kilometer maximum variance, 4202 out."

Tory and Donna anxiously awaited instructions in the darkened cockpit. The Spectrum's flat-screen instrument panel glowed with numbers and graphs that showed the aircraft's position, altitude, and other critical data.

Suddenly, an alarm sounded, followed by a calm voice warning them of imminent danger.

"Collision alert! Collision alert! Pull up. Pull up."

Tory glanced at the panel's radar screen that showed no aircraft in the immediate area. "What the hell is she talking about?" Tory commented to Donna, the warning alarms continuing, the computerized voice continuing to warn of an impacting collision.

"We better pull up to be on the safe side," Donna commented, to which Tory nodded in agreement.

Suddenly, the cockpit and cabin was filled with unbelievably loud sounds that sounded like bullets hitting the aircraft. Donna immediately went into combat mode and grabbed control of the wheel. The cacophony of alarms, computerized voices, and what sounded like bullets strafing them created a surrealistic atmosphere. Both women concentrated on the instrument panel to find out what was happening.

"I've lost the port engine!" Donna exclaimed. The blasting sound continued outside the aircraft. *"Pull up! Pull up! Pull up!"*

Tory's mind started connecting the dots. "It's a volcanic ash plume!" she yelled to Donna. "Cut the starboard engine!"

Donna looked at Tory like she was insane.

"Donna, cut the starboard engine. It's our only chance."

Donna complied. *She's as crazy as her father*, she thought. "Starboard engine disengaged."

The *Goose 2* suddenly went quiet. The pounding bullets of pumice lessened as the jet began to slow. Donna sat wide-eyed awaiting instructions.

"Fiji air traffic," Tory paged with no response. "Mayday, this is N4202-A. We have been damaged by a pyroclastic cloud. One engine is damaged, the other is manually shut down." *We're in the middle of the fucking Pacific Ocean*, she thought. "Mayday, Fiji air traffic. We are losing altitude." There was still no response. "Damn, I hope they heard us."

Tory extended the wing flaps to maximize lift as she thought of options on how to regain power to the aircraft. She felt the plane drop suddenly and then stabilize. *We are heading down*, she thought.

"Donna, tell the passengers to prepare themselves for a water landing." Tory commanded calmly.

"Yes, Captain," she replied professionally. "Jesus Christ, not again…" she muttered as she unbuckled her seatbelt and went back to the cabin to deliver the news.

****

Once safely on-board *Juventus,* Molly, Linda, Betty, Taylor, and Lukas sat together on the re-opened deck. The waves had calmed somewhat as the bulk of the storm was no longer a threat and the tsunami waves had disappeared. Lukas huddled over his satellite phone as he reviewed sequential space photos of the area during the time of the eruption.

"I find it odd that there was no preparation for the volcanic explosion. It's pretty easy to track seismic activity and warn people to evacuate," Lukas said.

"Remember that huge one that hit Tonga a few years ago? That explosion was heard thousands of miles away," Linda said. "The tsunami it caused was peanuts compared to the one that hit us."

"I'm no geologist, but that's what I thought, too," Lukas agreed. "The tsunami here was over thirty feet tall."

"It's not just the disruption but also the depth of the water that impacts tsunami size," Betty commented. "Any word on casualties?"

Molly shook her head. "I asked Baptiste, but I think he was in shock."

Lukas zoomed in on the photo. The satellite captured the magnitude of the underwater explosion. Something caught his eye, and he zoomed in further. "Huh, I wonder what that is?"

He passed the phone over to Molly, who handed it to Linda who peered at it through her reading glasses.

"It's something between two of the islands between the new volcano and Kiva Oa," she pointed out. "Could be a glitch." She swiped through the photo sequence. "Whatever it is happened before the eruption." She continued to study the images. "Strangely enough, it's not showing up on any of the other satellite shots."

"That's weird," Molly replied. "Maybe it was a cloud passing over."

Linda nodded, acknowledging the possibility but unconvinced.

Lukas quickly spotted something. "Hide the phone," he told his mother. Gael walked over to the group. He wore a tight-fitting sleeveless shirt that accented his muscular arms. Taylor, who had been dozing off, immediately sat up.

"How is everybody doing?" Gael asked with concern. "Can I give anybody a shoulder and neck massage?" He looked directly at Taylor. "I heard you had an adventure earlier."

Taylor smiled. "Okay, if you insist," he grinned as Gael sat on the sofa in a kneeling position resting Taylor's head on his legs. Gael began with a scalp massage as Lukas watched his husband drift in and out of lucidity, before heading to Taylor's shoulders and pecs. Taylor quickly drifted off, relaxed and exhausted by the stress of the tsunami. Molly slipped Lukas his phone she'd been hiding.

"Let's find a quick place to talk," she suggested to him. Linda and Betty nodded. The four of them walked toward the back of the ship.

"I'm next." Linda winked at Gael as she passed by.

****

They huddled at the stern. The sun was set, and everything around them was dark as they motored through Baptiste's archipelago. In the distance, torches flamed and flickered, casting reflections that reached into the surf.

"Looks like the tsunami knocked out the power," Lukas observed as he pointed into the distance. "I think that's Kiva Oa running on a generator."

Molly quickly cut to the chase. "Lukas, we think that was an explosion."

Lukas wasn't following her. "What explosion?"

"That white shape I pointed out between the two islands. That's what I'm talking about," she responded.

"Lukas, can your phone capture the same area now?" Linda asked.

"I guess." He was confused. "I can request photos of our location. What are you thinking about?"

"It's suspicious at best. Could be a pipeline or something like that," Betty commented.

Lukas looked over to the sofa where Taylor slept, exhausted from his massage and the fatigue caused by the high adrenaline rush he experienced earlier. Gael was nowhere to be seen.

For some reason, Lukas felt relief that Gael was not with Taylor anymore. The man was attractive as hell and basically a walking pheromone factory.

A vibration buzzed and he pulled out his phone. He studied the screen and saw the new satellite pictures of the area. He zoomed over the archipelago. Kiva Oa was relatively unscathed, Baptiste's compound still intact and undamaged, minus a dock or two and several palm trees.

"How many islands are in his archipelago?" he asked.

"I thought he said there were ten," Linda answered, "or maybe it was nine."

"I'm pretty sure it's ten," Betty confirmed.

Lukas continued to study the photo. "Ten is what I thought, too."

"What does the photo show?" Molly asked.

"Eight," Lukas answered flatly.

Pierre and Gael approached their group from the main dining area of the salon. Marc, Aleks, and Captain Kepler had made their way to the room.

"And what mischief are we up to tonight?" Baptiste asked with an edge in his voice.

"How is Kiva Oa?" Lukas asked. "Were there any casualties in your islands?"

Pierre's piercing gaze felt like a laser cutting right through him. "Everyone is accounted for and fine. I build structures that survive just about anything, including tsunamis," he boasted.

"What about the other islands?" Linda asked. "Are they okay?"

"Luckily the other islands are uninhabited," Pierre stated coolly.

"My family moved to Kiva Oa but used to live on one of the other islands," Gael added. Lukas noticed the icy stare Pierre had on his face as Gael spoke.

"Why did they move?" Betty asked, honestly curious.

"Dinner is ready," Baptiste told them, barely masking his frustration. "Oh, and Gael's family moved to Kiva Oa because they found work there. That's why the other islands are uninhabited. Gael's father built the small airport we have on the island. Now, he manages it."

"I didn't know you had a father close by," Lukas replied.

Kailani now joined them. "We were just learning about your father," Molly jumped in. Kailani seemed surprised by the comment, which Molly found to be a strange reaction. Both Kailani and Gael seemed uncharacteristically edgy and irritable since the tsunami. It was like they were wounded after a fight, licking their emotional wounds. Molly had no idea if this was the case, but the disposition of the two was definitely different.

Chapter 19

Something was wrong; she could sense it. Baptiste looked serious and troubled by something. Even as a master manipulator and chameleon who could shape his personality to what he intended, Molly sensed something bad had happened.

Marc Hammer, who was a surprisingly decent piano player, played some classical pieces that most would recognize but not be able to match to a symphony or orchestral work.

The *Juventus* crewmates watched Marc's unknown talent with surprise. The music, conversation, and soft lighting helped lighten the mood. The alcohol also helped. Servers walked through the crowd with trays of heavy hors d'oeuvres for the guests. Captain Kepler socialized mostly with her crew with cursory nods to Baptiste's guests. Marcel stayed close to Pierre, but bounded over to Taylor as he walked toward the group.

"Why didn't you wake me up?" he asked. "I'm gonna miss the fun."

"You looked so cute sleeping," Lukas responded. "You've had an action-packed day."

When everyone was seated, Pierre stood to make a toast.

"I know this voyage was not what you were expecting." He raised his glass to everyone. "But we all may be part of history soon by introducing the world to the secrets of extended life and youth."

"Until we got hit by a tsunami," Betty reminded him. "Is that your toast?"

"No, Betty, but thanks for keeping me honest," Pierre answered as his crew members laughed. "May fortune favor us on this quest."

"Why does he convince himself that we voluntarily joined him on this quest?" Molly whispered as she took a sip of her sparkling water."

"Always the salesman." Linda clinked glasses with her friend. "Knowing him, he'll keep saying that until we actually believe we joined his quest voluntarily."

Baptiste stood, patiently awaiting his guests to become silent so he could continue. Molly noticed that his demeanor had changed. A sullen frown etched his face.

"One thing I'd like to leave you with is a discussion about knowledge. What is the point of having youth if you don't have wisdom or experience to accompany it?" Baptiste posed to his dinner guests. "We have possibly found a way to extend our physical life, but it's the knowledge that we seem to lose and thereby must relearn generation after generation. I'm not talking about written history or storytelling. I'm talking about transferring collective experience from one generation to the next."

"I'm not sure I follow," Taylor asked.

"Let me put it this way," Baptiste continued. "Pretend there is a collapse of society and modern technology is somehow lost. Then years later, someone finds a book and learns about something called electricity, and how it used to light the world. That's history, reporting of what once was. Now imagine if that same person discovered the book about how to create and harness electricity. How to build a turbine, storage and transmission of electricity so it could be used. That's called teaching. Practical information that can be used to help future generations."

Molly, Taylor, and Lukas glanced at each other, their eyes expressing confusion over what Baptiste was talking about.

"Is society about to fall or something?" Lukas whispered to them. "Really random thoughts there."

"I think he's drunk," Betty whispered. "He's not making sense."

Taylor and Molly nodded in agreement.

"He makes a good point about civilizations having to relearn everything," Lukas concluded. "I'm not sure why he's talking about it now. Kind of out of the blue."

Marc served plates of food to Betty, Molly, and Linda.

"I wonder what they are serving us tonight," Linda wondered.

"Whatever it is, it looks good," Betty commented. "I feel like I haven't eaten for days."

"That's because we haven't," Molly retorted as she poked through her entree.

"I wonder if this moonstone treatment will allow me to eat as much as I want." Linda laughed.

Taylor and Lukas wolfed down their dinners, and then dessert. Kailani had joined them now and she observed Gael and Marc discussing something on the other side of the salon.

"We have been siblings and best friends for more than a century," Kailani responded as she watched her brother. "Gael told me he mentioned we are *mahu*."

"The two-spirit people, right?" Lukas asked. "I'm still not totally sure what that means,"

She rested her hand atop of Lukas' as he observed Gael and Kepler talking, Marc having departed the salon.

"It means we have two spirits inside us. I don't know how the shamans can tell just by looking at us as babies."

"Well, you are both beautiful inside and out," Lukas said with uncomfortable honesty. "Maybe they could see that in you as babies."

"I'm going to run to the restroom," Kailani said, distracted by something. "I'll be back in a minute."

Taylor joined Lukas at the table. "What were you two talking about?"

"Just a bit more depth on what *mahu* means and what that means for Gael and Kailani," Lukas answered. "She was starting to tell me more before she ran off. It was odd."

"Did I scare her away?" Taylor responded.

"I don't think so, but you almost gave me a heart attack during the tsunami," Lukas confessed. "I knew you would be okay, because that's who you are...you figure things out. But it made me realize how much I love you and how you are so interwoven with my soul and my life. For a brief second, right as I saw you guys go over the wave, a thought went through my mind about what I would do if you were gone."

"And? Speed-dialing the Chippendale dancers?" Taylor laughed.

Lukas gave him a wry smile. "Well, duh," he joked, before getting serious. "It made me wonder how my mom felt when my dad died. How everything they were together was just, over in a matter of seconds."

Taylor nodded. "I was worried about you, too. I figured with my luck, I'd survive in the tiny boat and *Juventus* would have been destroyed. I'm too young to be thinking like that, but I couldn't help it."

As the night progressed, the mood improved. Music played from the surround-sound audio system as the interior light display grew dim but colorful. Lukas and Taylor tapped their feet to a song they danced to at their wedding. The whole room looked relaxed. Marc and Aleks continued to stare at them with an intensity that made Lukas uncomfortable.

"I can't figure those two out," Lukas whispered.

"The whole crew is strange," Taylor opined.

"Plus the oddball in chief," Lukas answered. "I don't remember Baptiste being such a strange man. Never spent this much time with him."

"I need to get some fresh air," Taylor said. "Want to join me outside on the deck?"

****

They sat together, each with their hand on the other's thigh. The warm breeze cooled the night air as they surveyed the horizon.

"Can I ask you a question?" Lukas asked rhetorically. "If I died, would you get married again?"

Taylor gazed back at him. "Why on earth would you ask me that?"

"That's not an answer; that's evasion," Lukas pointed out half seriously.

Taylor thought for a moment. "No. I don't think I would get married again. Would you?"

"Why wouldn't you want to? Has this marriage been difficult?" Lukas asked.

"Lukas, why are you asking me these things?"

"Has it?" Lukas pushed. "Has it been difficult?"

"No, Lukas! It's not been difficult. Far from it. I wouldn't get married again because I married you and I can't even imagine being with someone else."

"Even Gael?" Lukas poked.

"Gael? What are you talking about?"

"I've seen the two of you talking closely. Then you were obviously enjoying him touching you during the massage. I just wondered."

Taylor struggled to keep his cool and not respond emotionally and took a deep breath. "Lukas, what's wrong?"

Lukas put his face in his hands. "I don't know what's wrong with me," he said. "I feel that everything has been knocked off center and way out of my comfort zone. I was nervous about the board meeting and secretly resenting my dad that he got what he wanted with me to be part of Phoenix and probably my mom's successor. He's gone and I can't talk to him about it. Now Tory is getting married, and we may be grandparents before we are parents…if we even become parents. Everything seems so out of my control and I'm feeling old and tired. Insecure."

Taylor sat silently for a few moments. "A lot has changed in the last year and a half," he agreed. "But you don't ever need to doubt the love, and a healthy amount of lust, I have for you, okay?"

Lukas nodded. "I don't think I realized how different I would feel without my dad. I'm suddenly very aware of my age and this moonstone has reminded me of how much time has passed when I look in the mirror every morning."

"I remember when my dad died," Taylor recounted. "I felt like the rug was pulled out from under me. Even though we weren't very close, it was just his presence that I missed, and..." Taylor cut off for a moment. "He was a generation ahead of me, my safeguard against my own mortality. When he died, I realized I was next in line."

"Hopefully later than sooner," Lukas added.

"I hope we have a nice long life together," Taylor reminded him. "There's always gonna be temptation out there, babe. Like Gael or anyone else."

"Were you tempted?" Lukas asked.

Taylor paused before he spoke, knowing his answer would be impactful. "Yes, I was, but not tempted enough to act on it." He decided on being fully honest, whatever the cost. "But I chose you years ago and still I choose to be with you, period."

"Thank you for being honest," Lukas answered. "That took courage considering your neurotic husband." He laughed. "But I was tempted, too, and the guilt has been eating me alive."

"Just let the guilt go," Taylor replied. "I'll eat you alive instead, if you know what I mean." He reached over to hug his husband. It was what Lukas needed to hear.

Chapter 20

A scream pierced the elegant atmosphere of Pierre's salon. Lukas immediately recognized the voice of his mother, followed by the hollow thud of someone falling to the floor. Dishes crashed onto the floor and all he could see was a commotion of cabin staff attending to someone or something. Horror gripped him when he saw Linda Eastman writhing on the floor, clawing at her neck and struggling to breathe. He darted over to his mother who was already trying to help Linda.

"Ma, what's going on?"

"Linda. She…she grabbed her chest and collapsed right after she had some food!"

Linda gasped for breath, her complexion darkening to a purplish-blue.

Taylor ran over to them. "Help me get her on the table," he yelled to Lukas. The two men lifted Linda onto her back. "What's happening to her?"

Another thud came from where they had just been standing. Betty wailed and stumbled, clutching her chest and falling to the floor. Lukas' eyes darted between the two fallen women, not fully comprehending what had happened.

Linda's body convulsed in spasms as her eyes rolled back and her skin continued to darken. Foam oozed out of her mouth as she struggled to breathe and clutched at her chest. Taylor saw Molly attempt to give

Linda mouth to mouth resuscitation. "No!" he shouted. "She may have been poisoned! You can't get near her mouth, or it may affect you!"

"She's having a heart attack! I can't just let her…" Molly cried.

Taylor straddled Linda and massaged her chest area to stimulate the heart. Trained as a first responder, Taylor grabbed a paper menu and created a barrier between his lips and Linda's. He breathed heavily into her mouth as her chest rose. *At least she's not choking,* Taylor thought. "We need to get oxygen! Where's sick bay?" Molly had already started pumping Betty's chest in hope of reviving her.

Lukas grabbed two waiters who had served them earlier. The younger of the two men stood frozen in shock at the spectacle of two struggling women. "Help me get her to sick bay, whatever it's called." The men left Linda prone on the tabletop and carried her out the double doors of the salon. Lukas kept one arm on Linda as he assisted in carrying her.

Taylor then ran over to assist Molly with Betty, who was struggling with similar symptoms as Linda. *They've been poisoned*, he thought. Molly's body weight pounded on Betty's chest while Taylor breathed into her mouth, hoping to bring her to consciousness.

"She's got a weak pulse. Same as Linda," Taylor announced. "We've got to stabilize them. I think they're in cardiac arrest!"

Kailani sprinted across the salon to assist Taylor and Molly as Gael followed Linda's stretcher. "We need to get her on a table," Kailani suggested and crouched to elevate Betty by herself. Taylor and Molly were stunned at Kailani's strength. Marc Hammer ran to assist, barking orders at his staff members to assist the two passengers. "Get her to sick bay!" he commanded Aleks.

****

As the chaos unfolded, Pierre Baptiste entered the salon in shocked silence. Known for his ability to remain calm in a multitude of business scenarios, Pierre stood rigid as the evening meal unraveled into a life-or-death emergency.

"Bridge! There have been two emergencies in the salon," he yelled into the intercom, his voice sharp with panic. "We need to get to a hospital immediately!"

"Sir," Captain Kepler answered. "Power is out across the country; buildings have been damaged by the tsunami. Kiva Oa has the only clinic in the archipelago, if it's even standing."

"Then take us there, damnit!" Baptiste barked in frustration. "Our sick bay will be stretched to handle two critical emergencies at the same time."

"I understand, sir," Kepler responded. "May I ask what happened?"

"Linda Eastman and Betty Bao collapsed during dinner. It appears they are in cardiac arrest! Taylor thinks they've been poisoned!"

On the bridge, Kepler held a quaking hand over her mouth. *Shit! Not now!* she cursed to herself. "I'll do what I can, sir. It's pitch-black outside and there's a volcano erupting underwater. There is a huge ash cloud which rules out an air rescue for the time being."

Baptiste suddenly called sick bay with his handheld device. He couldn't take the risk of two women dying onboard. He yelled in French to someone before disconnecting the device.

"I just spoke with Dr. Nevon. Their best chance is to remain on board and be treated in the *Juventus* hospital."

Chapter 21

Linda Eastman's body struggled against the ventilator. The sedative she was given had not yet kicked in, so she endured a challenging intubation while conscious. Her eyes were wild with panic and confusion. Dr. Nevon, Pierre Baptiste's personal physician and the de facto ship doctor, worked feverishly to get a read on what was happening to both Linda and Betty.

"The sedative is starting to take effect," he commented as he watched Linda's eyelids get heavier. Betty had never regained consciousness.

Mouth swabs and blood samples were currently being evaluated in the adjacent lab to detect if there was a triggering substance for cardiac arrest, and if so, what it was.

"Neither Linda nor Betty has a history of cardiac issues!" Molly announced to the room. "How can they both have heart attacks at the same time?"

"We don't know if that's what happened, Mrs. Halloran," Dr. Nevon commented. "Cardiac arrest can be caused by a number of factors."

"Like triggering substances?" Taylor interjected.

"Yes, that is one possible cause, Taylor."

"But they both dropped within minutes of each other," Molly commented. "That can't be a coincidence."

Dr. Nevon shook his head. "It's highly likely the two episodes are linked, but we can't rule out coincidence."

The evening had taken a tragic turn with both Linda and Betty clinging to life. Nurses and crew members did what they could to keep their patients comfortable as Dr. Nevon ran between sick bay and the laboratory, anxiously awaiting the test results. "Saliva test shows negative for any toxin," He breathed heavily as he announced the news. "Blood tests should be back soon."

"So that rules out poison?" Lukas asked.

"Ingested poison ruled out, most likely," Dr. Nevon responded.

"What can a blood test tell us about someone's cardiac arrest?" Taylor followed up.

"Abnormal levels of magnesium, potassium, and troponin can indicate a heart attack," Nevon responded. "I always run toxicology, too. I need to get some notes on what transpired."

"Could the moonstone have caused this?" Molly asked. "Because if it did, then you'll probably have more patients soon."

"I've never seen this reaction from moonstone," Nevon clarified. "Even so, it's extremely rare for a substance to bring upon cardiac arrest. Especially one applied topically."

Molly nodded. "But is it impossible?"

"Not impossible but highly unlikely. Unless she somehow took a large amount orally or intravenously," Nevon replied.

"Are Linda or Betty allergic to anything?" Lukas asked. "Mom, are you aware of something that could have triggered such a violent reaction? I can't believe they are not connected."

"Peanuts? Shellfish?" Taylor asked. "It's very strange this happened almost simultaneously."

Molly shook her head. "None that I'm aware of."

"That's a good question, Taylor," Dr. Nevon added. "I'll have their histamine levels checked, but as a precaution," He looked toward a nurse. "Give each of them an antihistamine injection."

Nevon went back to the laboratory to check the results of the blood test.

Lukas noticed his mother had gotten quiet. "Ma, everything okay?" he asked, but Molly didn't respond immediately.

"I was just thinking," she told her son. "This all seems surreal. Linda and Betty knocked down at the same time."

It wasn't a typical response, Lukas noticed. Molly had been rather clinical since the whole event in the salon almost an hour earlier. *Knocked down?* Lukas thought. *Odd way to phrase it.*

Dr. Nevon rushed back to sick bay. "It's a toxin," the doctor grimly informed them. "Blood levels of magnesium and potassium are high. Troponin is off the charts for both of them. I asked the lab folks to keep digging and are running the toxicity profiles through the database. The volcanic cloud is creating satellite interference, so our systems are slow."

Molly stared into nothing, again deep in thought.

"Ma, what's going on? I know that look in your eyes."

Molly returned to the conversation. "This reminds me of the night your father died."

"In what way?" Taylor asked.

"There are details about that night. Similar situation, like deja vu."

Lukas glanced at Taylor to see if he understood where his mom was going with her conversation.

"Ma, what's deja vu?" Lukas asked. "Dad died from the stress of a home invasion."

Molly paused for a moment but said nothing as Dr. Nevon came back into the room, harried with disbelief.

"It's TTX. An extremely lethal toxin," Dr. Nevon announced to the group. "They have a life-threatening amount in their bloodstreams."

"Shit, that's bad," Taylor exclaimed.

"What's TTX?" Lukas asked, but he saw that both Taylor and his mother already knew.

"Tetrodotoxin," Taylor sighed. "One of the most potent neurotoxins around. It explains their symptoms."

"Victims go into respiratory paralysis," Dr. Nevon explained grimly. "Patients die from suffocation as the muscles of the diaphragm seize up, or the toxin can stop the heart, which explains the cardiac arrest."

"Holy shit." Lukas sighed.

"It's good we were able to get them intubated," the doctor commented. "But there's something else about the toxin."

"What specifically?" Molly asked.

"It's not pure TTX. It's been modified somehow," Dr. Nevon explained.

"Modified with what?" Molly asked.

"I don't know to be honest." Nevon massaged the back of his neck. "My guess is that it's been genetically manipulated."

A troubled look appeared on Molly's face. "Ma,

what is it?" Lukas asked.

"What's their prognosis?" Molly asked Dr. Nevon.

"The fatality rate is quite high." He paused. "We need to keep them breathing artificially until the toxin is broken down. Their hearts are in arrhythmia, but still functional."

Dr. Nevon scribbled instructions on a chart and handed them to a nurse. "Put them on sotalol. It's all we have on board." He turned to face Molly. "It's a beta blocker."

"So will that save them?" Molly asked.

"I don't know," Dr. Nevon told them grimly. "Lungs, heart, and other organs can fail, but we have to keep them on saline, ventilators, and the beta blockers to even have a chance."

"How does one come in contact with TTX?" Lukas asked. "What's a neurotoxin doing on board *Juventus*?"

"It's all around us," Taylor explained. "It's often found in certain types of fish."

"None of us ate fish," Molly commented.

"One doesn't need to eat fish directly. The poison can be ingested, injected, or absorbed through an injury on the skin," Taylor continued. "It's a toxin that comes from a living thing that produces it as a defense against predators."

"Like a pufferfish?" Lukas asked.

"Pufferfish is one species," Dr. Nevon explained. "It is also found in porcupinefish, some triggerfish, some snails, salamanders and newts."

"How would two people be affected and the rest of us be fine?" Molly asked.

"It could be deliberate or accidental but targeted at a high enough dose to do this." Dr. Nevon pointed to the two victims.

"What about the blue-ringed octopus?" Lukas asked. "What kind of toxin do they have?"

"Well," Nevon said. "They are extremely toxic and also contain the TTX neurotoxin, but they are quite small and rare."

"And missing," Taylor jumped in. "There was one in the salon's aquarium yesterday and today it was missing."

"Are you sure?" Dr. Nevon asked.

"To be honest," Taylor thought, "I don't know, but it wasn't visible in the aquarium today. I checked a couple of times."

Chapter 22

Molly Halloran awoke on the cold sick bay floor, a dark blue blanket covering her. The rhythmic humming of the molten-salt reactor vibrated slowly on the decks below. Gael and Kailani sat next to her, cross-legged, asleep with their heads resting on each other's shoulders. Above her, Lukas stood with his arms crossed. Serious and no doubt pondering a solution to this nightmare. She always counted on Lukas' brilliant brain in times of emergencies like this. Ever since he was a boy, he had a knack for solving complex problems, often with results no one else could fathom. Molly prayed Lukas would do the same to save two of her best friends.

Linda and Betty slept peacefully, loaded with sedatives and fluids to keep their organs flushed. It was the noise of the ventilator that vexed Molly. The mechanical pumping and pulling of air in and out of their lungs created nightmarish, rhythmic sounds that Molly knew she wouldn't soon forget. Watching the bellows inflate and deflate was like being hypnotized by a macabre accordion.

Pierre Baptiste entered the room and asked for an update. "Both patients are stable," Dr. Nevon commented. "They are doing remarkably well considering their age."

The comment irked Molly, but she said nothing.

Dr. Nevon backtracked. "Forgive me. I misspoke. They are both remarkably healthy women, and their cardiovascular systems are strong."

"When will they be able to breathe without a machine?" Gael asked.

"I don't know." Nevon theorized. "We are bombarding their bodies with saline so their kidneys don't fail while processing and removing the TTX from their blood stream."

Baptiste had been on the bridge when the lab results came back. "TTX is a lethal biological toxin," he told Pierre proactively. "Our lab found it in their blood."

Pierre Baptiste stood silently and muttered, "Any idea how it got into their bloodstreams?"

Nevon shook his head as Lukas and Taylor listened. "It normally takes twenty-four hours to be detectable in the blood, if it's ingested. That is long after symptoms develop."

"How many hours after symptoms did you take the sample?" Baptiste quizzed him,

"The crew got them downstairs to sick bay quickly and I took the sample immediately," Nevon responded. "Probably less than ten minutes after initial symptoms. Not enough time for the toxin to circulate through the blood…unless…"

"We're all ears, Doctor," Molly pushed him. "Unless what?"

A serious look hung on Nevon's face. "Unless it was somehow injected directly into their bloodstream."

****

Juventus shuddered and groaned unexpectedly. The bow pitched downward, requiring people to hold on for stability. Lukas and Taylor held on to Molly as the angle of the floor increased. Panic surged through Lukas' body. He struggled to keep it together and tried not to think about what was going on outside in the deep water.

"What's going on?" Taylor asked.

Baptiste paged the bridge. "Captain, what just happened? Did we hit something?"

There was no response, so he paged Kepler again.

"We've got two sick women that need a hospital," Molly reminded him.

"What on earth is she doing?" Pierre grabbed the intercom and cursed at the person on the other end of the line. "Damnit, what the hell are you doing to my ship, Captain?" Baptiste growled. "It felt like we hit something!"

"Sir, I'm trying to maneuver. The ocean floor is shaking, it looks like another earthquake like the one that caused the incident earlier."

Baptiste knew better than to ask more in front of Molly, Taylor, and Lukas.

"Can you take us out to deeper water?" Baptiste asked emotionlessly.

"Aye, sir." She paused. "How far out do you want to go?"

"You know the territorial boundaries. Stay within those," Baptiste ordered.

"We are in an area of heavy seismic activity," Kepler reported. "The Fijians claim there are two volcanoes currently active. Tsunamis have hit the main island, in addition to your archipelago."

"What's the damage to Kiva Oa?" Baptiste asked.

"Battered but functioning," she replied.

"Damage to Viti Levu?" Baptiste inquired about the largest island in Fiji.

"Minimal, sir. They've closed the airport as a precaution. The ash cloud has already diverted over twenty flights to other countries. One flight appears to have disappeared from radar en route. There is a search going on now."

This news grabbed Taylor's attention. Lukas and Molly also froze. Instinctively, they knew they couldn't react while Pierre was around, despite the fact that any news like that struck worry in the hearts of anyone in the aviation business. Taylor smiled to cloak the worry that every parent experiences. *I hope that wasn't my kid.*

****

The *Goose 2* descended toward the Pacific Ocean. Since it was nighttime, Tory and Donna had to rely upon their instruments in order to maintain their spatial orientation. Darkness created confusion, especially over water where there were no lights. A pilot could easily become confused by the blackness of the ocean and the blackness of the sky. Tory had never experienced an engine failure like this, and now she had very few options. Her heart thumped in her chest while she fought fear to remain clear headed.

Both engines were off. One likely destroyed by volcanic debris, the other one purposely shut off to minimize damage and allow for what she and Donna would now attempt.

"How is everyone in the rear of the plane?" Tory asked.

"They trust us, but they're scared, of course," Donna replied. "Wilma is not a great flier anyway, and she has no idea of what's about to happen. Pepe trusts you."

"Well, that's sweet," she said, realizing how he also had no idea of what was about to happen. There was a knock on the cockpit door for formality only, and Pepe walked in.

"Are you okay, *cara*?" he asked.

"Si, caro." Tory attempted basic Italian. No telling if she'd have the chance again.

Even in a dangerous predicament, Pepe's boyish smile still beamed. "You've got this, ladies," he said, hoping to boost their confidence.

In less than a minute, Tory spoke to the plane. "I'm gonna be transparent. We've got one shot to restart at least one engine, so that's what we're gonna do. Donna and I will put us into a steep dive in order to increase our speed while we try to start the engines. If successful, we will continue our trip as planned. If not, we will need to land on the water, and if that's the case, we will have little time to prepare for that."

"Ready?" She looked over at Donna who gave her the thumbs up. "I'll take flight control. You try to restart the engine, okay?" Another thumbs up.

Tory pushed the yoke forward and the plane started to descend, nose first. Gravity pulled the jet toward the rippling black ocean, its speed increasing by the second.

"Speed is 450 miles per hour. We need to crank it up." Tory steepened the descent and the plane's speed increased to 550 mph. "Try starting the ignition," she commanded Donna.

"No luck. We're still too high."

Tory tilted the angle of decline to forty-five degrees, and they felt the speed of *Goose 2* increase.

"We're at 650 mph now. Try both engines and see what happens."

Donna tried again and the engine they purposely shut off came to life. "Engine 2 is running!"

Tory gave the thumbs up. "Worst case, we make it to Fiji on one engine. Not ideal, but we can do it."

"I'll continue to try Engine 1," Donna told her as Tory leveled off the plane.

"We're at twelve-thousand feet," Tory told her. "Keep trying please."

Within a few minutes, the second engine roared to life and the *Goose 2* was back at full power. "How much time to Fiji?" Tory asked.

"Less than two hours. We should land by 11:30 p.m. local time," Donna responded.

"Great, please radio Fiji air control and ask for priority landing due to the ash cloud strike."

Donna shot Tory another thumbs up, and the jet continued through the night sky toward Fiji.

Chapter 23

Inside the darkened sick-bay, Molly's face was etched in thought or worry. As Lukas approached her, she patted the chair next to her, an invitation to talk.

"They're not going to make it if we can't get them to a hospital, Lukas," she told him with morbid certainty.

"Ma, they're in good hands. Doctor Nevon said we need to wait until the toxin is flushed out. We just need to keep them breathing…"

"But they're not breathing. On their own, at least. Neither of them wanted to be intubated nor resuscitated. Iron-clad living wills. I'm torn on what to do."

Lukas was surprised to hear his mother's view on this. "Two more hours, Ma. We should know by then if the toxin has been filtered out of their systems."

"I know, I know. They are tough women, and they will pull through," Molly said trying to convince herself. "But I've got a bad feeling about all of this."

Lukas gazed at his mom. He had never heard her say something like this before and decided to change the subject. "Ma, how did they get poisoned? Did you see anything?"

Molly shook her head. "I wasn't paying attention, but there is something strange going on."

"It's pretty awful to see two women who could be your sisters go through something so violent, Ma. It's totally normal—"

"Honey, that's not what I mean," Molly interrupted, but paused, not sure of what to say.

"What do you mean then?" Lukas asked.

Molly stood. He could see she was antsy, preoccupied. "This reminds me of the night your father was killed."

Lukas nodded and decided not to argue the semantics of whether or not his father was killed or if he had a heart attack due to the stress of the home attack. "How so, Ma?"

"You will probably think I'm a paranoid old woman, but I'm…suspicious of everything going on here. First it was your dad, now Linda and Betty…"

"I'm not following you. Are you referring to all three of them going into cardiac arrest?"

"Yes. And I wonder if it was supposed to be me," Molly stated, prepared for her son to not believe her.

"Ma, why do you think that?" Lukas was genuinely surprised at her comment.

Molly faced her son. "Too many coincidences, and I was there for both incidents," she explained. "Maybe someone wanted me out of the way. They had a bone to pick with me, not John. And certainly not Linda or Betty."

"Sure. It's a coincidence, but who would want to do that to you?"

"Pierre Baptiste," Molly stated confidently.

"Whoa, Ma. That's crazy."

"Lukas, I need you to be very calm when I tell you this," she whispered. "Please keep a poker face as if I'm talking to you about the weather."

"Um, okay, Ma."

"I'm certain Baptiste was the board member who tried to steal the Poseidon technology back when your dad was kidnapped in Dubai a few years ago." His head raced at the bombshell theory, but he remained unemotional.

"You think Malik was working for him?" he asked, referring to the man who did the dirty work on the Dubai side of the project Poseidon.

She looked over her shoulder and noticed Gael and Kailani speaking with Taylor.

"Baptiste wanted to be CEO, and he's never forgiven me for it."

"Ma, seriously?" Lukas tried to suppress his voice. "Why do you think he would want to kill you and not Dad? Or anybody for that matter?"

"He had a motive. I was an obstacle to him, and he knows I don't buy his bullshit."

"Ma, you are freaking me out. Is this why Baptiste wanted the meeting to be here, in his floating palace?"

Molly nodded. "It was a set-up, but not for your dad. For me."

Lukas wasn't following her. "Ma, Baptiste invited you after Dad died."

"My thoughts are jumping, Lukas, but good question. I was referring to the original incident in Ocotillo Ridge. That was where the intruders mistook Dad for me. Are you following me now?"

"Ma, this sounds a bit cloak and dagger to me. Why would Baptiste go to all this trouble to kill you or Dad? He could have had Dad killed in Dubai…" Lukas paused as he put the connections together. "So why didn't he do it then?"

"Lukas." She tried to calm herself to sound

rational. "Your father kept me as the leading shareholder of Phoenix Equities for a reason."

"Like tax reasons, you mean?"

"No, because he didn't trust his own judgment all the time. He had a knack for scouting out new technology, especially those that could help humanity," Molly explained. "But your dad thought the best about everyone, at least initially. He trusted people at face value."

"That's one of the things that made him successful, isn't it?"

Molly nodded. "Yes, he was disarmingly open to meeting different people and hearing about their ideas, investing in them and nurturing them to success. That made your father unique. People trusted him."

"Exactly. Instead, Baptiste lured me over there with a bullshit kidnapping plot. That's the part that I can't reconcile. Lukas, listen to me. He did not want to kill your dad. It was me he's been after."

"But I don't understand something." Lukas replied. "Why would Baptiste go to all this trouble? He could have easily bought Phoenix Equities or any of its companies. He wouldn't have needed to kill anybody. He probably could have paid cash and been done with it. Dad would have jumped at the chance, so why all the theatrics?"

Jolts of memories from that night in Dubai came flooding back. The cat and mouse games, the choreographed kidnapping, and the easy clues as to what Malik's motive was, besides the family revenge part. The pieces started falling together and Molly saw a light of understanding twinkling in her son's eyes.

"Dad was the golden goose?"

"Yes, he was visionary, creative, well-connected, and incredibly ethical. He had a long line of companies that wanted to become part of Phoenix because they knew your dad's reputation and his tendency to let the entrepreneurs continue to develop the technology while Phoenix funded it. Trust was his currency and Baptiste had none, so he needed him."

"I never really looked at it that way. That's just who he is." Lukas exhaled.

"That conversation, business proposition, whatever it was about Baptiste offering to pay us to be the face behind the moonstone. It's further proof that Pierre coveted Dad's reputation as an honest, but tough businessman. Now he's hoping to use us for the same thing."

"Just like with Poseidon, Phoenix Equities' involvement brought instant credibility to the table. That was Dad's brand."

His mother nodded sadly watching her son absorb everything. "But there's more, Lukas."

"More? This has already rocked me to the core, Ma."

Molly caressed her son's face like she did when he was a child. Her touch always calmed him. She hadn't told any of her kids about her theory that John was killed and didn't die of a heart attack.

Lukas embraced his mother for the first time in a long time.

"Lukas," Molly whispered. "There is one more thing I need to explain."

"Yeah, Ma?"

"My instincts tell me there is something much bigger going on," she told him. "I don't know what it is, but every cell of my body is telling me there's another story."

Lukas knew his mother's intuition was usually accurate. "Ma, what is it?"

"Is there any way you can get video from the ship's logs?" she asked.

"Yeah, Ma. I can try once I get my laptop." He thought about the video footage from his and Taylor's stateroom when they woke up with Gael in their bed. "What are you looking for?"

Molly paused, her lips tight as she thought about what to say. "I believe your father was killed, and now Linda and Betty have also suffered heart attacks, simultaneously," she added emphasis. "It's too random."

Lukas didn't know what to say, but she had a point. "It's the TTX toxin, Lukas."

"I've thought about that, too." he replied. "But can the TTX create cardiac arrest?"

Molly glanced up at her son, the same worried look even more intense. "I need to tell you something, Lukas. Back in the Cold War, both the United States and the Soviets were busy developing technologies to kill each other's spies and prevent state secrets from being leaked."

"And you think they have something like that?" Lukas asked.

Molly didn't answer, but Lukas knew she was thinking about something. "Even after we left the CIA, we still heard about weapons in development, including one they called the HAG."

Lukas paused. "That's an odd nickname for a spy killer."

"HAG stood for a heart attack gun. Its name explains it," Molly continued. "It delivered a lethal dose of a toxin directly into an enemy's blood stream. The toxin quickly created symptoms that mimicked a heart attack, or cardiac arrest as we call it today."

"That sounds like something out of a spy thriller," Lukas commented. "How did the bullet not get discovered eventually during an autopsy?"

"Because there wasn't a bullet, nor were there any traces of gunpowder," Molly explained. "It was the ultimate stealth weapon to kill someone and leave no evidence behind."

His brow furled, Lukas thought through scenarios on how a weapon like this could actually work. *No bullet and no gunpowder?* he thought. "I'm at a loss, Ma."

"Well I never saw one of these guns, but I was told that they were small and concealable," Molly remembered.

"Then how did the toxin get into the person to cause the fake heart attack?" Lukas asked.

"It was a real cardiac arrest that killed people, Lukas," Molly told him grimly. "The toxin was so concentrated it immediately stopped the heart. Back then, we didn't have the technology to dig much deeper than a standard autopsy." Lukas could see the gears in his mom's head were turning. "Of course!" she exclaimed.

"What, Ma? What are you thinking about?"

"The gun didn't use gunpowder and was likely spring-loaded or battery powered," Molly continued. "Most likely the former."

"So it was a silent weapon?" Lukas asked.

Molly nodded excitedly. "Yes, and I think I know how the toxin was delivered to the victim." She paced excitedly. "Why didn't I think about this before? I could have checked your dad…" she trailed off.

"And?" Lukas asked, anxious to learn what his mom was thinking.

"It was frozen," Molly said confidently.

"What was frozen, Ma?"

"The toxin could have been delivered in a type of miniature dart made of ice." She continued to pace the floor. "Of course, it wouldn't leave a trace."

"Ma, you're losing me."

"Sorry, honey," she apologized. "I thought it was a joke when I heard about it years ago. The toxin was super-concentrated and the dart was so small, the victim would think they were bitten by a mosquito if they felt anything at all. By the time the victim was dead, the ice dart had melted, and the small entry hole was undetectable."

"This sounds wild." Lukas shook his head.

"It was the Cold War and both sides were very creative," she agreed.

"So how?" Lukas started to ask before his mother interrupted.

"We need to study the video from dinner," she continued excitedly. "I bet we'll find the weapon."

"And the shooter…" Lukas smiled at his mom. "And possibly the identity of the person who killed Dad."

Molly smiled at her son for acknowledging her theory. "Honey," she whispered. "If somebody used this gun to kill Dad, potentially Linda and Betty, then

there's something far more sinister behind all of this."
Molly paused. "I need to tell you something else."

Chapter 24

Lukas stared out the window of the *Juventus* observation deck. Sunlight rippled through the clean blue water, giving him a view of rocks, boulders, and a slightly curved mound of a bluish-white material he now knew as moonstone. They continued to cruise through Baptiste's archipelago, which he could swear had ten islands, but now had eight according to the satellite photos. "Maybe they were submerged by the tsunami and scrubbed clean of vegetation and were no longer visible from space." One thing that Lukas noticed was the absence of sea life. Where other locations teemed with aquatic mammals and fish, it felt strangely barren where he looked now. Instead, the ocean floor resembled more of a quarry than a sea life sanctuary.

The information his mother shared with him was still sinking into his head. Her theories rattled him and challenged so much of what he believed to be true. The concept that Molly Halloran could have been an assassination target floored him at first, but then he remembered a couple of occasions that with her newly voiced theories, could have some merit. To him, Molly was a rock of stability and unconditional love. She supported him and his sisters unflinchingly, protected them like a lioness, but also let them fall down, make mistakes, and learn. The thought that someone would want to snuff out her life was inconceivable. As he got older and learned more about his parents and life in general, he saw Molly's edgier side, facets he'd never seen before, and he had to adjust to these new insights.

But the second theory she shared was so bizarre, it was terrifying. His mother was serious, and he could see fear and stress in her eyes, but she was also practical, and rarely melodramatic. Lukas needed to process what she told him before he told Taylor. He was certain that what she told him had merit, and she told her son, both to protect him, but also so that he would push for answers to discover the truth, should she somehow end up dead, even from what could appear to be "natural causes."

Lukas remembered his rather predictable, mundane life as a tech entrepreneur until one day, several years earlier, he got news his father had been kidnapped overseas and suddenly everything changed. The event was a catalyst, he could now see clearly in hindsight, and potentially a harbinger for events to come. Now the world took on a new edge, one he'd never seen before because his parents protected him from it, until today. There was way more deception, treachery, greed, and selfishness in the world than he ever imagined. His mother pulled back a rug he never knew was there, and now he watched the world's exposed underbelly with morbid curiosity. He chuckled to himself when he remembered the insignificance of things that seemed important just hours ago. Molly had opened a window to a future that seemed inconceivable this morning.

Lukas reflected upon the first time he'd stepped aboard *Juventus* and was dazzled by the sea creatures living their lives in the Bora Bora lagoon. The last couple of days seemed surreal as he remembered awakening in his luxurious overwater bungalow, drinking an espresso, then diving into the aqua-colored water to swim with his husband. *That seems like weeks ago*, he thought. Until that morning, he had no watch or phone, he had no idea the time or day or where in the world they were. Adding to the disorientation, they were being held in a submersible yacht with a hologram-augmented reality interior, controlled daylight, and pixelated windows that could convey an outside view of icy glaciers or tropical lagoons instantly. In fact, he wasn't even sure if he was staring at an underwater landscape or if it, too, was a computer-generated image.

"Hey, baby." Taylor approached and sat next to him, his arm tossed over Lukas' shoulder offering comfort or protection. "What are you doing down here?"

"Thinking," he muttered sadly as he recounted the suspicions his mother had regarding Pierre Baptiste's disdain and the theory that the poison had been meant for her. "She's pretty certain she's the target." Lukas decided to not elaborate more as he was still processing it himself.

Taylor dropped his head. "This is a fucking nightmare."

Lukas nodded. "I know. I've been trying to figure out how we can help Linda and Betty, or at least try." A pause hung in the air as each assessed the other. "I wonder…if." He paused for a few seconds. "Never mind, it's a crazy idea."

"I think I know what is swirling around in that handsome head of yours," Taylor observed. "You want to see if the moonstone can help, don't you?"

"I've thought about it, yes." Lukas let out a sigh. "But what if it actually can work?"

Taylor shook his head. "It sounds like science fiction, but what if Kailani is right? Maybe moonstone can actually save them."

Taylor ran his fingers through his hair, a habit when he was perplexed. "From what I can see, the mounds and the geometric boulders will be the easiest to get at. They looked about four-hundred or so feet off starboard."

"You are thinking about taking out the sub?" Lukas asked, already knowing the answer.

"I don't know any other way. We'll need to get Baptiste's permission first," Taylor answered. "I have no idea how to open the hatch to launch it outside the ship."

"Before we solve that," Lukas asked. "Are you on board with this idea?"

Despite his healthy self-confidence, Taylor had to think for a second. "I've never piloted a submarine, so I'm a little worried about that to be honest."

"I'm sure someone on board can captain the sub," Lukas suggested. "Baptiste said it's like piloting a helicopter, remember?"

Taylor shook his head. "Maybe the controls are similar, but water and air are very different substances through which to pilot yourself."

"Are there any other people who could operate it on board?"

"I think it's worth finding out," Taylor responded. "We've got twenty-or-so crew members to ask, all of whom have a vested interest in getting their next fix."

"Baptiste made a comment about Marc having piloted a tourist sub in Mexico," Lukas pointed out.

"Sure, we can check with him and the others. There are two subs, so I can take at least one of them. Could open new job opportunities for me if I'm good at it."

"We'll need to check with Gael and Kailani so we get the right amount. And by we, I mean you," Lukas clarified. "Maybe they know how much we already have on board."

"Or what we are supposed to do with it. Other than removing wrinkles, it's probably a bit more involved process."

"I'll take that question to Gael and Kailani and be ready to go by the time you get back," Lukas concluded.

****

Marc Hammer, naked except for his underwear, sat on the edge of an unkempt bed. He threw his uniform over his head and fumbled with the buttons.

"Well I haven't felt like that in a while," Baptiste told him as he exited the en-suite bathroom, a towel cinched around his waist and shirtless.

Hammer stood to embrace him. "I gotta say, I like the new you. Jesus, you French guys know what you're doing."

"Lots of practice. It's nice to be back in this younger body, I must admit." Baptiste admired himself in the mirror. "I've got an assignment for you today."

"I thought the last hour was my assignment." Hammer laughed. Baptiste didn't.

"Kailani and Gael will recommend we use moonstone to cure Betty and Linda, and I need you to go out and pick some up for me," Baptiste told him.

"Uh, okay. Not sure how I'll do that."

"The mini-sub," Baptiste answered. "Aleks can give you a quick rundown but play dumb to it. I want Taylor to take the other sub alongside you."

"I'm not sure I underst—" Marc was quickly cut off.

"There and back, no dilly-dally," Baptiste added. "Olympus is within reach."

Marc looked at him, confused. "Olympus the mountain or the project?"

Baptiste pushed Marc down to where he was seated on the edge of the bed. "The project, dummy," he said as he cradled Marc's face in one hand. "Zeus needs his Ganymede to finish the job." Baptiste kissed Marc's forehead. Marc sighed, having no idea what Pierre was talking about.

"I don't get it," Marc replied as Baptiste gazed at his body while cloaking his irritation. "Where does Gael fit into all of this?"

Baptiste paused. "That depends upon Gael. Why do you ask?"

Marc stood off the bed and pressed his body against Pierre's. "Because I want to make sure I'm your number one."

****

Baptiste, Kepler, and Hammer marched in unison as they approached sick bay where they met Molly, Lukas, and Taylor watching over their stricken friends. Gael, Kailani, and Dr. Nevon huddled in a corner discussing something. Marc Hammer announced he was going to take a sub out, which explained why he was naked from the waist up, his lower half stuffed inside a black wetsuit.

"Ladies and gents," Baptiste interrupted. "We are going to attempt to resuscitate Linda and Betty with moonstone, but we need a larger supply. Marc here has volunteered to pilot *Jeune 1*, and we need a pilot for *Jeune 2*."

Eyes turned to Taylor. "You have piloted a submersible, correct? I saw in your early Air Force training you took instruction on a US Navy sub."

Taylor's face burned with surprise. *How does Pierre know about that?* "That's true, Pierre, but that was nearly twenty-five years ago."

"Well, I think that makes you more qualified than the rest of us. Even Marc hasn't had military instruction," Baptiste pointed out. "I think it was a tourist submarine you co-piloted in Cozumel, wasn't it?"

Hammer smiled coldly at Baptiste, his eyes daggers. "That's true, sir. I believe I can handle the basics of *Jeune 1*." His calm exterior cloaked his reaction to Baptiste's jab at his pride. It was part of Baptiste's game—reel them in, get them comfortable, and then destabilize the hell out of them until they were putty in his hands.

"Sir, may I suggest that we submerge and launch the subs from that standpoint?" Captain Kepler suggested. "It will be faster than launching them from the surface."

She braced herself for Baptiste's rebuttal, but it didn't come. "Captain, that's a wonderful idea." For a moment she thought she imagined that Pierre had given her a compliment. Kepler forced herself to stay cool as she processed what was probably the first positive response to one of her ideas in over a decade.

"Aye sir," Kepler said professionally while keeping her exhilaration from Baptiste's praise bottled inside, temporarily pushing aside the wounded teenager she normally felt like. "Just give the word and I'll begin the dive sequence."

"Captain." Baptiste approached her with curiosity. "Consider my word given."

Chapter 25

Baptiste laid out the plan for both of the mini-subs, one piloted by Marc and the other by Taylor, to travel no more than one-hundred yards from the now-submerged *Juventus*, collect approximately fifty pounds of moonstone, spread between the two subs, and return to the ship. The entire operation was expected to take no more than thirty minutes.

Marc Hammer, locked in a private changing room, squeezed his muscular body into a wetsuit. *I'll show Baptiste who can pilot a sub*, he thought. He was still pissed that Baptiste tried to humiliate him in front of everyone, but he knew this was his chance. Baptiste was so infatuated with himself and being the leader of the gods, or whatever the hell he was talking about when he called himself *Zeus,* that he failed to pay attention to what was happening around him. He was now too busy watching himself jerk-off in his new body to be aware of much more. To Baptiste, moonstone was a commercial opportunity to sell the fountain of youth and create a new class of demi-gods who lived for hundreds of years and didn't age, while the rest of the world bowed at their feet. *Not a bad idea for a creative old queen*, he thought. But Hammer had other ideas for moonstone that were far more useful. Now he got to see if moonstone lived up to the legends and can restore not only youth, but life itself. The two old bats in sick bay were an unexpected bonus, test rabbits to make sure the material worked before he collected his reward.

****

The team gathered on the launching deck. Marc Hammer and Taylor Pastore-Halloran were suited up and ready for their mission. The clock was ticking for Linda and Betty, still struggling and only kept alive by the ventilators. Aleks showed Taylor how to use the robotic arm to grab samples and place them into the storage containers on the side of the mini-sub. Marc was familiar with this and watched from the sidelines. Molly and Lukas closely watched the instruction Taylor was being given. Captain Kepler was there to make sure she understood her part, and also to voice her opinion on sea conditions as the seismic activity continued. Gael and Kailani stood by for the timing of the procedure and Dr. Nevon, temporarily away from sick bay, would monitor the patients' vitals while his staff prepared them for the immersion.

"There's a lot to do to get this ready. I hope the moonstone actually works," Lukas told his mother. "It's our last hope since the hospital on Kiva Oa is non-functioning due to the tsunami."

"I think we owe it to them to try," Molly commented. "If it doesn't work, they wouldn't want to go on living like they are now."

Taylor and Marc each stood by their respective mini-sub. Marc would take *Jeune 1* and Taylor, *Jeune 2*.

"Are you gentlemen ready?" Baptiste asked them.

Both pilots gave him the thumbs up.

"Splendid. They practically pilot themselves," Baptiste boasted. "The training you received should not even be needed. The entire mission has been pre-programmed and all you need to do is sit back and relax. We have artificial intelligence planned as a back-up."

"Let's hope our human intelligence was smart enough to program the artificial intelligence," Lukas jibed, hoping to burst Baptiste's sanctimonious bubble.

Lukas approached his husband. "How're you feeling?"

"You never know how tight these things are until you actually put one on," Taylor told him. "Do I look fat?"

"You look sexy, if I do say so myself," Lukas complimented him.

"Not bad for forty something, I guess. Not like *Mr. Underwear Model*," Taylor said, referring to Marc. "I had a six-pack once."

"Everyone looks good when they're twenty-eight. It takes work to look good as one gets older," Lukas said to his husband. "And I think you're perfect."

Both mini-subs were identical. While Taylor prepared and checked launch readiness, he marveled at the technical elegance that made up the *Jeune 2* cockpit. Energy efficient LED lighting gave the cockpit a calm atmosphere and could be customized to the occupant's preference. Taylor selected the indirect green lighting for some reason he couldn't articulate. There were no physical knobs, throttles, or buttons on the instrument panel. The entire cockpit control console was a giant touchscreen, glossy-black like a sleek manta ray.

"I designed it so that anyone, from anywhere in the world, would be able to use the graphic display. Any audio, automatic announcements, or text can be immediately customized to the pilot's mother tongue." Baptiste beamed with pride as he explained the features. "Studies have shown that when panicked or distressed, pilots can become confused or disoriented during an emergency when they need to translate instructions in their heads, rather than jumping immediately into action."

Baptiste proudly showed off the submersibles' features as well as evacuation options, including inflatable pontoons that could rocket the vehicle to the surface, and an encapsulated escape pod, complete with an ejector-seat.

"*Must be nice to be a billionaire,*" Taylor said quietly.

"I can assure you, Taylor, it is!" Baptiste smiled at his subtle reminder that even in here, everything would be recorded. "Godspeed, my friends."

Warning lights flashed as heavy doors opened on the floor revealing a swimming pool-sized submersible launching pond. Large yellow cranes, completely robotic, extended large claw-like appendages. Marc fastened himself into *Jeune 1* and Taylor saw the touch-screen console come to life, illuminating Marc's face while Baptiste ensured the small sub's airtight seals were operable. Taylor wondered if Marc's computer voice spoke English with a South African accent, Afrikaans, or some other language.

Aleks stood stoically by the launch cranes awaiting instructions.

"We normally launch one sub at a time, but we're going to do both of you at the same time." Baptiste spoke into a ship to sub communicator. "Aleks will operate both cranes that will be perfectly synchronized and place you into the launching pond. There are two doors to the launching pond. One is on the underside of *Juventus*, and the other one is there." He pointed to the double panel door on the floor of the launching bay.

Both pilots gave him the thumbs up.

"When the floor doors retract, you will see ocean water. Do not be alarmed, as the outer doors are closed. Then both doors are synched perfectly to drain water out the bottom while closing the deck floor so that you don't feel claustrophobic."

Taylor glanced over at Marc who discreetly rolled his eyes at, what he assumed, was Baptiste's lengthy explanation. The gesture made Taylor smile.

"Sub commanders, are you ready for the launch sequence?" Aleks shouted into his communication device.

Both Taylor and Marc gave their thumbs up approval as Lukas ran into the launch chamber and noticed his husband through the bubble-shaped transparent piloting window. Lukas anxiously ran to make sure Taylor saw him as the water level dropped. Taylor blew him a kiss as both subs were lowered down. Two large plate doors on the floor closed as the subs disappeared into the darkness.

"We have to close the deck before we can open the launch doors on *Juventus'* underside keel-hull," Baptiste explained. "Otherwise, we would flood this entire compartment."

"I'm ready to go if you are, J1 out," Marc called out to Taylor.

"Affirmative. Looks like everything works. You want to lead the way, or shall I? J2 out."

"As Pierre pointed out, I think you have the upper

hand in experience, sir," Marc responded. "I don't have twenty tourists on board, so I'm out of my wheelhouse. J1 out."

Taylor stifled a laugh. "I think this is the blind leading the blind, but I'm happy to lead. First stop is the moonstone field fifty meters away. J2 out."

"Which way? Port or starboard?" Marc chided him.

"Touché." Taylor laughed. "Be kind to your elders. Starboard."

Lukas watched from the glass window observation deck and wondered if both pilots knew their conversation was being broadcast. The submersibles bobbed like water bugs as the pilots got their bearings and attempted to stabilize their small vessels.

"Tell Baptiste this is much easier than flying a helicopter," Taylor spoke, knowing Baptiste could hear him. "A kid could pilot this thing, and it looks like one actually is!"

"Wheeee, this is like the carnival, daddy," Marc shot back.

"I'm not your daddy," Taylor joked.

"Ah, the day is still young," Marc replied sarcastically. "But you're a total daddy."

Baptiste laughed. "I'm not sure how much of these boys' schtick I can take. I'll be in my office. Please call me when they return."

Chapter 26

The jet approached Fiji airspace after a very dramatic and tumultuous journey across the Pacific Ocean.

"You want to switch to manual?" Donna asked.

"Let's keep autopilot engaged until Fiji gives us commands to approach," Tory answered.

"If I didn't know how well you can fly, I'd make a wise-crack about kids not being able to fly without the computer," Donna jibed her. "But I won't do that."

Tory smiled at her. "Have you been talking to my dad? He always tells me to fly manually as much as possible."

"Always listen to your dad," Donna commented. "He's a good man. Actually, both of your dads are."

Tory smiled at the compliment. "I'm a lucky lady."

"So are they." Donna fumbled as Tory snickered. "That didn't come out right, I know they're not ladies, ah shut up, Donna," she muttered to herself.

"I knew what you meant, Donna." Tory smiled.

The main island of Fiji was in a state of disorganized chaos as strong tremors continued to rock the land and create tsunami watches, warnings, and actual waves that were not huge, yet. Roughly a meter tall, each successive wave didn't have extreme height but was backed by millions of tons of displaced seawater. The government prepared to evacuate the southern part of the main island, which was expected to take the brunt of the waves. Some small villages on Fiji's barrier islands reported minor damage from higher-than-normal surf.

The streets were in pandemonium, with vehicles that swerved and honked angrily as drivers navigated congested streets with darkened streetlights knocked out due to power outages. Each jolt sent residents screaming in panic, only to be followed by an eerie quiet, punctured by aftershocks. Tsunami sirens wailed, warning residents to get away from the beaches and to move to higher ground. People were afraid, not sure if the situation was improving or if it was only the beginning of a long, terrifying night. Residents of Fiji had been through countless tsunami drills in their lifetimes. It was the tourists who were most at risk, huddled in their beachfront villas with no idea what was happening. Vacationers frantically called and texted friends and relatives, not sure if they would ever see them again. The rising water, the blackened streets, a typhoon lingering offshore, and the continued shaking created a stressful and frightening scene.

Fiji control crackled on the cockpit's speakers. "N4202, good to hear from you. We lost your signal."

"I shut down power temporarily as we tried to restart the engines. We hit a pyroclastic cloud that messed us up," Tory responded.

"Understood and glad you are all okay. The initial volcanic blast has disrupted flights all across the region and we need you to approach and land as soon as possible. Power outages are happening all over the island."

"Roger," Tory answered calmly. "Awaiting

approach instructions."

"Approach runway 2R at ten-thousand feet, then follow ground instructions. You will see one runway illuminated. We are running electricity from a generator, so shutting off non-essential lights," the control tower instructed. "Reduce speed and altitude. An escort vehicle will meet you at the taxiway to bring you to the terminal."

Tory took a deep breath. "Well, this will be a first."

"What will?" Donna asked, slightly nervous.

"Landing on an island, during a blackout, with earthquakes and tsunamis happening simultaneously." Tory half laughed.

"Between you and your dad, it's never a dull moment."

The Spectrum 7, its graceful wings, extended flaps, and its landing gear engaged like talons, resembled an eagle or hawk swooping for its prey. Being a relatively new model of business jet, its elegant form had not been seen by many, and the control tower staff studied intensely as the plane seemed to hover before it gently touched down on the shorter of two runways at Nadi airport. The plane automatically slowed as it neared the end of the runway and Donna pointed to the small SUV with a blinking *Follow Me* sign.

Tory and Donna expertly piloted the sleek plane to its stopping point and throttled back on the engines that whined as they powered off. "I hope we don't need a visa for Fiji. I didn't think to even check," Tory realized.

"I think we're fine," Donna replied with confidence.

The plane's wheels were chocked and a customs

officer knocked on the door. Pepe swung the door lever, and the cabin door popped open, revealing two smiling officials who asked to come aboard. Once they performed a quick inspection and reviewed each passenger's passport, they gave a thumbs up. One of the officials said something that was directed at Pepe, but he was unable to understand them. He then deduced the guys were making a comment about there being one single man and three attractive women on the plane. *If they only knew our story*, Pepe chuckled to himself. Tory asked about nearby hotels the customs officers could recommend. The immediate reaction confirmed her gut feeling; there were no hotels available.

After checking for options inside the airport, Pepe returned to the plane empty-handed. "The customs guys said we're free to sleep in the terminal until daylight," Pepe reported. "I suggest we sleep on the plane. It's way more comfortable."

"Agreed," Wilma said flatly. "And so does she." She winked at Donna.

"We've got plenty of food on board," Tory replied. "Let's get comfy. I don't think it will be a very long night."

****

Inside the observatory, Lukas watched the subs scour the ocean floor like aquatic bugs. He gripped his hands together, stressed at the situation and feeling completely out of control. The light banter between Taylor and Marc was more of a show, he felt. Taylor knew the seriousness of what they were doing as first-time submarine pilots, maneuvering through tectonic-generated turbulence to fetch samples of a mystery material that was supposed to make a miracle happen.

"Moonstone at two o'clock," Taylor uttered.

"Luckily I know what analog clocks are, old man," Marc teased him.

"I forgot your generation can't get out of a paper bag without a smartphone. Forgive me."

"Just for that, I'm going to make cricket references that I'm pretty sure no American can genetically understand," Marc replied.

"Try me. You might be surprised."

The two mini-subs slowed as they hovered over the field of moonstone. Taylor and Marc prepared to utilize their subs' robotic arms to grab samples off the ocean floor.

"Don't get anything bigger than a cricket ball," Marc suggested.

"Roger. Luckily I've been to a few cricket matches so I'm not completely clueless."

"I underestimated you," Marc said as his robotic arm started collecting samples. "This thing is very cool to watch. It's completely automated."

"There's a scale in the storage compartment that will tell us when we are at the proper weight." Taylor reminded him.

"Twenty-five pounds or kilograms? I can't remember." Marc asked.

"Either answer works. But technically it's pounds, smartass."

The two subs approached the field of moonstone boulders. Taylor noticed that each boulder was roughly the same size and shape. Hexagonal prisms of moonstone littered the ocean floor. Taylor stared at them, mesmerized by their identical shapes.

"I've never seen boulders that look like this,"

Taylor commented.

"They're from outer space, sir," Marc replied. "We're not in Kansas anymore."

Chapter 27

Inside sick bay, Gael and Kailani prepared the immersion beds for Linda and Betty. Kailani had noticed Gael's subdued behavior and watched with concern as he worked.

"Something is wrong, Gael." She didn't need to ask. "You can always talk to me."

Gael nodded. "Sometimes I wonder if moonstone is a blessing or a curse."

"It can be both, I guess, depending upon how it is used."

Gael continued to work silently.

"Is this about Mr. Baptiste?" she asked.

"Yes."

"He seems very confident now with his new looks," she commented.

"It is what I was afraid of," Gael told her, his voice tinged with anger.

"I'm sorry, brother, but Mr. Baptiste has always been that way. He always thinks of himself first, and now it is no different."

"Yes. You have always said that, and I've been a fool. He told me that when he became younger, we could be together, but he has hardly spoken to me since his treatment."

"Gael, listen to me. You must not let his actions blacken your heart. You cannot control what he does, only what you do. You have many gifts, and you are loved."

Gael sighed, but he could tell things were changing, perhaps ending in a way he had never imagined. "Thank you, sister."

****

With both of the mini-subs filled with their required weight of moonstone, Marc looked at his watch. "You want to go for a joyride? We are ten minutes early. Beats sitting under *Juventus* like a lamprey."

"Sure, let's look around, but the water is cloudy so let's not lose direction."

This time Marc was the leader. "We'll head west for five minutes and then do a one-eighty return to *Juventus*. Sound like a plan?"

"Fascinating. I'm at your mercy," Taylor replied in a comically deadpan tone.

The two subs propelled along the ocean floor, avoiding rocks and a reef or two, but Taylor was again surprised that there was no sea life anywhere, except for some occasional seaweed. About three minutes into their western jaunt, Taylor noticed Marc slowing down.

"You need brake lights on that thing," Taylor said as he watched *Jeune 1* come to a complete stop.

As he pulled alongside Marc's sub, he noticed what Marc was looking at in the distance.

"What the hell is that?" Taylor observed

"I don't know, but let's check it out." Marc accelerated *Jeune 1* and kept cruising toward what they both saw.

When they got closer, it was far bigger than they imagined. Before them was a towering pile of

Moonstone boulders, stacked in the shape of a pyramid. Taylor first thought it was an ancient ruin, until he noticed the hexagonal shape of the boulders along with their placement on the ocean floor. They were not placed there, he observed; they fell there. Marc and Taylor zipped around the perimeter of the colossal mound of boulders. Tucked between some of the rocks were trees and other vegetation, still green and fresh.

"What is it?" Marc asked.

"We've got to get back. They'll be waiting for us. It looks like a huge pile of moonstone," Taylor theorized.

"But what are all the trees doing with it? I saw some dead goats trapped under some of the debris. This looks recent," Marc asked, knowing Taylor didn't have an answer.

"Looks like rubble. Could the tsunamis have done this kind of damage? It's like the islands were shattered then collapsed into a pile of rubble," Taylor answered.

And then it dawned on Marc. *You've gotta be kidding me. How on earth?* he thought. "Let's get back to the ship, but I don't think we should talk about this."

Minutes later, they maneuvered beneath *Juventus* and it was the first time Taylor realized she had a double-hulled keel. *I'll be damned,* he thought. That explained *Juventus'* ability to hit high speeds, and combined with the X-bow sloped front, the ship could slice through waves and water either above the surface or below it. He also noticed the rear of the vessel where he spotted four massive water-intake panels to supply the hydro jet propulsion units *Juventus* used at high speeds. Three propellers, housed in sound-deadening shrouds, took over when *Juventus* operated below water or had to maneuver in port.

"*Juventus*," Taylor paged the bridge. "J1 and J2 are beneath the launching bay doors. Request permission to board."

Marc observed his formality. "Now you're showing off, sir."

This kid's pretty funny, Taylor thought. "It's military training. Thank you for noticing."

"Affirmative."

"Gentlemen, this is Aleks Borisov. I can only bring one of you in at a time. There is too much current under here to try and line you up without crashing into each other."

"Age before beauty," Marc offered sarcastically.

"A truer statement was never said. Thank you, my child."

Marc laughed but Aleks was confused.

"So who is coming first?"

"I'm under the doors Aleks. Marc is waiting behind me."

With Marc waiting and Taylor currently in the docking sequence with *Juventus*, he had an eerie sense of the vastness surrounding them. Plumes of a yellowish liquid and bubbles emerged from the seafloor. He pointed it out to Marc.

"J2 to *Juventus*, it looks like we have some volcanic activity below us. Hot spots, nothing huge, but thought you should know as the ship is parked right over it."

"Confirmed, J2. Thank you, and we'll keep an eye out," Captain Kepler answered.

The massive doors in the keel started to open and Taylor felt the mini-sub float upward in a very controlled way. The keel doors closed, and Taylor was plunged into complete darkness, sandwiched between the two levels of the ship. A crack of light appeared above him as *Jeune 2* floated into the launching bay, where he was greeted by Aleks, who had already started to fasten J2 to his active crane while the second crane positioned itself for *Jeune 1*.

The robotic crane gingerly placed Taylor's mini-sub onto the launching bay deck so that he could exit the vessel. Two crew members were already emptying Taylor's payload of moonstone with Gael standing by to begin the processing of it.

"I'm glad you had a safe trip, sir," Aleks said, rather formally.

"Mission accomplished, thanks. Marc is right behind me."

****

The second crane was ready to hoist *Jeune 1* when Marc bubbled to the surface. "I forgot how long that takes, jeez. I should have brought my cards so I could play a game of solitaire."

Aleks remained quiet, not sure if he was being admonished.

"Prince Charming is back." Taylor approached him. "The world is safe again."

Marc walked over to Taylor with his arms outstretched. "Come here, you big beast." he hugged Taylor in a way too familiar way. "Glad we got to work together." He unzipped the upper half of his wetsuit and pulled it off, revealing his bare torso that Taylor couldn't help but envy. Marc reminded Taylor of a prep schoolboy gone bad. There was a cocky arrogance combined with friendliness that he found interesting.

He noticed Marc staring back at him a little too long, before suddenly breaking his tense gaze.

Taylor motioned to Gael to pick up Marc's load of moonstone. As he neared the sub, he averted eye-contact with Marc but said nothing as he loaded the moonstone balls into a set of trays that would be taken to sick bay.

Kailani, Molly, and Lukas arrived and greeted the two men. Lukas gave an extra-long hug to his husband. "I'm glad you made it back in one piece. I've had too many scares this week." He kissed him quickly and they followed Gael as they knew the hard work was yet to get started.

Chapter 28

Linda and Betty each lay in a plastic, coffin-like container on top of their hospital beds.

The familiar in-and-out pumping of the ventilator kept them alive. Molly gazed at both of them, each struggling to stay alive, but most likely, not even aware of what was happening when Gael and Kailani entered sick bay with barrels of powdered moonstone dispersed in water. Each bed would be filled by one barrel of the liquid, their ventilators would be shut off, and the women, most likely, would die soon after. The four of them had made a pact when they worked together at Argonne and the CIA: *Don't keep me alive artificially and let me die with dignity.* At the time, they were twenty-something-year-old women with nothing but possibilities ahead of them. It was simple to make such a pact then, before the pounding of life had a chance to tenderize and humble them. Mortality at their age then was as foreign a concept as immortality felt currently. Molly, Linda, Betty, and Donna had faced death and life for nearly eight decades, and each woman realized there was no truer destiny for each of them.

As Gael pumped the moonstone liquid from the barrels into their enclosed capsules, Kailani softly hummed a song to them. Lights were dimmed and the capsules had been filled so that their bodies were submerged, except for their nose and mouth. Lukas stood beside his mother and tried to imagine what she was experiencing at that moment. Her husband was gone, and soon two of her best friends would be, too. Baptiste whispered something to Marc who sat against the sick bay wall, and Aleks stood somberly alone. Above each of the ladies was a screen that displayed metrics like heart rate, blood-oxygen and blood pressure.

Kailani gave Dr. Nevon a nod, which meant he was to remove life support. Once the ventilator was shut down, he removed the breathing tubes from each of the women. Molly's lip trembled as she saw both of her friends unmasked and she waited for their chests to rise and fall on their own. It didn't happen. Kailani and Gael prepared for their final task as everyone watched the vital signs of each woman slow down and eventually stop. Betty Bao and Linda Eastman were each pronounced dead at 7:42 p.m. Fiji Standard Time.

****

Pierre Baptiste and Marc Hammer sat side-by-side inside a plush lounge aboard *Juventus*. Baptiste normally did not utilize this space, as he would relax in his massive apartment, but after witnessing what he saw, he didn't want to be by himself.

"Let's see what the miracle material does to bring them back," Marc suggested.

"Or if it brings them back," Baptiste replied.

Marc paused for a moment. "If it doesn't, then we tell everyone it does anyway."

Pierre shot Marc a look of confusion and disbelief. "That's not how I operate."

"Where do you plan to get all of this moonstone? It sounds like you are preparing to have high demand.

What is the supply situation?" Marc provoked him. He wanted to know about those massive piles of moonstone he saw this afternoon.

"We've calculated and there's enough," Baptiste said dryly. "How is your father doing, Marc? Is he still stocking up for World War Three?"

Marc chuckled a bit, nervous. "Dad's been busy, ya know. Lots of conflicts around the world and rebels who need weapons."

Pierre sipped his cocktail, his mind somewhere else. "Have you ever thought about working for Rik?" referring to Marc's father's name. "It's gotta be more lucrative than what you're doing now."

Marc was taken by surprise. "Are you offering me a job?"

"I already gave you a job," Baptiste replied. "Are you interested in another one?"

"Depends upon the job," Marc answered.

"I only let people I trust work for me, Marc."

Marc was taken aback but struggled to maintain his composure. "Do you trust me?" he asked Baptiste. His throat was dry from nerves.

"That depends." Baptiste turned to him. "Tell me what you saw underwater today?"

Marc froze, not sure how to answer. His mind scrambled for the right thing to say.

"I saw a huge pile of moonstone," he answered truthfully, a bet he decided subconsciously. "But it was more than a pile. There were crushed buildings, trees, dead animals, and shit like that mixed in with the stone."

A sarcastic grin curled on Baptiste's lips. "It's terrifying what the gods can do."

Chapter 29

A cloudless blue sky stretched as far as the horizon. Sea birds dove and dipped as they hunted for fish. Dolphins jumped through the small swells that rolled across the blue Pacific Ocean. The calm water churned turbulent as a massive dark form emerged from the depths. A leviathan broke through the calm surface and seemed to appear out of nowhere. *Juventus* floated majestically with the morning sun reflecting off its deep blue hull and superstructure, dripping with ocean water that beaded off the sleek exterior and dribbled back into the depths.

Pierre, as was the ship's custom, was the first one to peruse the vessel's deck after a surfacing operation. It was one of his favorite things to do, celebrating the complex process of replacing the ballast tanks with compressed air and gently floating to the surface in a vessel as long as ten blue whales. The technology deployed for *Juventus* was more advanced than most military ships. The vessel was where he chose to live and to ride out the ebbs and flows of life, and possibly an apocalypse, should that occur, during his newly-extended lifetime. He no longer worried about months or years of life, and instead planned in decades and centuries. This gave him new perspectives and horizons he'd only dreamt about.

Mankind was slowly killing itself, as each

civilization somehow had an endgame pre-programmed into it. First the rise, then the golden years, and then the plummet into obscurity. But time and again, civilization would build back. It would ultimately look different than the cultures that came before, it would temporarily decline due to lack of knowledge passed on, but almost always come back stronger.

Two steps forward, one step back, Baptiste used to say to himself. Societal gains would peak, then regress and eventually build back differently, but better. Time and again, it always did. Pierre had studied history from the Egyptians, Greeks, Romans, Macedonians; they all followed the same pattern.

But Pierre had been working on something new that he called *Project Olympus*. He learned that individuals would be forgotten within two generations after their death, unless they happened to be famous. If they were famous, then their names might carry on for centuries like Akhenaten, Achilles, Socrates, Alexander, Caesar, and Washington, and like them, their generational contemporaries also died away, leaving no living witnesses to their actual lives.

Several of his billionaire friends became shareholders in his project, which had taken years to plan and begin to build so that when the inevitable crash of the current civilization occurred, they would be the survivors who possessed all the knowledge, technology, and wealth to guide the new emerging post-apocalyptic people like the new Gods and Titans.

Project Olympus stockpiled technology, data, medicine, genetic material, land, gold, and other things that would assist future generations with this task. Baptiste himself would lead the new Titans to be revered, worshiped, and feared by the struggling, emerging population. In return for their devotion, the new Titans would provide for the people. Moonstone would keep the Titans young for centuries, and the collective wisdom of billions of people who came before them would be stored in a massive artificial intelligence platform that would give them superhuman knowledge and powers. No longer would the sins and mistakes of the past have to be repeated over and over. Wars would be stopped. Earth would return to a cleaner, fresher planet like it had been eons earlier. With an estimated ten percent of the current world population surviving the societal collapse, resources would no longer be scarce. Food would be abundant, and it was a chance for a new start of the human race. Well, mostly human.

The past would be forgotten and the people who lived in the new present would be none the wiser. As Titans, they could exploit whatever and whoever they wanted. Baptiste daydreamed of having his selection of sinewy men and women share his bedchamber. Athleticism would replace obesity, and life would be simple again. The Titans would be the singular source of the truth and would leverage their massive databases and artificial intelligence when needed. Now, the Titans prepared to wait for civilization's inevitable collapse. They would watch the world unravel. Billions of people would die. Technology would be destroyed and knowledge forgotten. Those surviving would face a harsh new world of unimaginable challenges. There would be centuries of destruction after the collapse. Death, war, disease, and famine would push those survivors to the brink of extinction. A period of darkness would gradually start to show signs of light. People would yearn for knowledge and direction to explain their burgeoning interest in spirituality and a higher power. And when the time was right, Pierre Baptiste and the other Titans would emerge from the sea in their glorious vessel to save them all.

****

Even through the darkened glass of the Spectrum 7, Tory felt the heat radiating from the morning sun. She could tell it would soon be uncomfortably warm inside the jet and hoped the island and country had regained power since the devastating eruption and tsunami. Pepe slept shirtless next to her, his abdomen rising and falling with each dream-filled breath. Donna and Wilma slept on two adjoining flat-bed-seats. The four of them had been on a wild adventure as they searched for her dads and the rest of the party the last couple of days. Tory still remarked at how odd it was that their five friends had just disappeared without any communication from their billionaire host, Pierre Baptiste.

The unexpected collision with the pyroclastic cloud from a new undersea volcano, and their unique way to recover engine power, had left her drained. Full-on adrenaline moments followed by a crash of energy meant each of the four slept like logs for more than six hours, even with the heat and humidity in the plane's cabin. The last couple of days were about finding the haystack. Today and tomorrow would be finding the needles, her fathers Taylor and Lukas, Molly, Linda, and Betty. The first thing she needed was coffee and then she'd take a walk around the jet to see if the ash cloud left any permanent damage on the outside of the plane. Pepe and Wilma had done research on Baptiste and learned he owned a small archipelago off the coast. That would likely be the first place to look and hopefully she would get another electronic ping from her father's subdermal tracker.

Tory stood in line at the Fiji airport coffee shop and cafe. Pepe ran over to meet her with drink orders from Donna and Wilma.

"I don't think this will be the best coffee in the world, so prepare yourself," she told her fiancé.

"At least I can say I tried it. I've lived in America for five years, so I'm prepared for whatever I get." He laughed and said something in Italian that Tory couldn't understand.

There were four people in front of them ordering cold drinks, which made Tory question why they were ordering coffee in ninety-degree heat.

"*Caro*, can I ask you something?" Pepe asked. "Why don't we contact the Fiji Coast Guard or police for some help?"

"What would we tell them?" Tory asked. "As far as anyone knows, my dads went with Baptiste willingly. I don't believe they did, but we have no proof. Believe me, I've thought about this a lot and don't know what other options we have."

Within a few minutes, they gave the clerk their order. Surprised to see an Italian-model espresso machine, Pepe was excited and ordered his normal triple espresso. Tory thanked the clerk who delivered the four drinks to her.

"*Vinaka*," she uttered, hoping her one Fijian word was pronounced correctly.

"*Vinaka*," the man replied. "We use the same word

for thank you and you're welcome." He smiled at Tory, appreciative of her attempt to use local words.

She then asked him about how the island was after the violent volcano.

"The last couple of days have been difficult with earthquakes and the volcano. We will be okay now that we know to stay away from the beaches."

"Do you know where Pierre Baptiste has his home?" she asked knowing it was a random chance this man even recognized the billionaire's name.

"Ah yes," the man replied. "He owns islands, but I'm not sure which ones they are. We have hundreds of islands in Fiji."

"Were any of the islands damaged by the volcano?" Tory asked.

The man thought for a moment. "I think there was a big tsunami on an archipelago east of here." He tried to recall its name, and his eyes widened. "*Mataniciva archipelago*, that's the name."

"Mata…" Tory tried to repeat it.

"Ma-ta-ni-civa," the man said slowly. "It means *pearl* in Fijian."

****

Inside the cramped sick bay, Molly sat on a chair, a small pillow wedged between her shoulder and cheek somehow propping up her sleeping head. Kailani and Gael continued to massage the limbs of her two friends, both of whom died less than an hour ago. Molly's stoic face hid the guilt and remorse she felt for making the decision to terminate life-support for Linda and Betty, but at the same time, she believed her friends would have agreed with her decision. *You let us die, Molly,* swirled in her head, and the pit in her stomach told her what she really felt, despite all of the logic she tried to believe. The life-support monitors continued to display nothing but the flat lines of their vital signs. She stared at them hoping one would show a heartbeat starting. Nothing.

Taylor and Lukas entered to check on progress. Gael shook his head, meaning there was no update to their condition.

"How long does the moonstone take to work?" Taylor asked.

"It doesn't sometimes," Kailani answered. "But I would give it another fifteen minutes. If it doesn't work within the next hour, it has failed."

"Do they just wake up?" Taylor asked. "Or does it take a while for them to become conscious again?"

"It depends upon the person," Gael answered. "These ladies are healthy and should respond quickly."

"Healthy, other than the fact that they're dead," Lukas deadpanned.

****

Pierre Baptiste sat in an oversized chair. The transparent projection cube hovered in front of him, his face tinted slightly blue by the reflection of the screen and the faceless person with whom he was having an audio conversation.

"What time does your courier arrive tomorrow?" Baptiste asked the person.

"Three a.m., Fiji time," the man responded. "Please send your coordinates and preferences for transfer."

Baptiste looked over at Captain Kepler, her eyes wide with tension and excitement.

"My captain will transfer that information shortly." He nodded at Kepler in affirmation.

"Baptiste," the man asked. "Is everything on schedule with Olympus? I haven't heard anything of late."

"Everything is proceeding," Baptiste answered. "We had some delays with unexpected volcanic activity that changed our timeline a bit, but Olympus is unfolding as planned. Our two deceased subjects are marinating in the moonstone solution." He laughed at his own joke.

Kepler winced at the image of the two older ladies awaiting rejuvenation, if that was even possible. She moved to sit beside Baptiste, facing the projection cube. "Will you be on the courier vessel?" she asked.

"I will not," the man answered decisively. "I'll let my people do the dirty work."

"When will you have the treatment?" Baptiste asked the man.

"Soon, Baptiste," the man answered. "I'm intrigued by your Olympus project, yet quite doubtful of its effectiveness until I see it for myself. The cost is quite high, so due diligence will make me feel better."

"Of course," Baptiste agreed.

"How many of your prospects have signed?" the man asked.

"You would be number three," Baptiste replied.

"Hammer?" the man asked.

"Yes," Baptiste answered. "Rik, not his son. Marc still believes he will live forever and that his body will always be perfect."

"That bastard's a crazy fucker. I figured," the man said with a slight chuckle. "I'm in. Money'll transfer to you when the delivery is made, okay?'

"As agreed upon, yes," Baptiste concluded.

"Should you need more, you know how to find me."

"Looking forward to seeing how Olympus plays out," the man added. "Gotta hand it to you, Pierre. This is gonna be a game changer."

"It will, indeed," Pierre answered formally. "Would you like to talk to your daughter?"

Captain Diana Kepler brushed her hair behind her ears and sat attentively as she lined up with the projection cube. She hadn't seen him in over a decade. "Hi, Daddy."

****

Project Olympus was his brainchild. Baptiste's brilliant, but unconventional creativity helped him envision a society of God-like individuals who appeared to have eternal life, youth, and unearthly powers. Every civilization, no matter how advanced, eventually fell. Egyptian, Greek, Roman, Inca, Persian eventually ended because of disease, invasion, natural disaster, or climate-related issues that impacted the food supply. Baptiste now had the ability to extend his life, but he needed others to help orchestrate a collapse of civilization. He recruited other moguls like Philip Kepler, Hendrik Hammer, and others who would participate in the plan. Diana Kepler, his captain and Marc Hammer were on-board to assist with the planning. Baptiste called them nepo-babies, but ultimately they had so far proved useful. He needed scientific expertise, which is why he recruited Molly Halloran and her friends. Between them and Lukas, he would have the intellect, scientific, and mathematical abilities to help him during the next few centuries, assuming they played along

The next two priorities were still in progress.

Securing the supply of moonstone was already underway, despite some unexpected mishaps. Hendrik Hammer had provided some of the most powerful weapons ever built to blow up two of his islands to harvest the moonstone of which they were made. Underwater barges were now loading the hexagonal boulders and would transport them to another location. All of this had to be accomplished with the utmost secrecy. Baptiste now awaited the results of moonstone's folklore regarding reviving someone's life.

He was doubtful if it would actually work, and if it did, becoming a member of Project Olympus would become much more expensive. But none of these things would progress to Olympus' full potential until an inflection point where modern civilization began to crumble and fall. Only then could the new gods emerge to establish the new world order. He needed a catalyst to trigger the series of events that would lead to society's unraveling. Creative ideas to do just that swirled through Baptiste's warped mind.

Chapter 30

Diana Kepler strode confidently through the ship's main hallway running from Baptiste's salon to an open-seating area. Her mind raced with emotion after seeing her father on the video screen. He didn't look that different, but he was cold as usual. Philip Kepler was one of Hollywood's most wealthy and sought-after producers. On his third wife now, Philip had always been a man who got what he wanted, no matter the cost to anyone else. Diana found that out when wife number two clashed with her and the bitch ran to Philip with an ultimatum.

"Either she leaves or I leave, Philip," his second wife demanded after one of her and Diana's fights. "She's into drugs, sketchy boys, tattoos. I don't feel safe here!" she whined, despite Philip knowing Diana posed no threat.

"I'm sorry, dear. I'll have it taken care of," her father said as if Diana wasn't there listening to him.

I'll have it taken care of, circled through Diana's mind ever since then. *Just like you took care of Mom.* She remembered back to the mysterious car accident that killed her mother, Philip's first wife.

Marc Hammer passed through the lounge and saw Captain Kepler, approached her, and sat down.

"Yes?" she said to Marc, annoyed.

"How was it seeing Daddy?" he asked an irritated

Diana who shot him a look that could melt his face. "Pierre told me earlier your dad is part of Olympus."

"Pierre?" she asked sarcastically. "Already on a first-name basis?"

Marc shot her a cocky grin. "I didn't know your daddy had that kind of money."

"There are other ways to make money besides supplying weapons to terrorists and mercenaries," she said, pointedly calling out Marc's father.

"Are you in on it?" Marc asked. "Olympus?"

"I know a little bit. You?"

"I'm in. Both Baptiste and my dad want me on board," Marc boasted.

Diana bit her lip, not surprised that neither Baptiste nor her father asked her to be part of Olympus. "Good for you. I'm sure you two will be very happy together," she said flatly, her attempt to hide envy not very successful. "What I don't understand is how you all attempt to pull this off."

"Well," Marc continued. "We secured the moonstone, or it's in the process of being secured. Underwater barges are harvesting the rubble now. It's critical for us to execute the plan."

"I assume you need time, correct?" Diana asked.

"At least a century," Marc added. "Two generations need to die out before we can re-emerge."

"Why a century?" she asked.

"It's going to take time for civilization to collapse and much of the old world to be destroyed, and more importantly, forgotten," Marc said defiantly. "Then we come back as the unified Titans of the new world."

Diana laughed sarcastically. "I can't imagine how you'll grab the interest and following of ten billion people around the world."

"Oh, Diana." Marc chuckled, shaking his head. "There won't be ten billion people remaining."

She swallowed and tried to suppress her shock. "How many then?"

Marc rubbed his chin in thought. "Not sure what the big boys are planning, but I've heard a billion and change. People would survive and we would teach them how to rebuild."

"Ten percent?" she asked, hiding her alarm.

"About," Marc acknowledged. "Civilization's collapse has to happen fast. Survivors won't know what hit them. I won't lie, it's gonna be brutal."

"And then what? How will the world build back?" Diana asked him.

"*Archipelago,*" he responded. "It's Baptiste's AI platform he's been building for years."

"And he calls the computer Archipelago?" Diana clarified.

Marc laughed. "Archipelago is more than a computer Diana. It's the collective memory of every artist, musician, scientist, doctor, historian, physicist, and I can go on and on. Baptiste designed Archipelago to be the true God of the new world—the repository of all human knowledge and memories of key individuals throughout our history."

"And where does Baptiste come into this plan?"

"Archipelago stands for Archival Repository for Civil, Historical, Population, Legal and Governance Operations—and will be the brain behind the execution of Project Olympus. Baptiste will be the new world's Messiah."

****

Blue recessed lighting illuminated the sick bay where the two lifeless bodies of her friends lay marinating in moonstone liquid. It had been over forty-five minutes since they were declared dead, and Molly knew time was running out. Kailani gently massaged Betty's and Linda's shoulders and scalp while Gael prodded their feet. It was part of their ancient practice to keep the muscles limber and their blood from coagulating.

"Has rigor set in?" Molly asked Lukas as he felt for a pulse. He shook his head.

"Should begin two hours after..." Lukas caught himself, not wanting to admit that his mom's friends were clinically deceased. "Their muscles feel supple and body temperature has maintained normal."

"They will come back," Kailani reassured them. "The moonstone is regenerating their bodies. I think it will be a few more minutes."

Dr. Nevon had been observing the process since declaring Linda and Betty deceased. He watched with skepticism that anything significant would happen to them.

"If they do come back, I'm not sure they'll be so happy with me." Molly sighed.

"Ma, even if there's a chance, I think they'd want to come back," Lukas calmed her.

"Not me," Molly pronounced. "Leave me for dead."

Lukas glanced over at Taylor who had been holding vigil with them. He smiled slightly at his husband, whom he assumed must be as exhausted as he was. Two blissful days of a honeymoon that morphed into being abducted and held captive by an eccentric billionaire.

Molly's hand covered her mouth and Lukas thought she was crying, but soon found out his mother was suppressing a laugh.

"Ma?" he asked his mom, concerned that she may be having a mental breakdown.

"Oh my God, you poor guys," she said to her son and son-in-law. "I just had an image of you two skinny-dipping off your bungalow in Bora Bora and now you're here with two dead old-lady corpses waiting to see if they'll come back to life." Tears rolled down her cheeks as she tried to control her laughter, which was more of a stress-reaction than finding this situation humorous.

"I wonder where the souvenir shop is on board so I can buy a tee-shirt to commemorate it," Taylor snuck in, before he started nervously laughing, too.

"Donna and Tory probably flew out of dodge with their significant others in tow." Molly continued to laugh. "I don't know why I'm laughing but this all seems like a crazy dream. You can't make this shit up!"

Kailani and Gael continued their gentle massaging of their patients, too focused on healing to understand the irony of what was going on around them. Molly suddenly gasped.

"I just saw Linda's eyelids move," she shouted.

Kailani smiled but said nothing, her hands gently kneading the women's arms and legs now.

"Betty's eyelids just fluttered, too!" Taylor noticed as they hovered over their friends, waiting for a more defining sign of life.

Kailani and Gael, each with their hands on Molly's friends, stood quietly with their eyes closed, as if they were meditating. Or praying.

Dr. Nevon gasped when he saw blips of heartbeats registering on their monitors. "This can't be."

"They are coming back," Kailani commented. "We will see if they have changed."

Molly, Lukas, and Taylor glanced at each other, not sure what Kailani meant.

"Changed?" Molly asked. "Changed how?"

"Your friends had a traumatic event. They died. Temporarily, I mean," Gael answered. "There is no guarantee these events didn't affect them."

Lukas sighed and shook his head. "I wish we knew that."

"Would you have made a different decision?" Gael asked, his voice frosted and irritable.

"I would have made the same decision, Gael," Molly replied confidently. "It's just…an unexpected…"

"It's okay," Kailani answered. "You've all been through a lot."

Molly nodded and thought, *More than you know, Kailani.* "How much longer until they are conscious?" The second the words left her mouth, she realized what was going on. *Like people come back from the dead every day,* she thought. Her friends died and were potentially brought back to life using a special material that likely came from outside our galaxy and Molly was asking about time estimates, like she had a plane to catch.

"Sorry, that was an unreasonable question. Thank you for bringing them this far," she clarified to Kailani and Gael.

A muffled rumbling noise suddenly echoed through the ship's corridors. The ship rocked slightly.

"Sounds like that volcano again," Taylor observed.

"Never a dull moment," Lukas responded. "Hopefully no tsunami from this one…" His words were cut off by a loud hissing noise coming from inside the ship. "What the hell was that?"

A higher-pitched explosion reverberated through the hull of the ship. Kailani's placid face now looked distressed. Worry, anger, and fear etched her face simultaneously. *Juventus* lurched upward, riding what felt like a large wave, then suddenly plunged downward. Taylor's wide eyes betrayed his confusion as to what was happening.

"Feels like we're diving again," he told the group. "Hang on."

Juventus pitched steeply downward to the point that those standing had to shift their weight and stance to compensate for the steep angle. Ear-splitting alarms blasted throughout the ship. Something dramatic had happened.

"Are we sinking?" Lukas asked, afraid to know the answer.

Taylor shook his head, his muscular arms holding on to Molly to prevent her from falling. "Too controlled for sinking." He tried to sound confident, as the alarms and flashing lights added to the cacophony of confusion. Tension filled the air as *Juventus* leveled off. The alarms and flashing lights also died down leaving an atmosphere of relief and disorientation as to what had just occurred.

The captain suddenly appeared outside the sick bay doors, her face etched with stress. "Everybody all right?" she asked the group.

"What happened?" Lukas asked her.

"I'm not sure," Diana answered as she struggled to be calm. "But we hit something. It felt big."

"Why do you think that?" Molly asked her. Diana remained tight-lipped.

"I'm headed for the bridge," Diana informed them. "I will let you know what I find out."

"Wait, why aren't you on the bridge now?" Taylor asked.

Diana decided not to answer the question, knowing it would only make things worse. "I need you all to pay attention and listen for further instructions. If you hear seven short blasts of the ship's alarm, followed by one long blast, I need you all to prepare."

Taylor's face dropped, his face suddenly losing color.

Lukas immediately noticed something was wrong. "What do the alarm blasts mean?" he asked.

"Abandon ship." Taylor's emotionless response sent a chill through the room.

Lukas gasped as he tried to take the information in. "What?"

"Pierre already left," Diana told them. "That's why I came down here. I didn't want to alarm you."

"Alarm us about what?" Molly asked.

"It's a long story, and we don't have time," Diana continued. "Pierre promoted Marc to captain and relieved me of duty."

"Sorry to hear that, but…" Lukas asked.

"Baptiste is gone and so is Marc," Diana interrupted. "They took off in a shuttlecraft. I don't know where they went."

"But you can regain control of the ship, can't you?" Lukas asked.

Diana sighed. "We hit something big and we're taking on water. I don't know how bad it is," she explained.

"Are we sinking?" Taylor asked. "Why are we at such an angle?"

"It was an evasive move," she explained. "I'm pretty sure we hit another vessel."

"That's bad," Lukas commented.

"Baptiste has ships in and out of here, many of them submarines," she complained. "I can't see what's going on beneath the water."

Taylor thought back to the underwater barges loading up moonstone in order to ship it somewhere. *Shit*, he thought.

"There are only ten of us remaining on *Juventus*," Diana continued. "The rest of the crew is no longer on board."

"I don't get it," Lukas exclaimed. "Where did they go?"

Kepler shook her head. "Don't know, but two of the emergency evacuation vessels have been deployed."

"Deployed?" Lukas asked.

"Gone," Kepler explained. "Everyone has abandoned ship."

"Why are we still here, then?" Lukas asked, not wanting to know the answer.

Captain Kepler struggled to remain calm. "Baptiste set *Juventus* to auto-destruct in one hour. With us onboard."

Chapter 31

The blast echoed through the humid air like a bomb went off. Tory had never heard anything so loud, even though she could tell it came from several miles away. Her ears thumped as she struggled to regain full hearing.

"That was not a volcano," she said, not sure how loudly she said it.

"It was a concussion blast," Donna commented. "Couldn't that come from an eruption like that one in Tonga people could hear from thousands of miles away?"

"I'm not an expert on volcanoes," Tory responded. "It did sound like a concussion blast but not sure from what source."

Pepe stared at his smartphone. "I just read it could have been a steam blast. Sea water poured into the magma chamber and *boom*, instant pressure cooker."

Smoke stretched toward the sky from an unseen volcano. Pepe squinted in the distance at the thin, wispy plume. On his smartphone, he compared photographs of erupting volcanoes. The Tonga volcanic cloud was clearly visible from outer space, while the new volcano paled in comparison in terms of size and ash plume.

"Well, it looks small from where we currently are, but that ash cloud we hit coming here sure packed a punch." Tory's voice seemed rather small.

"The news stations are calling this volcano *Koro*," Pepe read to them. "It broke through the surface of the ocean two days ago." His voice was interrupted by another loud rumbling coming from offshore.

"That one was louder," Wilma observed. "Why are we hearing these loud blasts from miles away, but the volcano appears to have not changed in size."

"I was thinking the same thing," Donna backed her up.

Another rumble cracked through the air. "It sounds like war."

Pepe recounted and told the group about regional skirmishes he had seen during his military service in Italy. He had been deployed to airlift refugees whose boat capsized in rough seas. Pepe and his helicopter crew were ordered by the Italian Coast Guard to return the ten survivors to Tunis. At the time, the Tunisian military had been breaking up terror cells around the country. As Pepe and his Coast Guard colleagues walked back to their search and rescue helicopter, a terrorist bomb exploded near the airport where they were parked. Pepe lost full hearing for almost a week, and he never forgot that sound.

"I'm not convinced the rumbling concussion noise is coming from Koro," Pepe told the group. "To me, it sounds like a bomb."

Lukas had sent Tory a coded message two days earlier, and from what she inferred, both he and her other dad Taylor were somehow with or near Mr. Baptiste. The subdermal chip embedded in Taylor's scalp confirmed Fiji as their general location, but it was nothing like a tracking device. Donna, Wilma, and Pepe stood outside the Spectrum 7 jet and attempted to shade themselves from the blinding sun. They discussed a plan of action, but they had very little on which to base their plan. Without an exact location, they feared it would be like finding a needle in the great haystack of Fiji's islands and surrounding ocean. As they wolfed down a breakfast scavenged from the airport's overwhelmed cafe and vending machines, the team discussed options for how to find their missing friends.

"How far is Baptiste's archipelago?" Donna asked.

"About fifteen miles or so," Tory responded. "Part of the area has been cordoned off due to the new Koro volcano."

"How can we get there? Boat?" Wilma asked.

Tory's attention was diverted when her phone pinged. She walked beneath the plane's wing in order to read her screen.

"It's from Lukas," she told them, as she read through the message. "They are still on Baptiste's ship, but it's set to self-destruct."

"What the hell?" Donna exclaimed.

"Jesus, this Baptiste guy sounds like a maniac," Pepe commented. "Where is he?"

"Lukas sent his location," she enlarged the screen. "He looks to be about five miles from Kiva Oa, where Baptiste lives. Lukas said something about being on Baptiste's yacht that also appears to be submersible."

"What?" Pepe asked in confusion.

"That's what Lukas says," Tory clarified.

"You know, I'm really getting tired of billionaires," Donna exclaimed. "Too much money and too much time is a formula for the devil's work."

****

Taylor, Diana, and Lukas ran to the bridge and

found Aleks pounding the instrument panel frantically. Captain Kepler pushed him aside angrily.

"What are you doing on the bridge?" she asked.

Aleks continued searching for the source of the droning alarm that constantly buzzed. "I'm trying to stop the noise!" His hands covered his ears as he winced at the painful cacophony.

"How much time until self-destruct?" Taylor asked Captain Kepler. "How can we get off the ship?"

Diana's fingers frantically hit the touchscreen as she desperately searched for a way to reverse the auto-destruct. "Baptiste changed the network password! Damnit!" She huffed with frustration tinged with fear. "We can't do anything until we get into the system."

Lukas froze, desperately trying to remember his experience with password detection. He pulled out his satellite phone and attempted to log into the network again, hoping his phone would be recognized and automatically be allowed to join.

"Damnit!" he shouted. "I'm locked out. Look around for a laptop or mobile phone that is already on the network."

The group rummaged through cabinets beneath the instrument panel. They yanked open drawers and searched. Diana found a smartphone and held it up triumphantly.

"It's connected to the Wi-Fi at least," she shouted.

"Well, that's a start. At least we can get into the system login page and try from there," Lukas suggested. He shook his head at the simplicity of so-called *secure networks*. Passwords were relatively easy to discover on other devices, and the ability to hack adapted and evolved as quickly as security updates did.

Lukas thought back to the early days of his new IT business. One of his employees worked to generate security codes and protocols by day, held on-line seminars to existing and would-be hackers on how to bypass those same types of security codes after hours. As long as he didn't break protocol by hacking into Lukas' systems or sharing secret intelligence about their data, he was free to moonlight on the side.

When Lukas discovered this was going on, he decided to confront the employee directly. If he had a disgruntled teammate, Lukas wanted to know why. He came to find out that his employee, Scott, was struggling financially due to massive amounts of student debt, doctor's bills, and supporting his girlfriend and their new baby. Lukas was surprised by the state of Scott's life, as he never would have thought anything was amiss due to Scott's positive attitude and impressive work ethic.

The following day, Lukas called Scott into his office for a meeting. Knowing he was about to be fired, Scott boxed up his desk in advance so that he could be spared the walk-of-shame terminated employees faced when exited.

"You're my best coder," Lukas told him as Scott sat nervously across a glass coffee table from him, eyes downcast awaiting the ax.

"I'm sorry for what I've done. I was desperate and I wasn't thinking," Scott admitted. "You've been great to me, Lukas, and I let you down."

"Scott, how much do you owe in student loans?"

"About two-hundred thousand. It's gonna take me thirty years to pay off."

"I need to tell you this, Scott. Hacking is

dangerous, very dangerous. You're probably working with foreign operatives from Russia, North Korea, and other hacking hot spots. I don't want to see you or your family get hurt," Lukas said matter-of-factly.

Scott nodded his head, ashamed and embarrassed.

"So I'd like to make you a proposal."

"You're not going to fire me?" Scott asked.

Lukas didn't respond to the question. "I'd like to offer you a promotion to head of our cyber-terrorism team. All one of you," Lukas joked.

Scott stared at him, mouth agape, stunned.

"If you accept this, I will give you an equity stake in the company and your student loans will be paid off by me over a period of seven years." Lukas could have paid them off on the spot, but he also wanted to allow Scott to feel he earned this and it wasn't a bail-out. "I'll give you twenty-four hours to…"

"I accept," Scott interrupted him. "I don't know what to say."

"Cyber-crimes are doubling almost monthly. You have a lot to do, and this isn't a gift, Scott," Lukas replied. "Consider it an advance and an investment in you and your family."

That had been over a decade ago. Scott was now his Chief Technology Officer and Lukas' likely successor, something he needed to give serious thought to now that he was on the board of Phoenix Equities which considerably added to his plate of responsibilities.

Lukas' mind jumped back to the present, the challenge before him snapping him out of his walk down memory lane. He was able to enter into the *Juventus* operating network as the AI password generator tried multiple combinations of letters and numbers to break through the firewall. He still had access to the internet and instant messaging so he decided to send Tory another message, hoping their location would be automatically tagged.

It had been almost a week since Baptiste had pulled into the Bora Bora lagoon. Lukas sighed, attempting to stay focused and not think about the dire circumstances on board. The computer pinged when it got a password hit, which Lukas could unhide and he then photographed to keep a record of it.

"You're into the main operating system," Diana Kepler informed him. "I can take it from here." Diana's fingers deftly typed commands that got her to the main dashboard. "I've got to find the auto-destruct."

"Any idea where I can find a spare laptop?" Lukas asked her. "Is it inside a vault guarded by Dobermans? Baptiste always had a flair for the dramatic."

Diana pointed at a cabinet beneath the instrument panel. "Hate to burst your bubble."

Lukas grabbed the laptop, its battery charged, and fired it up. Using the password his program had figured out to log him into *Juventus'* operating system, Lukas was quickly able to clone Baptiste's credentials and log in as him.

"Is the bridge computer not slick enough for you?" she asked sarcastically.

"You'd think that with a billion-dollar yacht, he'd at least spring for some decent laptops," Lukas commented as he logged in to the ship's system.

Six electronic folders illuminated on the computer screen, each one labeled and dated. He clicked on one file called Surveillance and began to download the videos captured on their voyage, most importantly, the footage from their first night when they woke up ncxt to Gael. He made a note to himself to review these later, as his priority now was to stop the countdown to auto-destruct.

After downloading the folders, he searched for the ship's operating system commands that would hopefully give him an outlet for stopping the countdown. Taylor peered over his shoulder and Diana looked on.

"That's the system folder," Diana called out. Lukas maneuvered through the screens and found the ship's command settings. A digital clock slowly counted backward. "That's the countdown. Twenty-two hours left."

"That just seems weird," Taylor jumped in. "Why set an auto-destruct sequence that takes a whole day?"

"And why destroy a billion-dollar yacht/submarine that can literally hide anywhere in the world?" Lukas continued.

"That could explain why we're on the ocean floor," Diana replied. "It would muffle the sound and visuals of a ship on the surface."

"Which seems counter to Baptiste's desire for drama," Lukas offered another angle. "This all feels odd. If he were destroying his flagship, you would think he'd want the biggest audience possible."

Another jolting shook *Juventus*, followed by the hissing of something outside the hull. A massive explosion appeared on the exterior cameras. The group stared at the screen which showed a sizable explosion about a mile in the distance.

"What's going on?" Taylor followed the wake of

bubbles and swirling water as two projectiles shot into the murky distance before disappearing.

"Are those torpedoes?" Lukas asked, his hand pointing at what everyone could see. "Why would *Juventus* have torpedoes?"

A muffled explosion rumbled in the distance, but they could not see anything. The external speakers picked up more sounds in the distance that sounded like an avalanche.

"What the hell is going on?" Lukas' voice was cut off by another two torpedoes ejected from *Juventus*, following the trail of their predecessors.

Taylor stood quietly, remembering his trip in the mini-sub yesterday. *Destroying the islands?* he thought. "I saw huge piles of rubble, mostly moonstone, along with whatever debris came down with it."

A lightbulb went off in Lukas' head. "Are they destroying the islands made from the comet?"

"And using the erupting volcano as a decoy!" Taylor concluded. "Folks would assume the explosion and tsunamis came from the volcano, not Pierre blowing up his islands."

Diana remained tight-lipped, not comfortable to divulge Project Olympus to Taylor or Lukas. *Of course, they're harvesting all the remaining moonstone in order to hoard it for their multiple-century scheme they had been planning*, she wanted to say.

Lukas opened up his instant message app and began typing Tory a note.

****

Hey, favorite daughter, your dad, my mom, her friends, and I are underwater in Baptiste's yacht/submarine Juventus. We are near or in his archipelago and it appears he has left the ship and set it to self-destruct. Mom's okay, her two friends are very sick. Knowing you, you are already in Fiji or on your way here. Need emergency medical assistance for them. Location is on and we are logged into the ship's Wi-Fi as long as we are able. There's also T's chip. We will attempt to disarm auto-destruct. If that doesn't work we find a plan B. Love you, kiddo, Papa

Lukas hit send and hoped for the best. He was underwater and depended on some kind of satellite transmission that he didn't even know would work. Both his laptop and satellite phone were getting low on battery power. It was a longshot that any message sent from the ship would make it to Tory quickly, especially if she was in the air.

A chime pinged indicating he received a message that he assumed being bounced back as undeliverable. He scrambled to open the message.

WTF? Have your position marked. WFSO. In barrio. Stay dry. CTYA :-) VPH

Lukas smiled as he tried to decipher Tory's acronyms besides WTF, which he knew well. WFSO was probably *Will figure something out*. CTYA was likely *Can't take you anywhere* and she used VPH to sign her name with the initials of her legal name; Victory Pastore-Halloran.

Chapter 32

Lukas searched frantically for how to stop the auto-destruct countdown that descended menacingly toward detonation, with less than thirty minutes left to go until all hell broke loose. Baptiste hid it somewhere, cloaked behind an unknown app or screen in *Juventus'* operating system.

"Do you know where I can find the timer so I can stop it?" Lukas shouted to Kepler.

"Baptiste and Marc hid it somewhere. They left it for me to find before they escaped off the ship." She shook her head, acknowledging her misplaced trust in Pierre Baptiste. Diana raced through the applications on the ship's control panel while Lukas simultaneously searched his laptop that he had hacked into *Juventus'* operating system.

"Any luck?" he yelled to Kepler, who shook her head. "Me neither. Keep searching!"

Taylor ran back into the ship's bridge, panting. "Nobody else seems to be on board, besides us."

"Estimated number?" Captain Kepler yelled, her voice a high-pitched shrill.

Taylor counted. "Molly, Betty, Linda, Dr. Nevon, Gael, Kailani, and the three of us make nine."

"Did you check the crew deck?" she shouted.

Taylor remembered. "Aleks, what about Aleks? Anyone seen him?"

Lukas and Diana shook their heads.

"Make it ten then," Taylor shouted. "How many can fit on one of the lifeboats?"

"I was thinking that, too," Captain Kepler replied. "We'll be more than fine with just one of the evacuation vessels."

"Is that the new term for lifeboats?" Lukas asked Diana.

"At least for Baptiste it is," she replied, half smiling.

"Captain, we need to get to the surface," Taylor suggested. "We can't risk decompression if we launch from thirty meters underwater."

"Good point," Kepler responded. "I'll take her up." Kepler pulled back on the elevators and tipped *Juventus*' bow slightly higher. "Surfacing in seven minutes," she announced.

Juventus rose toward the surface. Countdown at twenty-five minutes. Taylor ran to sick bay to prepare the patients for evacuation. *Where is Aleks Borisov?* he thought.

****

Taylor entered the ship's hospital to calmly alert folks that they would be preparing to evacuate *Juventus*.

"We've got twenty-two minutes until auto-destruct," he informed Molly.

"Can we get them on stretchers and carry them to the escape boats?" she asked Taylor.

"I took a look at them on the way down from the bridge," Taylor told her. "They are actually what I would call escape pods, Molly. We are surfacing so they can be launched at the water level."

"How many people can each pod hold?" Molly directed her question at Dr. Nevon.

"I believe they are capable of holding up to ten people. It'd be a bit tight," Nevon responded. "They are well-stocked with food and water. Medical equipment not so much. We'll need to stabilize the patients before we move them."

"We better do that within the next ten minutes, then," Taylor replied.

"Good thing is they're breathing on their own," Nevon concluded. "We should be okay."

"Not that we have a hell of a lot of options," Molly responded to Taylor.

Dr. Nevon stood in shock as he saw Linda Eastman and Betty Bao flutter back to life. Their fingers moved and eyes stared at the ceiling above. Molly watched in disbelief as their bodies showed signs of animation, but no sign of her actual friends.

"How long until their personalities return?" she asked Kailani. Watching her friends' bodies animate with none of their spark for life was disconcerting. *Patience, Molly*, she thought to herself. "When will we know they are truly back, not just alive?"

While Kailani appeared serene, she noticed that Gael seemed agitated, jumpy, and distracted. Molly noticed Gael kept checking his smartphone, an action she hadn't seen him do before today because he'd never used his phone around her. Gael's forehead creased as he stared at the screen on his phone. He then said something to Kailani and rushed out the door of the sick bay. Kailani's downcast eyes were dark with anger, fear, bewilderment, or a combination of several things. She noticed Molly watching her with concern.

"Gael received some urgent news." She smiled at Molly. "He will be back shortly."

****

Juventus rose and finally surfaced, like an enormous nine-hundred-foot whale displacing thousands of tons of water as the cobalt blue hull glistened in the sun. The external video cameras channeled outside video of a serene blue sea.

"Camouflage engaged," Captain Kepler said calmly.

Lukas turned his head to her. "What does that mean?"

Captain Kepler did not respond, but Lukas was busy downloading all of the files to his laptop. As he searched for more surveillance video, he came across an app that stood alone on the screen. The app, represented by a navy-blue tile adorned with a capital A in the middle intrigued him, so he clicked on the tile to see what was inside. Lukas was immediately drawn in. His eyes were wide with whatever he was reading. Fingers typed commands as he frantically absorbed the information he found. From what he read, he decided not to download anything as potentially dangerous as the file labeled *Archipelago*.

Lukas' head hurt as he speed-read, and attempted to absorb, the information inside the Archipelago file.

Holy shit, he thought as he felt blood drain out of his head as the reality of Archipelago began to materialize in his throbbing head. He slammed the laptop shut. Lukas couldn't afford to be distracted by such a complicated story. They were seventeen minutes to auto-destruct, and he still could not find a way to stop the countdown. He had to put learning more about

Archipelago on hold. Suddenly the lights dimmed, and the cockpit glowed a sinister blue.

"Hello, my friends," Pierre's insincere greeting echoed throughout the entire ship. "I hope you are all doing well and enjoying your adventure. It's been a wild ride, I know, but I promise it all leads to something."

Lukas glanced around the bridge. Taylor clenched his jaw. Captain Kepler's face remained stoic and unemotional.

"By now you realize everybody is off the ship, but you." Baptiste chuckled sarcastically. "But it's not too late to make a choice."

Baptiste's voice echoed through sick bay where Molly, Kailani, and Dr. Nevon continued to attend to the awakening of Linda and Betty.

"Pierre," Lukas shouted at the speakers. "How do I shut off the ship's auto-destruct? Why are you doing this? What's on board that you have to cover your tracks, Baptiste?"

A sinister laugh came through the speakers. "What makes you think I'm destroying my precious *Juventus*?" Pierre asked as if everyone knew his plans. "Maybe the plan is to just destroy all of you." He laughed menacingly.

Lukas clenched his jaw so the words he wanted to shout were silenced. "Why do you want to do that, Baptiste?"

"You are such a downer, Lukas. Do you know that? Just like your father," Baptiste mocked him over the intercom.

Lukas' jaw protruded as he looked for Taylor to no avail. "Where are you, Pierre?"

"Oh, very close by, Lukas. I've been supervising the collection of the moonstone from the bottom of my ocean."

Suddenly Taylor ran onto the bridge. He had heard Baptiste's last comment. "And where did all the moonstone come from, Pierre?"

Baptiste chuckled over the intercom. "Marc tells me you saw something, so don't ask me rhetorical questions, Taylor. What do you think happened?"

"*Juventus* has been firing missiles at your islands in the archipelago. I'm not sure what you're using, but the islands have collapsed beneath the sea. That's what caused the tsunami, isn't it?"

"I can't confirm anything, Taylor. But it's possible. Marc's father got me a great deal on some TBs," Baptiste continued. "They brought down the islands precisely as we had hoped."

"What's a TB?" Lukas asked.

"Thermo Baric," Taylor responded. "They are the largest non-nuclear conventional weapons used. So powerful, they can cause earthquakes."

"And tsunamis apparently?" Lukas asked, not wanting to know the answer.

"I had them specially modified to be used as torpedoes," Baptiste evaded the question. "The Russians have been eager to work with me. The islands are mine, anyway. I can destroy them if I want. The material they are made of is much more valuable than the island real estate intact. I've still got five islands left."

"How the hell do you blow up an island?" Lukas asked.

"It's basically a massive concussive force," Taylor

explained. "Imagine a bomb that doesn't explode on impact, but rather right before impact, sends a massive force of energy, and obliterates anything within its blast zone. The blast breaks the moonstone's crystalline structure into smaller blocks that collapse into the sea."

"How do you know about these?" Lukas asked.

"Air Force. They were designed as satellite guided missiles," Taylor said. "Sounds like Pierre has modified them for water."

"And nobody thought it might cause a tsunami?" Lukas asked.

Silence. "Perhaps," Baptiste muttered. Taylor nodded and mouthed the word *Yes*, confirming the explosion most likely triggered the massive tsunami.

"An enormous amount of water is displaced as you can imagine," Taylor explained.

"How much moonstone will make you happy, Pierre?" Lukas asked sarcastically.

More silence hung in the air as Pierre Baptiste refused to answer the question. Seven minutes remained until the countdown ticked away to zero.

"Look to your starboard side," Baptiste said coldly.

"Stop the countdown, Pierre!" Taylor ordered, knowing his demands were futile. Again, silence reverberated off the walls.

"I've done what you requested," Marc Hammer's voice echoed through the cabin.

Lukas glanced up from his laptop and a thumbs-up confirmed the countdown had stopped.

"Now go to the starboard window," Baptiste commanded them.

About one-hundred feet away, a large, malevolent shape rose above the waves. Waves lapped its sinister black hull from which two delta-shaped wings appeared stretched outward, their ends capped with winglets. The craft did not appear to be affected by the waves, rather it almost appeared to be a landmass or a huge marine animal. What Lukas assumed was the cockpit glowed like a cycloptic eye in the center of the black mound.

"What the fuck is that?" Lukas asked. Taylor was equally awed.

Baptiste's voice crackled over the speaker. "It's the newest member of my fleet. Also the largest and the fastest."

"Tired of *Juventus* already?" Taylor asked.

Baptiste let out a laugh. "Why would you ask that?"

"The auto-destruct command was one of the first clues," Lukas snapped back.

"Ah, I see, Lukas. Black and white thinking. I gave you more credit than that," Pierre Baptiste sneered. "Rest assured, I'm not destroying *Juventus*. She has a long life ahead of her, but I needed *Olympus* for a larger group of people. It's more…residential."

"What the hell is he talking about?" Lukas commented

"*Olympus* is the name of the new ship," Diana Kepler stated, surprising Taylor and Lukas.

"Then why have you set *Juventus* on an auto-destruct sequence?" Lukas asked.

"As I told you, the auto-destruct is for the remaining passengers, not the ship, my friends, It's much cheaper and easier to get rid of you all. The *Juventus* plays in important role in my future" Baptiste said matter-of-factly. "You all, not so much. But you can still decide to join me. If not, you're too much of a risk."

Anger etched their faces as Lukas and Taylor froze, not sure whether Baptiste was serious or bluffing. Diana Kepler stared straight ahead, emotionless.

"I need to get my mom up here," Lukas said to Taylor, who quickly darted out of the room to get her.

Kepler and Lukas were alone on the bridge, not sure of what to say to each other.

"I don't know where you fit in all of this," Lukas said to Captain Kepler. "Not sure if I should trust you or not."

A thin smile etched Diana's face. "I'm not sure you should either. Pierre wants me to kill you."

Chapter 33

Tory and Pepe scoured the airport for a vessel that could take them out to Baptiste's islands. Their search nearly exhausted, they stumbled into a dark hangar littered with aircraft parts and incomplete carcasses of helicopters.

"Is this a helicopter chop shop?" Tory whispered to her fiancé.

Pepe noticed movement toward the back of the hangar and confidently walked toward who he hoped was a friendly person. From the darkness, a man emerged wearing only coveralls. Wispy gray hair sparsely covered his head. The man smiled as he welcomed the young Italian man to his domain.

"Hello young man," he said politely in accented English.

"Good day, sir." Pepe went for a more formal approach to introducing himself. "My name is Giuseppe. You can call me Pepe." He offered his hand to the older man.

"Pepe." The man scratched his chin. "Where have I heard that name before?" He wasn't able to recall and extended his hand back to Pepe. "Jone," he responded back, the Fijian pronunciation sounding more like *Chonah*. "What can I help you with today?"

"I need to rent a helicopter. A big one." Pepe decided to be direct.

"Oh?" Jone asked. "May I ask what for?"

"We have some friends stuck on an island by the new Koro volcano. I would like to go get them and bring them back."

"I see," Jone spoke. "Can you fly a helicopter, young man?"

Pepe fidgeted at the awkward interchange. "No, I cannot, but my friend can."

"Your friend? I see." Jone pondered. "The only craft that can make it that far would be my Pelican." He walked Pepe through the cavernous hangar. Opening a door, they entered into another small bay. "That's my Pelican." Jone pointed proudly.

A large helicopter was illuminated after Jone flicked on the lights. His Pelican was an old Sikorsky model, probably at least forty years old by the looks of her. Paint had flecked off the craft and floated onto the hangar floor.

"Isn't she a beauty?" Jone emphasized. "I hope your friend can fly her. She hasn't been out for a good six months."

"How much?" Pepe asked him.

"How much for what?" Jone asked.

"To rent your…Pelican. Just for a day."

"Oh, I don't rent the Pelican to people," Jone explained. "But I will fly it for you. How does one-thousand Fiji Dollars sound?"

"Fine. When can we leave?" Pepe asked, not even sure of the exchange rate.

"Well, I will need to find another pilot," Jone explained. "It's Fiji law just in case something happens to me while in flight."

Pepe was about to stall Jone for a few minutes

when he heard heels on the shiny floor, approaching him from behind.

"I can fly her." Pepe spun around to see Donna standing confidently next to Tory. "Assuming she's air-worthy."

"Oh very air-worthy, ma'am," Jone replied with excitement.

A loud ping echoed through the hangar after something metal dropped off the fuselage.

"Let's hope that wasn't anything important," Donna commented with sarcasm.

****

Linda's eyes fluttered open. Molly ran to her side so that Linda would see a familiar face and not be frightened or disoriented.

"How was your nap?" Molly asked her, half kidding.

Linda's mouth moved but produced no sound. Betty became conscious next, equally disoriented in the darkened room that hummed with hospital equipment. Both women scowled with confusion, their eyes taking in a room they didn't recognize.

Their hands had been tied to the bed rails so that they did not pull out their ventilators, and now that they appeared to be breathing on their own Molly and Dr. Nevon removed them.

Dr. Nevon worked in stunned silence. "This moonstone material is unbelievable. Thirty years as a physician, I've never heard of someone returning to life after being deceased for nearly an hour. It's a miracle."

Molly nodded. "A miracle Baptiste wants so he can exploit people's vanity."

Nevon remained silent, not sure how much Molly

knew. "I've advised him against that." He continued to take pulse readings from the arms of both women. "This material is quite amazing, but it needs to be studied, but I doubt he'll listen to me."

"My guess is that he won't." Molly tried to maintain a friendly tone.

"Probably not." Dr. Nevon sighed. "That's why he's a billionaire and I'm just a ship's doctor."

Linda began to cough, expelling liquid from her lungs after the ventilator was removed.

Molly leaned over her bed and stroked her hair. Linda's post-moonstone youth had disappeared, and she returned to looking closer to her actual age.

"How are you feeling?" Molly asked her friend.

Linda struggled to respond, her lips forming an answer. She just couldn't get it out, so she raised her thumb to signal she was okay. "Hugnee," was all she could say.

"I think she's hungry," Molly translated for Dr. Nevon.

"That's a good sign," the doctor agreed.

Betty grabbed at the bed rails to pull herself up to a seated position. Her mussed hair covered her upper forehead and eyes. "Excuse me, I need to use the restroom," she said clearly.

Molly stifled a laugh thinking how she would explain this situation to her friends when they were fully recovered.

Betty struggled to get her feet over the rail. "I need to get to the goddamned bathroom."

Dr. Nevon rushed over to help her. "How do you feel, Mrs. Bao?"

"I'll feel better when I get to the damned

bathroom!" Betty was clearly in need, so Molly joined Dr. Nevon to escort Betty to the facilities.

The restroom door slammed, and Molly stood against it, relieved. "She just made it."

Dr. Nevon smiled. "Now you see what nurses go through."

"I've spent a lifetime cleaning up shit, vomit, whatever from kids. I can't do it for an adult without gagging."

Betty remained in the bathroom for several minutes until they heard the toilet flush. After washing her hands, Betty stepped out. "What's for lunch?"

"It's good to see you walking," Dr. Nevon addressed her.

"Thanks," Betty replied. "Who the hell are you?"

Chapter 34

Baptiste's voice pierced the speaker. He sounded agitated. Impatient.

"I'm giving you my third and final offer to come aboard *Olympus*. I could very much use your skills for our project."

Silence.

"My preference is that you and your friends join me. *Olympus* and *Juventus* will be home to us for the next several years, protected and living in luxury while we ride out the events of mankind."

"Events? What events?" Taylor asked.

There was a pause for half a minute as Baptiste, always the showman, did his best to build the suspense.

"Have you heard of the Doomsday Clock? World events, political disruption, natural disasters, human-created shortages, pollution, and climate change all contribute to it."

"I've heard of it," Lukas answered. "I didn't know it was a real thing."

"It is, and the human race is at 23:59 hours. Literally one minute to midnight," Baptiste explained. "We have never been this close."

"This close to what?" Lukas asked.

"The apocalypse," Baptiste stated calmly.

****

Within a few minutes, Baptiste's crewmen returned

to *Juventus* to escort off those that agreed to go to the *Olympus* ship. Taylor, Lukas, and Molly stood in the *Juventus* cockpit. Betty and Linda, more alert but still weak, sat in chairs they had brought them from the lobby. They watched as Gael, Kailani, Aleks, and Dr. Nevon were escorted to the edge of the deck and met by a shuttle that came from Baptiste's new ship, *Olympus*. Once they boarded the shuttle, it turned and propelled its way toward the larger vessel. Captain Kepler stood emotionless as she watched her colleagues calmly escorted off *Juventus*.

"Are they coming to get you?" Molly asked.

"I don't know, ma'am." Her stoicism masked her deep disappointment that it was highly likely her father had abandoned her. Again.

Two crew members entered the bridge, each one holding a pistol. One of the men motioned to Diana while the other one went to escort her off the ship.

"I guess that means I'm going," Diana commented to Molly.

"You are welcome to stay with us, but you'll probably live longer if you go with them." Molly tried to lighten the mood as Diana Kepler furled her brow and prepared to leave.

"I'd like to say goodbye to my friends, first." She approached Lukas, gave him a big hug and kissed him on the ear before repeating the same for Taylor and Molly, reserving a wave to bid goodbye to Linda and Betty.

Lukas, puzzled by the sudden affection and a meaningless message she whispered in his ear, watched as Diana Kepler prepared to disembark *Juventus*. He thought he saw Diana wink at him but brushed it off as his imagination.

As the crewmen escorted Kepler to the door, she quickly turned her head, smiled at them, and gave a brief wave. The cockpit door slammed behind her and in a few minutes, they watched as Diana was escorted onto the shuttle and departed *Juventus*.

Now they were alone. Five people, two of them still recovering, were confused and agitated by what would befall them.

"We need to get to the escape pods," Lukas told them urgently. "They're down one deck level. Taylor, can you get them downstairs?"

"I'll do that, babe," Taylor responded. "Did the countdown restart?"

"Five minutes," Lukas said. "It will take you three minutes to get Donna and Linda downstairs and secured into the pod. Mom and I will be right behind you."

Suddenly, a new voice came over the speaker that rattled Lukas and Molly to their core.

"You guys better hurry up," the voice of John Halloran echoed off the steel walls. "The end of the world is coming quickly."

"Dad?" Lukas exclaimed. "How are you…?"

"Alive?" Halloran's voice echoed. "Are you surprised to hear me?"

Molly, her eyes wet with tears, looked up in disbelief.

"I'm waiting for you on the *Olympus*. Come join me. Baptiste and I have lots of work to do, and we need your help."

Lukas and Molly fought back tears as they struggled to make sense of what they were hearing. *How can dad still be alive?* Lukas thought to himself.

"Honey," Molly choked. "I saw you dead on our terrace. Why didn't you tell me this sooner?" Her voice was tinged with sadness and anger.

There was almost fifteen seconds of silence, which felt like precious time with only four minutes left on the countdown. "It's been secret. My death was staged because of the important work Pierre Baptiste and I have been working on a project and I needed to concentrate on it."

Molly was puzzled. *Her husband fakes his death and tells nobody? He did all this to work with Baptiste?* "I'm surprised you didn't at least try and tell us," Molly stated, her emotions frozen beneath a calm veneer. "A lot of us have been quite sad since you supposedly died."

Lukas approached the speaker as if it were John himself.

"Dad, when is my birthday?"

"April 15th. Tax Day," he answered without a pause. Lukas smiled at that. His father always told him his birthday was also Tax Day. He would be an adult before he understood what his dad meant.

"Our anniversary?" Molly shouted.

"June 30th," John replied as Molly smiled

Lukas continued to ask a series of questions to verify this was actually his dad. He peppered him with questions. Address, birthdates of his grandchildren, the type of car he had at the time of his faked death, the name of the hotel they stayed in for their honeymoon, and several other questions of events both recent and long ago. He answered every question correctly.

Lukas glanced at his mother, her lip trembling in disbelief and confusion. Tears ran down her cheeks as she remained stoic.

"Dad," Lukas asked. "I have one more question for you. This one was never recorded or has any data associated with it, okay?"

Silence from John.

"What was our secret word, Dad?"

"Our secret word?" John asked to clarify.

Baptiste's voice interrupted. "Lukas, what game are you playing?"

Lukas shot his mom a look that she understood immediately. *Go*, he mouthed to her. *It's not Dad.* Her face dropped in disappointment, but she trusted her son.

"It's not a game, Dad. You gave me a word so that you would know it was me if I called you on the phone and needed help?"

"I can't remember that word. It was a long time ago." John answered flatly. "Lukas, I've had some memory loss from a fall. I'm sorry, buddy."

Lukas' eyes narrowed. His dad never used the word *buddy*.

Molly realized it, too. Her face drained.

There was more silence. Lucas looked at the speaker. "Dad, our word."

After a few more moments of silence, John perked up. "Now I remember. We had two words, one you gave me and one I gave you."

Dad, don't put memories in my head that aren't there, he thought.

"The word I gave you was…Well, I just can't remember."

Lukas wanted to cry and scream at Baptiste for creating such a nasty trick but knew that would get him nowhere. The ruse was clear. It wasn't his dad.

"Bye, Dad," was all he could mutter.

"Otemanu," John's voice said flatly.

Lukas gasped. *How could he possibly know?* he thought.

"I look forward to seeing you aboard *Olympus*," The AI-generated voice of John Halloran said as if it were a bright sunny day to meet in the park.

****

Lukas pushed the sadness out of his mind so he could focus. He ran down a flight of stairs and saw Taylor, Linda, and Betty standing by what looked like a door.

"It's locked," Taylor said. "I keep inputting the numbers Diana whispered in my ear and it doesn't open."

"She gave me a set of numbers, too," Lukas replied.

"Me too," Molly confirmed.

"Let's try all three sets." Lukas suggested. "I'll go first since she hugged me before you two." Lukas went over and plugged in the five numbers Diana whispered to him.

"Taylor?" Lukas said, checking his watch. Less than a minute remaining.

"Mom, your turn." Molly input her code. The door didn't respond.

"Shit," Lukas exclaimed as he pushed the hashtag key. The green lights flashed, and the door opened.

Forty seconds.

Taylor climbed in first and helped pull Linda, Molly, and Betty into the luxurious escape pod before Lukas jumped in and slammed the door.

Twenty seconds.

"Now what?" Taylor asked, frantically searching for possible controls inside the escape pod. Lukas spotted a graphic on the pod's ceiling that depicted a forward arrow and a seatbelt.

"Sit down and put on your seat belt!" Lukas yelled as he ran to buckle Betty and Linda. Taylor and Molly did theirs and he jumped into his seat, fastened his seatbelt, and the escape pod slowly launched from *Juventus*.

They braced themselves for a massive explosion.

"How far are we away from the ship?" Molly asked. "Maybe it has a safety override if another ship is too close." The minute she said it, she laughed. "That makes no sense. Sorry."

As the escape pod continued its slow drift away from *Juventus*, it became more and more unlikely the ship was going to self-destruct. Taylor rummaged through the storage area of the control panel and found an operating manual of drawings on how to operate the escape pod. The console contained two levers that protruded vertically, and Taylor assumed they were joysticks for controlling the craft. He soon discovered these were used to maneuver the escape pod left or right. There was also a single button that hovered over a pictogram of what appeared to be stylized waves.

"This thing only goes up from the looks of it," Taylor told Lukas. "How are you doing with…?"

"I'm okay, babe," he said. "I'm trying to keep my mind focused on what we're going to do next." Lukas grabbed his phone out of the rucksack he took that contained his laptop, both of his phones, and about a pound of moonstone rocks.

Taylor broke the silence. "That was just mean.

Baptiste pretending to be your dad."

"He's a first-class asshole, Taylor. Nothing surprises me," Lukas said angrily. "But it wasn't Baptiste pretending to be my dad."

"What was it then?" Molly overheard Taylor's question and joined them.

"It was Dad, well at least somewhat," he replied to Taylor's and Molly's collective shock.

"Lukas, what are you talking about?" his mother asked him.

"It was dad's voice, synthesized with what were probably actual recordings of dad over the years. Artificial Intelligence is advancing to the point that we can virtually recreate people who have passed away, at least from a digital perspective."

"I'm not sure I understand," Molly said. "Are you saying that Dad is still alive somehow in the digital world?"

"Ma, this is such new technology, I'm not sure how to answer your question," Lukas replied. "I mean at its simplest, knowledge is data. Our brains store experiences as data. That data, if repeated and reinforced, is ultimately stored as something we know to be true," Lukas explained. "Now imagine, if we were able to somehow digitize all of the archives, speeches, personal diaries of someone famous, like Abraham Lincoln. We could theoretically, using AI software, predict what Abraham Lincoln would do in a certain situation today, based upon all of that recorded data."

"Honey." Molly rubbed the back of her neck. "This hurts my head to think about but let me throw out something to make sure I understand. Using this AI platform, we would be able to extrapolate from all the data we have on Abraham Lincoln, how he might respond to a modern-day challenge?"

"Yeah, Ma. Theoretically," Lukas answered her. "But Lincoln lived before the age of computers, video, and other technologies we use today, so imagine what data is available in today's world."

"So back to your dad," Taylor continued. "If someone had digitized all the known data about John Halloran…"

"And the recordings of hundreds of his speeches, television appearances, his internet bios, even his search history," Lukas added. "That could be synthesized into a predictable and probable output of what he might say, think, or do."

"So, you said that the voice of your dad was not recorded, but his actual voice?" Taylor asked for clarification.

Lukas nodded.

"Then how did you know it wasn't him?" Molly asked.

Lukas thought about it for a second before answering. "Ma, remember when I asked Dad to remind me what our secret word was?"

Molly nodded. "But he, or the computer, couldn't remember the secret word, right?"

"Ma, Dad and I didn't have a secret word. I totally made that up to see how he would react," Lukas explained. "He tried to get around the question, tell me he couldn't remember, and then, when I was already onto another topic, do you remember what he said?"

"Otemanu," Taylor replied. "The huge volcanic mountain on Bora Bora."

"Exactly," Lukas said with excitement.

"Somewhere in his digital brain there were images of Mount Otemanu and maybe diary entries, search history, whatever to warrant the AI software to choose the secret word as something he and I talked about. The AI platform was able to use reason, predictability, and other factors and it basically took a guess, but wasn't able to lie."

"You mean about you and your dad having a secret word?" Taylor asked.

"That was my lie," he told the group. "But Archipelago didn't know that, so it took a guess, and a damned good guess."

"But not a correct guess," Molly concluded.

"Sounds like it works like a human brain," a groggy Linda commented, still sleepy.

"That's extraordinary," Betty said.

"Welcome back, Linda and Betty," Lukas said warmly. "And yes, it's extraordinary, but not clever enough to detect a lie from a truth with no data behind it."

Chapter 35

Jone and Donna sat in the cockpit of the Pelican while checking off their pre-flight protocol. The estimated flying time to Baptiste's Jardin Archipelago was just shy of an hour. Despite Donna and Tory offering him to use their computer tablet for navigation, Jone scoffed at the idea and insisted on using his normal flight maps.

"We take off and fly for about ten minutes over Viti Levu, and then we are over water for the rest of the flight," Jone explained. "Please make sure you have a life vest on, or at least, ready to put on. The Pelican is a good Heli, but she's up there in age, so we need to be prepared."

Wilma and Pepe glanced at each other warily and picked out their own life vest to have on hand should they need it. An old flare gun tumbled off a rack and Tory caught it before it hit the floor of the chopper.

"You have my permission to shoot me with that if we crash," Wilma said with a mixture of seriousness and jest. "Being eaten by a shark is my biggest fear, so just put me out of my misery."

"She's not kidding," Donna piped up. "This is why we always do land vacations."

As the rotor started, the blades began to squeak as they turned. Black smoke billowed out of the Pelican's ancient engine and exhaust pipe, but soon the rotors were spinning rapidly as Jone prepared for lift off.

"Seatbelts please." Jone pretended to sound like a flight attendant as a flagman directed the Pelican as it lumbered to the takeoff point. Jone's thumbs up was responded by Donna's and they both pulled back on the throttles and slowly lifted into the air.

****

The Pelican hovered over the airport while Jone fiddled with the controls.

"You looking for something?" Donna asked, slightly nervous.

"Nah, I'm good." Jone piloted forward, circling the populated areas before heading out over the Pacific Ocean.

"Fiji is more mountainous than I expected," Wilma shouted from the back seat.

Jone nodded. "It's all old volcanoes and coral worn down over centuries," he shouted back. "Kind of like me!" Jone laughed as Wilma gave him a thumbs up.

The blue ocean appeared to be impossibly endless from each direction. Donna had a brief sense of vulnerability as the Pelican left the safety of land. Tory and Pepe also looked more stressed than normal. None of Jone's passengers was nearly as familiar with helicopters as they were with traditional airplanes. There was something about having wings and the ability to glide that all of a sudden was not an option in a helicopter. That, plus the fact that the Pelican was older than both Tory and Pepe unsettled them.

"Next stop is Kiva Oa!" Jone shouted. "About forty-five minutes away."

"I thought Kiva Oa was Pierre Baptiste's private island." Tory asked. "Do we need permission to land

287

there?"

"All the airports are still under jurisdiction of the Fiji government, so as long as we have clearance from them, we're good," Jone responded.

A bank of clouds approached. The Pelican bounced through the turbulence created by the temperature difference between clouds and ambient air. Pepe hung on tight, alarmed by the knocking and rattling each air pocket created and the overall shaking of the old aircraft. Tory put her hand on his knee, sensing he was a bit nervous.

"It's definitely a different ride, isn't it?"

"That is very true," Pepe replied as he tried not to think about it.

****

"The concept, in theory, is incredible. It's called Collective AI." Lukas explained. "It's one of the most amazing and frightening technologies to come in a long time. The United States government is on high alert, to put it mildly."

"Can you explain collective artificial intelligence in a few sentences that won't completely boggle my mind?" Molly asked.

"No promises, Ma." Lukas smiled. "But it's pretty simple. Imagine that an AI platform was able to network with thousands of other computers around the world, with or without the owner of that computer being aware."

"Is that even legal?" Taylor asked.

"Depends upon who you ask, where you live, and whatever the mood of the day might be," Lukas said with slight sarcasm. "In other words, there aren't any definitive rules."

"But it's data protection, right?" Taylor asked.

"Technically, I think so," Lukas responded. "But some lawyers argue that ideas, experiences, and creative problem solving are not data; they are outcomes from data."

"Kind of more like IP then?" Betty asked.

"Closer, but with intellectual property there must be an owner of that property," Lukas explained. "And technically collective AI, since it comes from multiple sources of data, is difficult to identify the actual owner of the product of the data."

"Jeez, this makes my head hurt," Linda groaned.

"Welcome to the new frontier of digital law," Lukas said. "At some point, artificial intelligence could be considered sentient and possibly have rights."

"You know," Betty said. "When I hear stuff like this, I'm glad I'm closer to exiting this life than entering it."

"Unless moonstone has guaranteed you'll live for centuries," Molly jabbed.

"If I do, I will spend those centuries tormenting you." Betty laughed.

****

The escape pod continued slowly, just about ten feet below the surface of the ocean to remain as visibly undetectable as possible. Molly reported that she noticed they might be approaching land as the contour of the ocean floor started to slope upward. Taylor estimated the water depth to be about seventy feet.

"What's that behind us?" Lukas noticed a large shape in the distance that hovered in the murky water.

"I don't see anything," Molly answered. "Maybe I'm not looking in the right place."

"Could it be a whale? Are there whales in Fiji?" Lukas asked.

Betty and Linda shrugged.

"Maybe we should head to shallower water," Taylor suggested. He piloted the pod using its weak thruster motors that slowly followed the sloping bottom. "I think we're heading in the right…"

A whoosh shook the escape pod followed by a turbulent trail of swirling water and bubbles about fifty feet off the port side of the vessel.

"What the hell was that?" Molly asked.

Taylor squinted in the distance as the mysterious dark shape became clearer. "Oh, shit!"

The bow of *Juventus* materialized, still murky but slowly coming into focus.

"What's *Juventus* still doing here?" Lukas asked. "I thought…"

Another whoosh flew by the escape pod, this time about thirty feet from their hull.

"Damnit, these guys are firing torpedoes at us!" Taylor yelled. "I'm coming about."

Taylor used the left and right joysticks to turn the craft one-hundred-eighty degrees to face the massive ship which seemed to be hellbent on destroying them.

"How many torpedoes can that thing hold?" Lukas asked, not expecting an answer.

"I'm guessing those were warning shots," Taylor responded. "No explosions followed, so the torpedoes didn't have payloads."

"Not yet," Betty commented.

"Always the ray of sunshine," Linda jibed her. "Why are you facing *Juventus* head on, Taylor?"

"Strategic placement," Taylor answered her. "We

have no guns so we're gonna have to maneuver our way through this."

Juventus continued its slow, intimidating approach toward the escape pod.

"What do you think they'll do?" Lukas asked.

"There is nobody onboard *Juventus* currently. "I'll put money on it. It's being controlled remotely." Taylor theorized.

"Like a drone?" Molly clarified.

"Like a nine-hundred-foot-long, heavily armed drone," Lukas offered. "Taylor, are you planning what I think you're planning?"

Taylor's eyes didn't move, locked on *Juventus*. "Seatbelts, everyone. Now."

"Oh God," Linda commented. "That doesn't sound good."

Both hands gripping the joysticks, Taylor waited patiently. He knew this maneuver was his only option, should it come to that.

"We'll have to see if they sh—"

Before Taylor could get the word out, two torpedoes launched from *Juventus* and raced toward them at high speed.

"Hang on!" he yelled as he pushed the joysticks to dive almost straight down.

Lukas watched the approaching missiles, unsure of how Taylor would respond. He sat beside his mom, seatbelts secured, ready for whatever was going to happen.

Taylor drove the pod straight down toward the sandy ocean bottom. Noticing a coral outcropping the size of a house, he aimed the pod toward it and drove the vessel rapidly toward the seafloor, the torpedoes missing the escape pod by a few feet and continuing toward another target. As they whizzed by, Lukas was surprised at their size and speed and he also assumed *Juventus* was not finished firing at them.

As the escape pod tucked itself behind the coral and rock, Lukas felt his ears pop with a strange sensation that his head was filled with water, but his hearing was crystal-clear. The image he saw racing toward them filled him with dread, as his mind struggled to make sense of it.

The pressure wave hit them with the force of five locomotives. The escape pod rolled like a discarded beer can being kicked through an alley. He noticed there was no screaming, and the passengers kept their heads tucked down as the pod crashed along the ocean floor. In the distance he saw a massive explosion of muddy water that raced toward them again. Chunks of coral, dead fish, and other animals flew past them. The coral and rock outcropping held, despite them having rolled several hundred feet. The outcropping acted like a shield that blocked the bulk of the massive explosion and helped keep the capsule intact.

So this is what a thermobaric bomb feels like, Lukas thought. He struggled to stay conscious while he wondered what in the hell would happen next.

Chapter 36

The Pelican closed in on Kiva Oa as it chopped above the waves. In the distance, the smoking cone of the Koro volcano continued to belch gas, earth, and lava into the sky. Tory noted its size, and even from the air, it had significantly grown since the news reels she saw yesterday. Lava sloped down the steep sides of the cone, flowing into the water in a steamy showdown between earth and sea, the net result being a new island. When they flew over the Jardin Island chain, Jone began to descend as he approached the Kiva Oa airport. The passengers noticed the rotors slowing slightly and peered out their windows to catch a view of the smaller islands as they made their approach.

Tory noticed an unusual wave pattern running almost perpendicular to the waves lapping the islands' beaches. For a second, she thought it was maybe a dolphin or a shark either being chased or in pursuit. She quickly grabbed her smartphone, snapped some pictures and started recording video. Tory noticed the perpendicular waves, two side by side, were heading directly toward one of the islands. Her first concern was dolphins or other sea animals beaching themselves on the island, but she soon realized this was no animal seconds before the whole ocean turned a frothing white.

A massive explosion sent plumes of seawater skyward like a field of geysers. The shock wave reverberated upward and interfered with the helicopter's approach to the airport. Tory continued to film in horror as the impacted island split in two before collapsing into the waves. It all happened so quickly and thoroughly that Tory thought maybe she had imagined it. She noticed one more perpendicular wave racing at an incredible speed toward the island. Tory rustled her fiancé to watch what she was witnessing. Jone, Donna, and Wilma were also engaged in watching what was going on. Another massive shock wave blew at the outer perimeter of the reef sending a cascade of bubbling water hundreds of feet into the air and rattling the island so violently, it collapsed into the sea in less than a minute.

"What the hell was that?" Donna yelled, having watched the island disappear before her eyes.

"It looked like a missile," Tory answered. "The first two weakened the island and the third one brought it down."

"*Dio Mio, guarda!*" Pepe yelled in Italian, his native language all he could summon as he pointed at the remaining islands. Several lines of waves began rising about a kilometer offshore from Kiva Oa. They were significantly taller than the surrounding waves and began racing toward the islands. Hundreds of feet of coral reef and seafloor became exposed as the tide pulled back from the incoming strength of a tsunami. Pepe watched in horror as it looked like the tsunami wave slurping all available water surrounding them and growing by the second.

"This is gonna be bad!" Donna yelled from the cockpit as she watched the succession of waves line up to pummel Kiva Oa, and after that, hit the fledgling

Koro volcano. "This could be a shit show."

"Put on life vests!" Jone yelled.

"Why? We should be okay, right?" Wilma asked.

"Just put on the vest just in case." Jone's tone went from friendly to direct.

"Just in case what?" Wilma asked out of curiosity.

Jone pointed at the instrument panel.

"Oh shit, seriously?" Donna commented when she saw the fuel gauge bouncing toward the empty mark.

"We only had gas for one way," Jone explained. "Kiva Oa was going to fill us up for the return, but…"

"Look!" Pepe yelled as the occupants of the helicopter watched the horror of a fifty-foot wave crash toward Kiva Oa like a runaway bulldozer.

Jone pulled up on the yoke to abort the landing as Kiva Oa was engulfed in water, destroying buildings, ripping boats from their moorings, and covering the island with a mound of water that only allowed some of the taller trees to be seen.

"Holy shit!" Donna yelled. "It was like the island wasn't even there." The succession of waves continued to assault Kiva Oa but rushed onward toward their next landfall, the Koro volcano.

"No more islands!" Jone yelled as the helicopter rotors began to sputter. "We not going to make it back to Fiji mainland!"

"Maybe the water will recede on Kiva Oa!" Donna yelled back.

"Maybe. But I don't think so," Jone responded.

"How much fuel do we have?

"Ten minutes, maybe," Jone answered Donna.

"Shit, keep circling this area," Donna commanded. "There has to be an island down there somewhere."

****

They hung upside down from the chairs that used to sit on the floor of the escape pod were now dangling with five occupants luckily seat belted in.

"Everybody okay?" Taylor asked.

"Ma? Betty? Linda?" Lukas called out to the older women. The emergency lights were on and despite the tossing around, the pod looked to be relatively intact. "At least no leaks," Lukas commented to Taylor.

They were still in the light-zone, less than thirty feet below the ocean's surface, so lighting was okay enough to see the basics.

"What happened?" Molly asked.

"It was a hyperbaric bomb, most likely," Taylor answered. "Baptiste is blowing up his islands to harvest the moonstone. That's what likely caused the tsunami a couple days ago."

"Looks like we had one again," Lukas pointed to the soupy mix of silica, dust, and debris clouding the normally crystal-clear water.

"So what do we do now?" Linda asked.

"Personally, I'd like to get out from under the ocean," Betty suggested.

"Second that." Lukas followed, his mom raising her hand in agreement.

"Agreed," Taylor informed them. "I'm going to find the inflator, once I get myself out of this seat."

In a few minutes, both Taylor and Lukas had unstrapped themselves from their seats and gently lowered themselves down onto what was once the ceiling. They then, in tandem, lowered Linda, Betty, and Molly to a similar position.

"I suggest you all stay seated while I look for the

inflators. I'll let you know when I find them." Taylor motioned to Lukas to search for one of them. "Don't activate it obviously."

Lukas gave Taylor a deadpan look. "Okay." He had no need to get defensive under water.

"Sorry, the Air Force commander comes out at the least convenient times."

Both men felt around the inside of the escape pod. "What exactly am I looking for?" Lukas asked him.

"Could be a hook, something with a key, even an enclosed button."

Lukas continued to search. "Like this?" he pointed to a recessed button covered by a plastic plate. On the plate the word INFLATOR was stenciled.

"Very funny, dear." Taylor chuckled. "I'll find the other one." He had started to feel warm, which meant they were likely running out of oxygen. He decided to keep that to himself for the time being.

When Taylor found the second inflator, he counted down and he and Lukas pushed their respective inflator buttons. Nothing happened.

"Let's try it again." Again, there was no response. *Shit!* Taylor thought.

"Oh boys?" Molly called. "Maybe it's this one." She pointed to a single knob, red and something to be pulled.

"Go ahead and…"

Molly pulled the knob and immediately the pod righted itself and the inflator curtain sounded as it started to fill with air. Almost immediately, they started drifting toward the surface.

"Good job, Ma."

"Our resident physicist comes through again,"

Taylor complimented her.

A rumbling noise echoed through the vessel seconds before the seafloor began to shake and heave.

"Better get going! Head toward the sloping shore. It's probably an island."

As they rose to the surface, more rumbling sounds emanated from outside. Fish scurried in confusion, darting back and forth, as if unsure of where to go.

"Something's happening outside," Linda yelled.

"Head for that island!" Molly shouted as the pod crashed through a rocky barrier reef. A large wave pushed them over the top and the escape pod rolled through the shallow tide pools as the inflatable bags ripped and hissed as gas escaped. Taylor and Lukas kicked at the hatch, which was dented from the roll. After five kicks and a coordinated push that included Molly, the hatch popped open. Sunlight flooded the partially submerged escape pod as quickly as the seawater.

"Everybody out!" Lukas yelled as he helped the women out safely and then followed them. Their shoes helped them walk over the sharp coral and rock toward the sandy shore of the island.

"Shuffle as you walk," Taylor shouted. "It'll scare away lionfish and stingrays so you don't step on them!"

"Great," Betty whispered to Linda. "I've already died once this week and now I'm back in the hornet's nest."

The sun was painfully bright, his pupils not adjusting fast enough. Lukas heard a sputtering noise above him. Looking up, he was blinded by the sun and had to look away. In the distance, the plume from the Koro volcano seemed to be even larger and profuse.

"Incoming!" Taylor yelled. "Heads up!"

A relic of a helicopter, its rotors moving slowly as it fell through the air, plummeted silently toward Kiva Oa.

Chapter 37

Taylor and Lukas trudged through calf-deep water as they ran toward the wreck, a metal heap of twisted metal and glass, its rotors half submerged into the wet white sand.

"No fire so far!" Taylor said, breathing heavily as he hurdled through the tidal pools with Lukas close behind. "We need to get people out."

They ran up the beach toward the hulking wreck. Lukas searched the area. *We were just here a couple of days ago,* he remembered. Scoured of all buildings and most trees, Kiva Oa looked like a different island, but as they ran uphill away from the water, Lukas noticed the sand was still wet hundreds of feet from the normal waterline.

Taylor trudged up the wet sand embankment toward the downed helicopter.

This thing's a relic, was the first thing he thought when he saw the make of the vessel.

The cockpit windshield was a spiderweb of broken glass, one of the panes completely missing. He noticed movement inside and saw an older gentleman slumped to the side, his bloodied hand outstretched and reaching for something.

"Hey!" Taylor yelled. "Hold tight and don't move! You'll hurt yourself."

The bloodied hand raised and signaled back with a

thumbs up. "Survivor," he yelled to Lukas who continued toward him. "Let's get him out."

As Taylor approached one side of the cockpit, Lukas ran to the other side and attempted to muscle the side cargo door open.

"Lukas!" a familiar voice called out.

He thought he may have imagined it until he saw the origin of the voice. It was Donna Rivero strapped into the front seat next to the pilot. Lukas forced the cargo door open a few inches and saw inside. Tory, Pepe, and Wilma stared back, a bit in shock but unhurt.

"I've got Tory!" he yelled over to Taylor, knowing that hearing his daughter's name would get his attention and give him a burst of energy.

Molly, Linda, and Betty, dripping wet but otherwise okay, continued slowly up the beach toward the wreck. Taylor and Lukas forced the jammed cargo door open with their combined strength as Tory jumped into her father's arms.

"I'm engaged!" was the first statement out of her mouth. She hadn't seen her dad since the momentous occasion over a week ago.

"Baby, are you hurt?" Taylor asked while Lukas helped Donna and Wilma out of the downed aircraft. Pepe followed escorting an older man who looked like a local.

They hugged each other, revolving from one to another. Jone stood alone, smiling quietly.

Taylor and Lukas immediately attended to his wounded arm, which Jone brushed off as no big deal.

"Papa," Tory informed her dads, "someone blew up some islands nearby."

"I know. I'll explain later," Lukas responded.

"How are you not hurt?"

"Jone is a master pilot." She pointed to him. "He circled until we ran out of fuel and the waves receded. Somehow, we're all safe."

Taylor approached Jone and gave him a hug, which surprised the Fijian man. "Jone, thank you for saving my daughter."

"Your wife is a good pilot, too." Jone responded. "She knew exactly what to do and it was her idea to drain the fuel tank. Risky, but it worked."

Donna heard this comment and laughed and walked over to join the conversation. "Jone did it all. I just helped out," she told the group. "And Jone, just for the record, Taylor is not my husband. He's his." She pointed to Lukas.

He nodded and smiled. "*Mahu*. I see. My son is *mahu,* has strength like no man I've ever met. We need to find high ground, Koro is angry."

"What do you suggest?" Molly asked him. "I don't see much high ground here."

"That." Jone pointed to a rock peak that didn't look high enough. "That's the best chance when tsunami hit. Follow me."

Jone headed toward the center of the island and stood aside as he let the others pass.

Linda led the pack. "I hope I don't get us lost."

"You can't get lost, ma'am. Straight up the mountain," Jone replied with encouragement.

"He doesn't know Linda," Betty wise-cracked to Molly and Donna.

"I heard that!" Linda shouted from the front of the line.

Lukas had been so focused on the rescue of the

helicopter passengers and the subsequent trek to higher ground to escape a potential tsunami that he forgot about the escape pod and all the food, water and supplies that were contained inside.

"Shit, we're gonna need food and water," Lukas informed them. "I'm gonna run back and try and secure the escape pod or at least what's in it."

"I'll go with you, sir," Pepe volunteered, the younger man already scurrying down the hill back toward the beach.

"Guys," Jone called out. "It's not worth the risk."

"Pepe!" his fiancée called out. "Get back here!"

Shirtless with his tee-shirt tied around his head, Pepe stopped and shrugged. "What, *cara*?"

"This is the part in the movie where the hero does something heroic and gets killed. Get your ass back up here! Now!"

Taylor glanced sideways at the Herb Society. "I have no idea where she gets that behavior, by the way," he said sheepishly. Pepe and Lukas scampered back up the hill in response.

"Fine. Don't cry to me when you don't have food or water." Pepe exhaled.

"We find plenty of both up on the hill. Do not worry." Jone reassured him as they reached the pinnacle of the hill.

"We're up a couple hundred feet," Taylor estimated. "If Koro blows…"

****

Taylor's voice was drowned out by the sonic boom over thirty miles away. All ten people instinctively ducked to the ground and covered their ears as the explosion's sound waves traveled rapidly across the ocean. Even with his hands over his ears, Lukas had never heard anything so loud. Now he couldn't hear anything, other than a white noise similar to when listening to the inside of a conch shell. His eyes reflexively closed which gave him an odd feeling of being removed from the world, unable to hear. Unwilling to see. He decided to open his eyes and imagined the worst was yet to come.

****

Jone, knowing they were almost out of fuel, and witnessing the man-made destruction of one of Pierre Baptiste's islands, radioed the Fiji Coast Guard. Whatever happened to him and his passengers, the alert would direct the Coast Guard to perform either a rescue or a recovery mission, depending on the outcome of his flying skills. Luckily, his co-pilot Donna had performed the autorotation maneuver many times in the United States Army. The concept centered around using the un-powered propeller blades to create wind resistance and give the pilots some control to the plunge from the sky. Together they got everyone safely on the ground.

From the high point of Kiva Oa, Taylor spotted two transport helicopters headed toward them. In the distance, a massive plume of smoke snaked its way toward the sky and beyond. If there was an end to the smoke trail, he couldn't see it. The tsunami he'd predicted was mostly directed in the opposite direction, and even so, was less than two feet tall and created little to no damage. There was clearly still a risk, as volcanic eruptions rarely were single-incident events.

One Coast Guard helicopter touched down on Kiva Oa, while the other flew on to check on other islanders. Lukas rummaged through the escape pod and collected whatever he could regarding personal property, electronic equipment, and any documentation needed to fly out of Fiji or into the United States. Remarkably, the contents of the escape pod remained dry and operational. Jone informed Lukas and Taylor that a Fiji Coast Guard cutter and a Navy patrol ship were dispatched to the area to investigate the alleged intentional destruction of the islands. With all ten people, plus the two pilots, the Fiji Coast Guard ship took off from Kiva Oa and headed toward the main island of Viti Levu.

From the air, the Koro volcano appeared much differently. A massive crater protruded out of the ocean, black and smoldering cinders darkening one side of the slope while orange lava slid down the other side. The pilot, curious to see the spectacle, got within three miles of the new island. The passengers craned their necks in awe of the majestic sight in the distance. Earth was renewing itself as it always had. Destruction brought creation. Death brought new life. The eternal cycle, despite man's attempt to change it, somehow continued.

All eyes were on Koro until they were too far away to see anything but a plume of smoke. The transport helicopter turned and headed back toward the main island and international airport.

"Twenty minutes until we land at Nadi," the pilot announced, referring to the country's major airport.

"Can we actually get a hotel tonight?" Betty asked. "I'd love one night of sleep on something that isn't moving."

"I'm with her," Linda replied.

Jone smiled. "I set you up! Don't worry." He picked up his mobile phone and began speaking to someone on the other end. "All settled."

"I really hope we're not sleeping on his cousin's sofa," Donna whispered.

"All I want is a shower," Molly replied. "I'll sleep in a hammock if needed."

Taylor sat across from Pepe and smiled when he noticed Pepe's arm draped around Tory's shoulder as both nodded in and out of sleep. Lukas rested his own head on Taylor's shoulder.

"Welcome to the family." He smiled when he saw Pepe awaken briefly.

Pepe smiled back. "Is this a typical family vacation experience?" Pepe attempted to bring some levity to the previous week's adventures.

"Each new family member has to add to future adventures," he said as Lukas briefly woke up.

"It's true. Our trips were pretty boring until Taylor came into our lives," Lukas replied, his ears still ringing and not sure how loud he was speaking.

"Sounds like a challenge," Pepe replied. "Tory and I will plan the next trip."

Epilogue

Jone had set them up at a five-star hotel owned by his son and his husband, right on the beach about twenty minutes' drive from the airport. Fiji sun warmed the tarmac as they loaded their luggage into the *Goose 2* and said their goodbyes. Jone, his wife, and his son and husband stayed to see their friends off, bringing fresh fruit and homemade food for the long trip ahead.

"Make sure you eat all the fruit before you land," he told Taylor and Lukas. "Customs will nail you, otherwise."

"Thank you for your hospitality and for taking care of our friends and family." Lukas hugged him as though they were long time friends.

"You're always welcome in Fiji. My son said he will make sure you get the best room in the house." Jone bade them farewell.

"I think we already got that last night. Thank you, Jone."

****

Hours later, the Spectrum 7 raced high above the Pacific Ocean. Donna and Tory sat in the cockpit to allow Taylor some time to rest and recover from a harrowing journey. Molly, Linda, and Betty napped in the luxurious soft leather seats. Wilma sat awake and pored through a book, illuminated by an overhead lamp, the only light in an otherwise dark cabin. Lukas heard

Taylor's rhythmic breathing. He knew that sound from the hundreds of nights he'd slept next to his husband. Taylor was exhausted, but even in deep sleep his hand rested upon Lukas' thigh. It was his connection he made to Lukas while he slept. Taylor always had to have contact with his husband in order to sleep soundly.

Lukas' laptop illuminated his face. His eyeglasses reflected warped images of the computer screen as he flipped through the surveillance videos from *Juventus*. He fast-forwarded through the images of Pierre's salon and the holographic light show from the first evening aboard the ship. The sped-up video added a comical view of what had been a surreal experience on Baptiste's mega-yacht. He searched for the date and located the recordings from their first night aboard *Juventus* and scrolled through the various staterooms until he found his and Taylor's

A deep breath in and out as Lukas braced himself for what he'd find on the video footage. He knew he was making a big deal out of this, but he had to know if he and Taylor had hooked up with Gael. He glanced down at his sleeping husband and told himself that no matter what happened, they would deal with it. He clicked on the file and only saw video footage of them walking around the cabin, getting dressed, using the toilet, and taking a shower. He fast-forwarded and stopped when he saw an image of Marc Hammer and Aleks carrying Lukas into the room and hastily flopping him down on their bed. He and Aleks took selfies with a sleeping Lukas that just seemed weird. They repeated the strange ritual with Taylor as if this was a high-school sophomore overnight camp.

Finally, Gael walked into the stateroom fully

clothed. His lips moved but there was no audio in the footage. Gael became immediately angry at Marc and threw a punch before being knocked out by a taser. The three men lay naked, none of them conscious. Aleks returned with Kailani who cut Gael's neck cord, containing the moonstone pearl, and tucked it into her pocket. She rubbed all three men with the moonstone solution, focusing on Lukas' arm and leg injuries from earlier that day. Marc, Aleks, and Kailani then exited the dark stateroom and closed the door. There was no indication they hooked up with Gael, who was knocked out by a taser. But the scenes with Marc turned his stomach. Lukas felt like a hazing victim of an awful fraternity prank. He would eventually tell Taylor but decided to let him sleep.

Lukas perused the next set of videos. His mother had gotten up to stretch and walked by on her way to the lavatory.

"What are you working on?" she asked her son.

"Watching video surveillance of *Juventus*," he explained. "I want to see what happened during the dinner when Linda and Betty collapsed."

"I'll be right back," she told him. "I want to look for that weapon I told you about."

A couple of minutes later, the lavatory door was opened and Molly motioned to Lukas to join her in the back of the plane. He closed his laptop and gently maneuvered his way off his seat without disturbing his husband before joining his mom.

"If it was the HAG weapon like I explained, then…" she paused.

"You mean that heart attack gun, Ma? That sounds like something from a spy movie."

Molly grabbed her son's hand. "I know it sounds like fiction. You don't have to believe me."

"Of course I believe you, Ma," he reassured her. "I have a hard time believing a weapon like this could have been developed over fifty years ago."

Molly chuckled. "It was a time of unbelievable technological developments. Much of what we have today is due to technology invented before you were born. We just didn't have the ability to leverage and scale it."

Lukas continued to maneuver through the video footage of Pierre's salon. He fast-forwarded to the dinner where Baptiste was making a speech.

"Here's Baptiste pontificating about something," Molly pointed out. "It was dinner after that first tsunami hit."

"Massive pressure explosives can do a lot of damage," Lukas commented back.

Molly watched the video frame by frame. Linda and Betty stood, talking to Kailani and Gael before Kailani excused herself to use the lavatory. She passed Marc, who reached out to hug her, for which she stopped only briefly. Gael followed her and stopped to chat with Aleks and Marc while Kailani was in the bathroom.

"Zoom in on those three," Molly asked Lukas, as he increased the focus on Gael, Marc, and Aleks. Another figure came into the shot. "It's Baptiste," she pointed out.

Lukas zoomed out again and saw that Baptiste stood near Linda and Betty. He panned the camera angle and caught Taylor and him walking back from the outside deck. Next, Diana Kepler entered the room and walked toward Baptiste. As she approached him, Lukas saw that Linda had started to stumble and grab her chest followed by Betty doing the same.

"Stop!" Molly yelled. "Can you back up and zoom in?"

Lukas did what his mom asked and played the surveillance video slowly. Molly's eyes scoured the screen for any detail that seemed out of place.

"There, stop the video," Molly commanded. "Now rewind." Lukas smiled thinking about when his mom was a spy they actually used reels of video tape they actually had to rewind.

Molly's mouth hung open in shock or disbelief. "Did you see that?" she asked her son. "Rewind again."

Lukas played the zoomed-in video in second-by-second sequence and rewound to the point that Kailani and Gael left for the restroom.

"There!" Molly shouted in excitement as Lukas froze the frames in ultra-slow motion. Kailani walked past Marc, and he slipped something into her pocket. Kailani walked to the restroom and then Gael approached Marc, who appeared to give him something. Frame by frame, they studied everyone's movement. When Baptiste was within two feet of Linda and Betty, Molly pointed out what she spotted.

"I'll be damned, Ma. Good eyes."

Lukas and his mother stared at the screen in disbelief. Two figures in the background pulled out small pistols, about the size of a child's toy. They took aim, possibly fired, and tucked their small guns away before exiting the salon. The video showed Linda and Betty collapsing and everyone in the salon running to their aid.

In the distance, they saw the same two figures exiting the salon while everyone else went to aid Linda and Betty. Lukas smiled and sat back in his chair while Molly took it all in. "How? Why?"

Lukas shook his head. "Don't know, Ma. They're the last two I suspected."

Molly snapped screenshots of Lukas' laptop while Lukas shook his head in disbelief. He couldn't break his gaze from the two figures exiting the salon immediately after Linda and Betty collapsed. He couldn't see their faces, but he knew. The unmistakable forms of Kailani and Gael made a dash to the exit.

Next, he clicked on the file he downloaded simply titled ARCHIPELAGO. Inside were hundreds of files that overwhelmed his tired brain. He couldn't process anymore and promised himself he'd read them when he had more time.

****

As the *Goose* entered United States airspace, Lukas made a phone call to his office. He spoke softly to the person on the other side, smiled, and disconnected.

"I'm having Scott, my IT guy, run the security film from your house the night Dad died."

Molly's eyes grew wide with excitement. "Do you think they'll have a video of what happened to Dad?"

"I don't know, Ma," Lukas answered. "But your theory was directionally correct. There is likely a HAG or two out there. Baptiste could be the connection."

"That wouldn't surprise me one bit," Molly responded.

"I know he's one of your favorites, Ma. If we can get the video from your house and compare, who knows what we'll find?"

"Thanks for believing me," she told her son.

"You're usually right, Ma."

A buzzing sound echoed through the cabin as Lukas' smartphone seemed to blow up with arriving text and email messages.

"I guess that's what happens when you spend a week underwater." Lukas laughed. He turned the phone over and saw a number of messages and missed calls. "Someone's been trying to get a hold of me." Then he saw the caller ID and almost went pale. "Ma, I've got to make a quick call. Can you go and wake up Taylor and tell him I need to speak to him fast?"

Molly walked toward the front of the cabin and within a few minutes, a very sleepy Taylor lumbered toward the back of the plane, yawning and rubbing his eyes. His hair stuck out at odd angles, resembling a palmetto or some desert plant.

"Can we make a quick call from the crew bedroom?" Lukas asked him. "I don't think we should wait until we land." He turned the phone screen to face Taylor, who when recognizing the number had to steady himself.

"Oh my God." Taylor's voice was muffled by his hand covering his mouth.

****

A week after they landed in Washington, D.C., Scott sent over the video footage he was able to retrieve from the Halloran's Ocotillo Ridge home server. From their Arlington penthouse, Lukas and Taylor watched the grainy film taken from a security camera mounted on the top of the Halloran home. Frame by frame, they combed through hours of footage. After an hour, they arrived at the file recording of the night of the home invasion.

Three dark figures crept in from the desert, completely dressed in black and treading lightly to avoid making any noise. The intruders silently hopped over the adobe wall and hid behind some large bushes and trees. Lukas watched as his mom got up off the sofa, threw crumbs or something into the burning fire pit and walked toward the house. Within seconds of her leaving, the figures closed in on an unsuspecting John, who appeared to be drinking some wine.

One of the dark figures jumped in front of John, startling him, and pulled out a small gun, the size of a child's toy, aimed it, and within thirty seconds, John collapsed grabbing his chest. The other intruders began shooting up the back terrace, popping out lights and shattering pottery. Lukas could see his mother approaching the glass door to see what was going on when suddenly the glass windows and doors shattered and splintered. He could hear the police sirens approaching and the three figures ran toward the desert, but one person turned back to look at the carnage they'd left behind.

Lukas froze the screen and zoomed in. The figure that stopped to look back had a familiar gait and stature. As Lukas and Taylor improved the resolution, they were able to get a read on the man's face, which was almost entirely cloaked by a black balaclava.

"No fucking way," Taylor exclaimed as they both recognized that the man staring back at them with deep and inquisitive eyes had a piercing through his eyebrow. It was in the unmistakable shape of a trident.

****

Taylor and Lukas sat nervously in the dank waiting

room. The unupholstered furniture was uncomfortable and slightly sticky in the early morning heat. Lukas unconsciously pumped his leg like it was a piston for his thoughts. It was a sign to Taylor how much Lukas had processing in his brain at that moment.

"Are you sure you want to do this?" Taylor asked as he placed his hand on Lukas' knee, attempting to calm him.

"You're seriously asking me this now?" Lukas was uncharacteristically edgy and his husband, while calming him, liked to throw a few playful jabs at him to break the cycle of his spinning thoughts.

"Just calibrating." Taylor used a phrase he learned from Lukas, hoping it would resonate while his mind was in overdrive.

"Thanks, babe." Lukas broke out of the spin. "I'm okay, just running a billion scenarios in my head simultaneously."

"This is gonna be messy," Taylor told him. "It always is, even for the strongest couples."

Lukas nodded as he stared at the floor. His knee started tapping against the linoleum floor.

"Mr. Pastore? Mr. Halloran?" a smartly dressed woman in her mid-thirties approached them with her outstretched hand.

"I'm Martina Ramirez," she introduced herself. "I'll be handling your case today. The judge is ready to see you."

They walked slowly down the dimly lit hallway as they approached the courtroom.

"It's weird to hear our names separated," Taylor mentioned. "I guess it's good we never officially combined our last names. Makes things a lot easier."

Lukas said nothing. They hadn't told anybody what they were about to do. Molly was off visiting her daughters and their families. She hadn't seen them since his father had died. Linda and Betty were recovering from their experiences. Linda was at a celebrity-filled spa for two weeks, while Betty hiked the Andes. Wilma and Donna were on a safari in Kruger National Park, a bucket list destination on which they compromised with a more luxurious upgrade to full glamping mode, much to Donna's chagrin.

Martina held the door open and allowed Taylor and Lukas to enter, despite both men insisting she go before them.

"My mother wouldn't be happy if she saw that." Lukas tried to bring levity to the impending situation.

A bailiff announced the entry of the judge as Elena Somerville and the court stood as expected. Elena looked to be in her mid-forties. When she sat, the audience did the same. She said nothing as she flipped through documents and case files, her reading glasses balanced on the tip of her nose.

"Are you sure you guys really want to do this?" she asked both men. "It's a big decision that will affect you for the rest of your lives."

Both men nodded.

"I need a verbal answer," she retorted.

"Yes, your honor. We want to proceed," they said in unison.

Judge Somerville sat back in her chair, her hands clasped and resting in her lap. "I see you both have had counseling, both alone and together." She flipped through the pages. "There's no guarantee on any of this and you can't undo it, despite the hundreds of times you will undoubtedly want to, at least in your mind." She smiled. "My ex-husband wouldn't likely be my ex-husband if…well, you don't need me blabbering. Please stand."

The bailiff stood and walked slowly to a door that led to a room behind the judge. He opened it and two young children ran toward Taylor and Lukas and nearly toppled them over, hugging and kissing them. A social worker followed them carrying a baby about a year old.

Tears streamed down Taylor's face. His own adoption that he was too young to remember suddenly felt very personal. He saw the energy and excitement of the two boys who jumped up and down wanting their new dads to pick them up. He fought to hold back tears to no avail.

"Why is papa crying?" the oldest boy asked Lukas.

"Because he is so happy," Lukas choked out before the tears streamed down his own cheeks.

Judge Somerville smiled and wiped tears from her own eyes. "You guys are brave," she complimented them. "These kids are very lucky."

Lukas composed himself. "We are the lucky ones, your honor."

Her gavel came down, heavy with finality. Suddenly the courtroom filled with people. Adoption consultants, social workers, and others who had desperately worked to find these three orphaned children a home stood by with balloons, toys, and flowers for the dads. An assistant wheeled in a large sheet cake. Lukas and Taylor walked over and noticed there was blue frosting and pink roses decorating the cake.

The Pastore-Halloran family
Tomas, Matteo, Ana
Dad and Papa

"Guys, we have some cake," Taylor announced as Tomas and Matteo fought over a yellow dump truck toy, completely oblivious to Taylor.

The social worker handed one-year-old Ana to Lukas. Ana smiled, recognizing both Lukas and Taylor from their visitation outings with the social workers who watched how well the kids bonded with their potential new dads.

Lukas popped Ana in the air and smiled. "You're gonna be the boss one day," he told her, as both he and Taylor laughed at her side-eye glance toward her boisterous brothers. Ana smiled and laughed at her two dads.

Judge Somerville descended from the bench and congratulated both Taylor and Lukas. "I hope you guys can take some time together as your family gets settled. They are beautiful kids."

"Thanks, your honor." Taylor responded. "We will definitely do that."

Somerville smiled, yet they could see she had a touch of sadness in her eyes. "And most importantly, make time for each other. Have your alone time, go out to dinner, and keep yourselves strong physically and mentally."

"I have to admit, I've suddenly forgotten every single thing I thought I would do when I was a parent," Lukas added.

"Welcome to parenthood," Judge Somerville interjected. "We strive to be the best parents the world has ever seen, but these kids will take you down a few pegs, believe me." She laughed at her own memory. "Then you realize we do our best to keep our kids safe and healthy while not losing our own minds. And then, in what feels like a few minutes, they're grown up."

****

It had been several weeks since Taylor and Lukas heard of Pierre Baptiste's death. He and his crew of *Juventus* experienced a catastrophic explosion, and the massive ship disappeared into the depths of the Tonga Trench. With a maximum depth of almost thirty-six-thousand feet, no rescue was attempted, nor was a salvage operation even considered. The likelihood of any survivors at that depth was zero.

After hours outside with lots of play, their kids slept soundly in the spare bedroom as Lukas and Taylor watched news coverage of Pierre Baptiste's life and the story of how he went from a street kid in Marseille to hitting the trillionaire mark in his business and financial life. Details on his fortune and where it would go were kept under wraps. His assets and properties transferred to his many trusts, all controlled by his estate manager.

"You know he's still alive," Lukas told a sleepy Taylor as they stretched out on their sectional sofa. No mention of the larger ship, *Olympus*.

"Probably, babe. This isn't over. I'm just too tired to think about it now."

"When you're more awake, I'd like to tell you what I learned about ARCHIPELAGO. I've got my tech team working on it."

Taylor perked up. "What did you learn?"

"It is very complicated, but quite simply Baptiste has interlinked his network with billions of computers around the world. He's connected to archives, museums, libraries, and even personal computers containing digital memories of their deceased loved ones," he explained.

"And none of them know they are connected to Baptiste?" Taylor asked.

"That's the thing. It's more like a digital version of *phone a friend,*" Lukas explained. "The connections are sporadic, quick, and then quickly dropped. Very hard to trace. It's almost like a community," Lukas mentioned. "If one computer needs another idea or point of view, it's like going to the neighbor for a cup of sugar, but instead of sugar, it's knowledge, data, and facts that help it solve a problem."

"And what problem do you think it's trying to solve?" Taylor asked. "Hypothetical ones humans may face when the Olympus team is three-hundred years older?"

"Maybe." Lukas bit his lower lip. "Or something a whole lot scarier."

A lightbulb went off in Taylor's head. "No way."

"All of Project Olympus depends upon the crumbling of society. An apocalypse, as Baptiste referred to it." Lukas paused. "Maybe he wants ARCHIPELAGO to figure out and maybe even execute the collapse of civilization."

Taylor sighed. "It feels very different to hear that now that we have children who could live in that destroyed world. Maybe it won't happen."

"Look at the world, Taylor." Lukas grabbed his husband's hand. "Society is angry. Trust is low and strong political figures are manipulating masses of people."

"It does feel like the world has been getting darker

and scarier," Taylor added.

"Imagine if ARCHIPELAGO has the ability to conspire against humanity," Lukas said with pessimism. "It may be orchestrating the early stages of societal collapse right now."

A word about the author…

E. William Podojil has worked as a writer, advisor and international business executive while living in the Netherlands and the United States. He studied screenwriting at UCLA. His first novel was published in 2004. His latest novel, The Poseidon Project, was published by Wild Rose Press in August, 2024 as the first book in the Herb Society Mysteries series.

Podojil currently resides in Northeast Ohio with his husband and three sons. He travels extensively and writes about his experiences on his website www.ewpodojil.com.

Thank you for purchasing
this publication of The Wild Rose Press, Inc.

For questions or more information
contact us at
info@thewildrosepress.com.

The Wild Rose Press, Inc.
www.thewildrosepress.com